Rebelli T0011605

Finishing school was ... *aristocratic ladies...but these four friends can never be contained by society's expectations!*

To conform to what society deemed correct for females of their class, Amelia Lambourne, Irene Fairfax, Georgina Hayward and Emily Beaumont were sent by their families to Halliwell's Finishing School for Refined Young Ladies—which they soon dubbed "Hell's Final Sentence for Rebellious Young Ladies"!

Instead, the four found strength in their mutual support to become themselves, and a lifelong friendship was formed...one they'll need to lean on when each young woman faces the one thing they swore never to succumb to—a good match!

Read Amelia's story in
Lady Amelia's Scandalous Secret

Read Irene's story in
Miss Fairfax's Notorious Duke

Read Georgina's story in
Miss Georgina's Marriage Dilemma

And watch for Emily's story,
coming soon from Harlequin Historical.

Author Note

Miss Georgina's Marriage Dilemma is the third book in the Rebellious Young Ladies miniseries, featuring four unconventional young women who became firm friends when they met at Halliwell's Finishing School for Refined Young Ladies.

As the daughter of a wealthy industrialist, Georgina Hayward takes pride in the fact that she has only one skill: enjoying herself. While her parents expect her to marry a titled man, she prefers to spend the Season making sport of the men who pursue her so they can get their hands on her generous marriage settlement.

Then she meets Adam Knightly, the Duke of Ravenswood, an impoverished widower with three children, who is in need of a wife. Georgina's commitment to only marry a man who loves her and is not interested in her dowry is severely challenged.

I hope you enjoy *Miss Georgina's Marriage Dilemma* as much as I enjoyed writing it. I love hearing from my readers and can be reached at evashepherd.com and Facebook.com/evashepherdromancewriter.

EVA SHEPHERD

Miss Georgina's Marriage Dilemma

HARLEQUIN
HISTORICAL

If you purchased this book without a cover you should be aware that this book is stolen property. It was reported as "unsold and destroyed" to the publisher, and neither the author nor the publisher has received any payment for this "stripped book."

HARLEQUIN®
HISTORICAL™

Recycling programs for this product may not exist in your area.

ISBN-13: 978-1-335-59595-9

Miss Georgina's Marriage Dilemma

Copyright © 2024 by Eva Shepherd

All rights reserved. No part of this book may be used or reproduced in any manner whatsoever without written permission except in the case of brief quotations embodied in critical articles and reviews.

This is a work of fiction. Names, characters, places and incidents are either the product of the author's imagination or are used fictitiously. Any resemblance to actual persons, living or dead, businesses, companies, events or locales is entirely coincidental.

For questions and comments about the quality of this book, please contact us at CustomerService@Harlequin.com.

Harlequin Enterprises ULC
22 Adelaide St. West, 41st Floor
Toronto, Ontario M5H 4E3, Canada
www.Harlequin.com

Printed in U.S.A.

After graduating with degrees in history and political science, **Eva Shepherd** worked in journalism and as an advertising copywriter. She began writing historical romances because it combined her love of a happy ending with her passion for history. She lives in Christchurch, New Zealand, but spends her days immersed in the world of late Victorian England. Eva loves hearing from readers and can be reached via her website, evashepherd.com, and her Facebook page, Facebook.com/evashepherdromancewriter.

Books by Eva Shepherd

Harlequin Historical

"The Earl's Unexpected Gifts"
in *A Victorian Family Christmas*

Rebellious Young Ladies

Lady Amelia's Scandalous Secret
Miss Fairfax's Notorious Duke
Miss Georgina's Marriage Dilemma

Young Victorian Ladies

Wagering on the Wallflower
Stranded with the Reclusive Earl
The Duke's Rebellious Lady

Those Roguish Rosemonts

A Dance to Save the Debutante
Tempting the Sensible Lady Violet
Falling for the Forbidden Duke

Visit the Author Profile page
at Harlequin.com for more titles.

To everyone who enjoys a happy ending

Chapter One

Somerset, England, 1895

After successfully negotiating five Seasons, her single status firmly intact, Georgina Hayward could not believe her parents were still trying to match her with supposedly suitable men.

What was wrong with them? Were they incapable of understanding the simple fact that she did not want them to find her a husband? She'd thought by now they would have realised she would not be married off to some fortune-hunter who fell in love with her immediately on hearing the size of her marriage settlement. Nor would she marry a man with a title just to advance the family's position in Society.

She paced her bedchamber, her fury growing with every step.

Her father was not an unintelligent man. After all, the grandson of a humble baker did not become one of the richest men in England without having a certain amount of intelligence.

Her teeth clenched more tightly together. And it might be better if they weren't so rich. While she loved all the nice things money provided, if her father hadn't bought all those properties, businesses and whatnot in an endless quest to get richer and more influential, and if her mother had been content to remain in that quaint Park Lane house where Georgina had been born, rather than aiming to have the best estate, the best balls, the best everything, maybe life would be easier. At least for Georgina. Then she wouldn't be paraded in front of an endless stream of men who were all but salivating at the thought of getting their hands on her dowry.

Georgina shuddered. Why, oh, why could her parents not understand the simple concept that if Georgina married—and that was an *if*, not a *when*—it would be to a man of her choosing? A man who loved her and she loved in return. A man who wanted her for herself and cared nothing for her dowry, unlike all those grasping men she met during the Season.

She stopped pacing and glared out of the window, as if showing her anger to the entire world, then recommenced pacing the well-worn path across the Oriental rug.

When she had informed her parents at the beginning of the first Season what her conditions regarding marriage were to be, they had looked at her as if *she* were the simple one.

Unbelievable.

Instead of doing as she emphatically commanded, they had tried to interest her in Baron this, the Earl of that or the Viscount of something else.

And they were still at it.

Even more unbelievable.

The Season hadn't even begun and they had invited some penniless, widowed duke to their estate in Somerset, and told her he was absolutely perfect for her, when they all knew the only thing perfect about him was his title.

Well, her parents and that toothless old codger were going to have to be taught a lesson. It was time to take action and show them she was not to be trifled with.

The Duke would arrive, expecting to find a docile young woman who was bedazzled by the prospect of becoming a duchess. Meanwhile, she would be hundreds of miles away, entertaining anyone who would listen with a daring tale of how she had thwarted her parents' plans yet again and put a grasping member of the nobility firmly in his place.

But first, like a princess imprisoned in a tower, she had to escape her evil captives.

Fortunately, unlike most princesses in towers, she was not helpless and knew exactly how to gain her freedom, and she didn't need a handsome prince to help her do it.

To that end, she bundled up her skirt, leant out of the window and looked down at the gardens below. She had climbed out of this window countless times as a young girl to flee from her mother, her nanny and her annoying older brother. And she could do it again now. After all, it was only two storeys.

Only two storeys.

A knock at the door caused her to drop her skirt and stand up straighter, as if proving she was not guilty of the crime she was yet to commit.

'Miss Georgina, please, you must let me in so I can

finish dressing you,' her lady's maid pleaded through the locked door. 'And your mother wants to talk to you in the drawing room as soon as you are ready.'

'I'm perfectly capable of dressing myself, Betsy.' She looked down at the frilly dress her mother had insisted she wear to meet the Duke, bedecked with ribbons, ruches, laces and a ridiculous number of pearl buttons.

That was the problem.

That was why climbing out of the window seemed so daunting. When she was a child, she would have worn a plain dress, one that caused less hindrance when climbing trees, or down the occasional drainpipe.

She had to change, but did not need a lady's maid in order to do so.

'Oh, miss, you're not going to do anything foolish, are you?' Betsy pleaded.

She stared indignantly at the closed door. 'No, I certainly am not.' Betsy's lack of faith in Georgina never failed to amaze her.

'Please, miss.' The lady's maid rattled the locked doorknob.

'And tell Mother I will be down presently.' She smiled to herself. She was not lying to Betsy. She *would* be down presently. She just wouldn't be using the stairs to do so and would not be appearing in the drawing room.

The doorknob turned again. That was followed by a *hmph* of disapproval, then Betsy's skirts swishing off down the hallway.

Georgina rushed to the wardrobe, pushing aside gown after overly ornate gown to find something more suitable to wear.

Then she saw it, stopped her frantic pursuit and smiled in triumph.

She pulled out the uniform she had purchased from the chambermaid for what she suspected was an exorbitant price so she could play a prank on her brother, Tommy, a few weeks ago. It was perfect.

With much wriggling, squirming and squeezing, she eased herself out of her gown and corset, pulled on the simple brown dress and placed the floppy white cap on her head. Then she flipped off her embroidered silk slippers and tied on the much more practical black boots.

There was nothing stopping her now.

She looked back out of the window. The side of the house appeared to have grown higher while she had been distracted. But she had been left with no other choice. She pushed up the sash window as high as it would go and climbed onto the windowsill.

She edged herself over the sill, turned onto her knees and angled her body in an attempt to reach the first bracket on the drainpipe. As a child she had been able to scurry down this drainpipe like a circus acrobat. Surely it would be easier now. After all, her legs were much longer. But it seemed her bravery had diminished at the same rate at which her body had grown.

Slowly, tentatively, she edged her foot along the outside wall until it made contact with the drainpipe, then just as slowly, just as tentatively her foot slid downwards to find the first bracket that attached the cast iron pipe to the outside wall.

She sighed with relief as her foot reached its destination. Not looking down, she edged herself slowly out of the window, her feet steadying her as her hands left the sanctuary of the windowsill and grasped hold of the drainpipe.

There was no going back now. She clung to the drainpipe as if her life depended on it, and tried not to think about how her life did literally depend on it. Now was also not the time to think about how she weighed so much more than she had when she was a slip of a girl. Nor was it time to wonder whether the drainpipe would cope with her added weight. And it was certainly not time to admonish herself for eating all those cream cakes and chocolates that were responsible for the added weight.

She looked down at the ground swirling beneath her, gripped the drainpipe tighter, stared at the stonework so close to her nose and told herself to never, ever look down again. Instead, she looked up, at the window above her.

Should she return to her bedchamber? Even as a child she had not mastered the art of climbing back into her room, and there was no wisdom in trying to learn a new skill now at the advanced age of three and twenty.

Down it would have to be. Her hands scrabbled down the pipe until she reached the next bracket. Once she had a secure grasp, she slid her feet further down until she made contact with the bracket beneath. In this awkward manner she slowly made it down the pipe.

When her feet reached the firm ground she took a brief moment to celebrate her victory, then dropped down behind the shrubbery.

She was still not free. She had to escape the estate. Maintaining her crouched position, she moved along the side of the house. It was inelegant, and she suspected she resembled a waddling duck, but it was the only way she could avoid being seen by anyone who might look out of one of the multitude of windows at the front of the house.

Her father had been so proud when he had moved the family into the Somerset estate he had purchased from an impoverished viscount. Georgina had also loved the house and had enjoyed playing in the enormous gardens, but with her thighs screaming as she continued her awkward progress, she wondered why a house needed to be so big, why it had to have so many rooms, and why the windows on the lower floor had to be quite so close to the ground.

Finally, she made it to the corner of the building. She stood up, shook her legs to release the tension, then sprinted to the large, red brick building that held her final means of escape. She entered the stables and said a silent thanks to her brother for providing her with a way to race across the countryside as free as a bird. Her parents had disapproved of the gift, claiming no good would come of it. They were wrong. Much good was to come of it. It would allow her to put as much distance as possible between herself and the greedy old Duke.

She quietly wheeled her bicycle out of the stable and down the path, holding her breath as if that would somehow quieten the sound of rubber on gravel. The moment she reached the elm trees that lined the path, she mounted her bicycle and pedalled faster than she had ever pedalled before.

Not stopping to see if there were any carts or carriages travelling along the country lane, she flew around the corner and continued pedalling. Her lungs cried out for a rest, but her legs kept pumping. She would not stop until she reached the village. Then she would take a train and travel as far away from Somerset, the Duke and her irritating parents as it was possible to travel.

Sailing around another corner, she smiled to herself. Freedom was near at hand.

Her smile disappeared. She stopped pedalling and whirled to a halt. Where was the village? When they travelled by coach it was always such a short distance. She couldn't remember there being so many corners, so many long stretches of road. But there was nothing for it. She pushed off again and forced her legs to continue, albeit at a less hectic pace.

She reached another corner and still no village, just another long stretch of hedge-lined country road.

Wheezing to a halt, she climbed off her bicycle, threw it into the hedge and glared at it. It was supposed to be her ticket to freedom and instead she was stuck on this country road, miles from anywhere, her legs aching, her lungs gasping, and by now her family had probably noticed her missing and were mounting a search party.

She looked back down the lane and her blame turned towards her father. He had probably bought an estate so far out in the country for just this reason, so she would be trapped. She sank down beside her abandoned bicycle and placed her head in her hands. It was all so unfair.

Adam Knightly, the Duke of Ravenswood, looked out of the carriage window as it drove along the country road and told himself, yet again, that he would not be dispirited. He was resigned to his fate. He had to be. He had been left with no other choice. If he'd been given some warning, he might have been able to find another, less desperate solution to his predicament. But with his father's sudden death he had not only inherited the Dukedom, but also the burden of seemingly insurmountable debts. He needed money, and he needed it immediately. Too many people's livelihoods depended on the Ravenswood estate. Too many tenant farmers and villagers risked losing the tied cottages their families had lived in for generations. Too many tradesmen were owed far too much money and risked going into bankruptcy. They could not be left to suffer because of his father's profligate ways.

Despite his resolve, he huffed out a despondent sigh. He had to marry an heiress. That was the only answer. He tried to take some small solace in the knowledge that he was not the first aristocrat to have to resort to this method to save the family fortune. Nor would he be the first man who had to marry for duty. He would finally be doing just what his father had expected of him when he had first taken a wife.

The old Duke had been furious when Adam had gone against his wishes and not only married a woman with no dowry but had fallen in love with and married the daughter of a tenant farmer. Now he knew why. It wasn't an objection to his beloved Rosalie that had angered his father. It wasn't because the old man was a snob, although there were definitely elements of that. It was because the Duke knew the family was desperate for money.

Well, now Adam would have to do what his father wanted. He watched the scenery pass him by, his mood sinking lower the closer he got to the Hayward estate.

Marriage. It was the last thing he wanted. When Rosalie had been taken from him so early and so cruelly, he had known he would never marry again, and had vowed he would love her until the day he died.

And now, a short five years since her death, he was already being forced to take another bride.

He had married Rosalie for love, and no one would ever replace her in his affections. He still loved her with all of his heart and she never left his thoughts. This marriage was not a complete betrayal of his vow, but it certainly felt like it.

He would do his duty, as would Miss Georgina Hayward. Just like countless couples before them, they would find a way to make this work. And from what Mr Hayward had said, she would make a suitable bride for a man such as himself.

Her father had described her as a dutiful young woman, one who only wanted the best for her family and was honoured to have the opportunity of becoming a duchess. He had said she was amiable, gentle and would make a perfect mother for his three children. If he had to marry again, he could want for nothing better than such a young woman.

His carriage turned a corner and out of the window he spied a maid in a state of some distress. He signalled to the coachman to stop.

As he climbed out of the carriage, Adam told himself he had stopped because it would be wrong to pass by a female in need of help, but deep down he knew there was another reason. He'd welcome any delay if it could put off the coming ordeal, even for a few moments.

'May I be of assistance?' he asked the dishevelled young woman.

'Yes, yes, you can,' she said, standing up and giving him a beaming smile. 'I have to get to the village and I'm afraid I've run out of puff.' She pointed towards the abandoned bicycle.

She did indeed give the impression of someone who had run out of puff. Her cheeks were a bright shade of pink and her strawberry blonde hair, most of which had fallen out of her bun, was stuck to the top of her forehead and neck. Adam also couldn't help noticing she was rather pretty, with dimples on each flushed cheek and a somewhat delightful smile.

But something about this scene was not right. He looked from the maid, who was now brushing down her uniform, to the bicycle, tossed carelessly into the hedgerow, and back to the maid. The shiny black bicycle was new. Could a maid afford such a contraption? Her accent was not what he would expect of a servant, and the way she boldly looked him in the eye was not the usual behaviour of a maid.

And young women did not usually ask strange men for a ride in their carriage, or even speak to men without a formal introduction.

Her uniform restored and her hair tucked back into her cap, she looked back at him. Her smile quivered slightly as he watched her with growing curiosity, and she bobbed a belated curtsey.

'I'd be ever so grateful for your assistance, sir,' she said, her accent suddenly taking on a curious Irish lilt.

Whatever was going on, Adam had neither the time nor the inclination to work it out. She was a young woman, alone in the countryside, and she wanted his help. That was all that really mattered.

He signalled to the open door of the carriage. Her smile returned and she climbed in.

'What of your bicycle?' he asked as she settled herself on the padded leather bench.

'Oh, don't worry about that. Someone will pick that up later.'

Again, it made no real sense, and again it was not Adam's business. He signalled to the coachman and climbed back inside and took his seat on the bench across from her. The carriage was now filled with the delicate scent of lily of the valley. This maid, it appeared, was not averse to helping herself to her mistress's expensive perfume.

The coachman manoeuvred the carriage on the narrow country lane so they could go back to the village. They travelled for a moment in silence, the young maid looking out of the window, still with that pretty smile on her lips.

'May I ask why you need to get to the village with such urgency?' he asked.

The smile faded and she frowned. 'I had to get away from the Hayward family.'

She now had his undivided attention. If something untoward had happened to this young maid at the Haywards' home he was eager to know. The father had seemed like an honourable man, but how a man acted when he was conducting the business of securing a title for his daughter and how he treated his servants could be two very different matters.

'Were you treated badly?'

She nodded rapidly. 'They're terrible people. Tyrants. The things they expect me to do, it's appalling. I'm not a piece of chattel. They don't own me and I won't do it.' She lifted her chin in defiance.

Adam's fists clenched so tightly his nails dug into his flesh. This was an abomination. Servants, particularly young female servants, could be so vulnerable.

'Then you did the right thing in running away.' Adam knew for a young woman in her position, that was all she could do. The law would always be on the side of the master, never the servant. If she had stolen a bicycle so she could flee for her own safety, then in his eyes there was no crime, even if the constabulary might not see it that way.

She leant towards him, as if including him in her conspiracy. 'I plan to run away, as far as I can. I'll take the first train that comes along and hopefully make it all the way to one of those islands at the top of Scotland, or maybe I'll leave the country. No one will ever find me if I run away to America.'

'I believe you need a better plan than that.' He doubted the Haywards would pursue an errant maid all the way to the Shetland Islands or abroad, and it would be unwise for a young woman to travel such a distance unaccompanied. Particularly this young woman, who hadn't even made it to the local village without throwing herself on the mercy of a complete stranger. 'Is there not someone closer at hand with whom you can stay? A family member or a friend?'

She nodded slowly. 'Yes, you're right. I'll take the train to London and hide out with Irene Huntington.'

Adam frowned. 'You know the Duchess of Redcliff?'

She stared at him, her eyes wide, those flushed cheeks turning a deeper shade of pink. 'Well, no, not as such. I mean, well, you know, I worked in her house and—' she shrugged one shoulder '—I know the housekeeper and I'm sure she'll give me employment.'

'That sounds like a sensible idea.'

'Hmm,' was all she said in response, and she looked out of the window, her blushing cheeks now becoming almost scarlet, and the colour moving down to encompass her neck.

Again, it was a peculiar reaction, and again it was none of his business. All he had to do was to make sure she was safely on her way.

The carriage arrived at the station, and he asked her to wait while he bought her a ticket to London. She opened her mouth to object, but he held up his hand to still her words.

He was soon back, with the ticket and some bad news. 'I'm afraid the next train does not leave for another hour.'

'Oh.' She frowned and looked over her shoulder as if expecting to see the Haywards in pursuit. 'Oh, well, never mind. I suppose it won't matter. And thank you so much for buying my ticket. You didn't have to, you know. I do have money.' She patted her pockets and frowned, obviously finding them empty.

He helped her down from the carriage. 'Perhaps we can have a cup of tea in the tearoom while we wait.'

'Oh, are you going to stay with me?' Her face lit up with a pretty smile, and those dimples deepened. She really was too sweet, too pretty and too innocent to be left alone in the world.

'Yes, and perhaps I should send a telegram to the

Duchess of Redcliff so someone can meet you at the station upon your arrival.'

'No, no need,' she said. 'I wouldn't want to put you to any more trouble. Let's just have that cup of tea, shall we?'

With that, she took his arm in a surprisingly familiar manner and led him towards the tearoom, as if taking a gentleman's arm was a perfectly acceptable thing for a maid to do. But her odd behaviour mattered not. He would buy her a cup of tea, put her on the train, perhaps provide her with some money so she could get transport to her new employer's residence, then forget all about her and get back to his real reason for being in Somerset.

'Good morning, sir,' the woman behind the counter said. 'What can I get for yourself and Miss Georgina?'

Adam looked back at the young maid, who was seated at a table and staring out of the window at the travellers and railway workers passing by along the station platform.

'Miss Georgina?' he asked, turning back to the tea lady. 'Are you familiar with my companion?'

'That I am. My sister works up at the Hayward estate. Is Miss Georgina on her way to a fancy dress party or on her way home from one?' She smiled at him, her eyes bright with anticipation as if about to hear an amusing story.

'Yes. She is in fancy dress.' It was all he was prepared to say to the disappointed woman as he placed his coins on the counter then returned to his seat.

Miss Georgina smiled at him. He had been duped, and not just by this so-called escaping maid. He remembered clearly how Mr Hayward had described his daughter.

She was amiable, gentle, would make a perfect mother to his children and was excited about the prospect of marriage to a duke. The man was lying on all counts. Nothing about her behaviour was that of a young lady eager to marry. Quite the reverse.

Thank goodness he had seen the real Miss Georgina Hayward and knew how desperate she was not to wed. Otherwise, they both could have made a terrible mistake. But he had been inadvertently drawn into her strange charade, and that was a situation that needed to be put right immediately.

Chapter Two

This was all going rather well. Georgina decided she should disguise herself as a maid more often. It provided one with so much freedom—she was all but invisible. This gentleman hadn't even asked for her name, which was fortunate because, in her haste to escape, she hadn't thought far enough ahead to come up with an alias. She looked out of the window at the country station, at the people clasping their suitcases and waiting patiently for the train to puff its way around the corner. If anyone on the train should ask, she would say she was Agnes Bull, or perhaps Molly Scunthorpe, or maybe Bertha Ramsbottom.

She looked back as the gentleman took his seat, and wondered whether she should introduce herself now and try out her name. She smiled across the table at him. Her rescuer really was rather dashing, and so handsome, with those dark brown eyes and coal black hair. If she had to be saved by a man, she could think of none better than one with chiselled cheekbones and a strong jawline. It would be better if those sculptured lips smiled on occasion, but perhaps heroes who rescued damsels in distress weren't supposed to smile or laugh.

'As the train is going to be another hour, it might be best if I took you to the next station so you can get a connecting train to London,' he said, his expression still deadly serious.

Georgina was about to say it was no bother to wait, but he was right. The sooner she was out of this village and on the train to London, far away from her family, the better. And if she was being honest, she was rather enjoying her time with her dashing, earnest saviour and was more than happy to prolong her time in his company.

'That would be ever so good of you, kind sir. If it's not too much trouble that I'm putting you to,' she said, remembering to use her new maid's way of speaking.

With no further explanation, he stood up and walked towards the door. She looked over to the counter, where the woman was still preparing their tea. It was all a bit rude, to both her and the tea lady. But now was hardly the time to give him a lesson in manners, so she stood up and dutifully followed him out of the tearoom. And, bad manners aside, what choice did she really have but to follow along? After all, he still had her train ticket and she had foolishly left home without her reticule.

She scowled slightly. Father was, unfortunately, right about *one* thing. She really did need to start thinking things through a bit more carefully. Next time she staged a daring escape she would make sure she had plenty of money for the journey. Then she would not have to rely on the kindness of strange men. She could have sent her own telegram to Irene, and the message would contain no confusing mention of maids, unknown men or the request for employment. But then, if she'd planned ahead, she would not have met this kind and not the least bit strange man. She nodded in satisfaction. It had all worked out in the end and Father was wrong to criticise her yet again.

He strode across to his waiting carriage and opened the door. She waited for him to offer her his hand. No hand was proffered so she clambered inside. He joined her, shut the door and signalled to the coachman. Her knight in shining armour had suddenly become a bit of a grump, but not to worry. She would soon be miles away in London. Away from her rescuer, away from the greedy Duke, away from her family and away from attending yet another insufferable Season.

She gave a little shudder at the thought of the looming Season. If she went into hiding at her friend Irene's London townhouse, she would not endure being placed on display yet again. She would not be subjected to all those down-on-their-luck nobles assessing her flaws and attributes to see whether she was worthy enough to become their bride.

And to think the first Season had started off so promisingly. Her father had pulled strings and called in favours so his daughter could be presented at Court. She had been so excited when she had lined up in her white gown with all those daughters of the aristocracy and taken her curtsey in front of Queen Victoria. She had then expected to be the belle of the ball, that men would be lining up to dance with her. She had expected to have fun flirting with countless handsome men and to be inundated with proposals from love-struck suitors.

Instead, the only men who'd paid her any attention were those everyone knew were in desperate need of money. Yes, they flirted and charmed, but in such a manner she would have to be a halfwit not to see the real reason behind their interest. And even if she had been a half-wit, she would not have been able to ignore a conversation she'd overheard between the Duke of Cromley and his eldest son.

'I don't care if she is the most vacuous woman you've ever met. And if her looks don't appeal to you, then think of the vast fortune she will bring to the family and all we can do with it. Now, ask her to dance again, before one of those other blackguards bags her dowry.'

Georgina had been flabbergasted. She hadn't even wanted to dance with John Cromley, and certainly would not consider marrying him. He was such a bore. And yet he thought she would be flattered by his attentions, just because he would one day become a duke.

After overhearing that outrageous conversation, she had been unsure whether to give Cromley a stern telling off, or to thank him for opening her eyes to what the ball was really about. It was merely a place where men could scrutinise what was on offer that Season so they could make the most advantageous marriage.

Well, if all those men were interested in was her marriage settlement, then she wanted nothing to do with any of them.

She blinked away the annoying tears that had sprung to her eyes and looked out at the scenery. Then she saw a sight that drove out all thoughts of Cromley, Seasons and dowries.

'What?' she gasped as she pointed out of the window. 'We've just passed my bicycle.' She turned in her seat as her abandoned bicycle disappeared from view around a corner. 'We need to turn around. We're going the wrong way. This is not the way to the next village.'

'Perhaps now would be a good time to introduce ourselves,' he said, rather than informing the coachman of his mistake.

'What? Now? Yes, all right. I'm Agnes Ramsbottom. How do you do?'

'No, you're Miss Georgina Hayward and I am Adam Knightly, the Duke of Ravenswood.'

Georgina's lips formed an O shape, but no words came out. He continued to stare at her, those dark brown eyes boring into hers while Georgina racked her brain to come up with an explanation for her behaviour. None came. She lurched forward to pull open the door. She had never tried leaping from a moving carriage before, but desperate times called for desperate measures, and this most decidedly counted as a desperate time.

The handle didn't move. She wriggled it harder. It still didn't move. And neither did the Duke. He sat completely still, his face expressionless, those brown eyes still staring at her without pity.

'You've locked the door. Are you holding me prisoner? What sort of man has a lock on his carriage door?'

'I have a lock on the door to stop my son from trying to climb out of the carriage when it is moving.'

'You have no right to lock me in.'

'I made the decision to do so as it appears you are just as likely to do something foolhardy without thought of the consequences. Just like my son. He, of course, does have the excuse of being only five years old.'

She scowled at him. She had thought him kind and considerate, but he wasn't. He was arrogant, rude and as awful as she'd expected the Duke of Ravenswood to be. Although she hadn't expected him to be so young. What would he be? Late twenties, early thirties? Nor had she thought he'd be so handsome, but none of that mattered, not when he had the audacity to actually hold her captive.

'Stop this carriage now and let me out,' she demanded.

'I will take you home to your parents, where you belong.'

'So you can marry me and get your grubby hands on my dowry?' She looked down at his hands, which were definitely not grubby. In fact, they were rather attractive hands, strong, with long lean fingers.

Her gaze flicked back up to his face and she lifted her chin high. 'Well, that is not going to happen. I am not one of my parents' chattels and I will not marry anyone just because they say so.'

'I'm returning you home to where you will be safe. And you can rest assured I have no intention of marrying you or anyone else against their will.'

'Good,' she stated defiantly. It might have been nice if he'd put up a bit of an argument, but still, she had what she wanted and should be content. 'Now that we've agreed there will be no marriage, you can let me out, and go back to wherever you came from.'

'Dorset.'

'What?'

'That is where I come from.'

'Good, well, go back there. Now.'

'Your parents invited me for the weekend, to meet

you and to see whether a courtship between us would occur. I accepted the invitation. It would be remiss of me not to arrive.'

'But I have no interest in being courted by you or anyone.'

'I am well aware of that. And you will be pleased to know that I too have no interest in a courtship.'

'Why not?' Georgina blurted out, affronted by so immediate a rejection. He wanted a dowry. She had a dowry. Wasn't that all men like him ever saw when they looked at an unmarried heiress? Or did he think himself too handsome, too grand, too superior for the likes of her?

His long, tapered fingers indicated her attire.

She looked down at her dull brown, sack-shaped uniform, which was far from flattering.

'I'm not really a maid, you know. I don't usually dress like this, but I could hardly climb down a drainpipe dressed in a fancy gown, now, could I?'

One eyebrow rose slightly. 'I am now well aware that you are not a maid. But I am also aware that you are... how shall I put this...rather impetuous and indulge in behaviour that is perilous. I have a young son and two impressionable daughters. I need a wife who will be responsible and a good influence on them, not someone who climbs drainpipes.'

Georgina glared at him, although it was hard to deny she was impetuous or that she did, when the occasion demanded, behave perilously. Not when she was sitting across from him dressed as a maid, having just admitted to him the manner in which she'd escaped her home.

'But I come with an enormous dowry,' she said instead, her words dripping with sarcasm. 'That's usually enough for most men to overlook my long list of flaws.'

'I'm not most men.'

Georgina could not argue with that. He was definitely more attractive than any man she had met before. And more something else. Manly? Commanding? Something she couldn't quite put her finger on. But, whatever it was, it did not excuse his rude dismissal of her.

'But you don't deny you were after my dowry.' He had criticised her, now she was determined to show him up for the sort of man he really was. One who had no right to look down his nose at her, albeit a rather elegant, imperious nose.

'No, I don't deny it.'

Georgina frowned. How could one argue with a man when he agreed with one?

'Well, I think it's appalling to marry someone just for their money,' she said. That was what she would focus on—self-righteous indignation—and not the fact that he did not appear to be the slightest bit insulted by her accusation.

'I agree.'

'You do not. You already said you were after my dowry.'

'I agree that it is wrong to marry just for money.' He huffed out a deep sigh. 'Unfortunately, my financial position means I have to marry a woman who brings with her a substantial amount of money.' His jaw tightened, although his exasperation no longer seemed to be with her.

'Why? I suppose you gambled away all your wealth and now you want to do the same with mine.'

He flinched at the accusation. Good. She had hit the

nail on the head, as they said, and shown him up for the man he really was.

'You're right that the family fortune was gambled away, but not by me. I have never entered a gambling den, attended a racecourse or shuffled a pack of cards in my life.'

She didn't doubt it. He was far too humourless for that.

'It was my father who was the gambler, and as a result I inherited a dukedom collapsing under the weight of crushing debts, one carrying mortgages more than ten times the size of the estates' annual incomes.'

'Well, why don't you just sell them?' she fired back, determined not to feel sorry for him. 'Wouldn't that be the decent thing to do, rather than marrying for money?'

'That is exactly what I would do if legal restrictions did not mean no part of my inheritance can be sold and it all has to stay in the family. I inherited debt, but I do not want to pass on that burden to my son, nor do I wish to put at risk the futures of the tenant farmers, whose families have lived on the estates for generations, by selling off the land on which they live.'

'Then get a loan from someone, a bank or something.' Georgina lifted her chin higher, pleased that she knew about such things. 'That's what Father always does when he starts a new business venture.'

'Do you not think I have tried?'

She shrugged. Money, banks, finance… She knew such things existed, but that was the limit of her knowledge. Arguing with her father for an increase in her allowance was the closest she ever came to such matters. But the Duke's money troubles did not mean she would forgive him, although whether she was still annoyed with him for seeking an heiress or rejecting her, she was no longer entirely sure.

'Banks lend to your father because his businesses are viable propositions that will make them a good return on their investment. They do not loan to dukes who already have enormous debts throughout the land, whose estates are unprofitable because they are still using farming methods that have changed little since the Middle Ages, whose home is in desperate need of repair, whose...' He sighed loudly. 'No bank or financial institution will lend money under such conditions. So I am forced to marry an heiress who is desirous of a title.'

'Oh...' was all Georgina could say.

'But, as I am to marry again, I also require a wife with whom I am compatible, who is content with this arrangement, and one who will make a good mother for my three children.'

'Oh,' she repeated.

'Your father assured me you would be agreeable to this arrangement, but you are correct. You are not a chattel and I will not marry anyone against their will.'

'Hmm,' was all she could say to that. Then she turned back to him as another thought occurred to her. 'So how do you intend to find your perfect heiress now that I've failed to live up to your expectations?'

He hissed out a sigh through clenched teeth. 'I will do what every other unmarried man in search of a bride does. I will attend the Season and see who is available.'

His doleful expression suggested he found the thought of attending the Season as pleasurable as she did.

'They're awful, aren't they?' Georgina said, dread of what was to come driving out her irritation with him.

'I have never attended, so can't say.'

'Really? But how did you meet your first wife?'

'It wasn't during the Season,' he said, turning to look out of the window as if to inform her that the manner in which he'd met his wife was none of her concern.

'Well, you're about to discover just how truly horrible the Season can be. Everyone dresses in their finest clothes, all being so terribly polite, while at the same time manoeuvring and manipulating to catch the man with the highest title or the lady with the biggest dowry.' She gave a mock shudder to emphasise the horror.

He did not respond nor did he look happy.

'If it's any consolation, while you're in search of your heiress I'll be fending off men after my fortune.' She frowned at the thought. 'Men who don't care about my countless faults or whether I want to marry them or not.'

He still made no response but continued staring out of the window. Apparently, her problems were no consolation at all. Well, he was soon going to discover for himself how ruthless mothers and debutantes could be, particularly when there was a handsome unwed duke for the taking.

She smiled to herself as a wonderful source of amusement occurred to her. 'I could help you,' she said.

He didn't answer, merely turned to look at her, his eyebrows raised, as if he couldn't possibly see any way in which she would be helpful.

'If you tell me all the qualities you are looking for in your heiress, I can let you know which young lady possesses those qualities. Believe me, debutantes can be very deceptive when they're looking for a husband. They'll all pretend to be the perfect bride for you, until they get you up the aisle. Only then will you discover what a terrible mistake you've made. Oh, the stories I could tell you. There was one young lady who—'

'I believe I am perfectly capable of seeing through deception.'

'Really? You thought that I was a maid who needed your help.' She sent him a satisfied smile.

He merely hmphed in response, then drew in a deep breath and exhaled slowly. 'And if you do help me, what will you be expecting in return?'

An image of the Duke taking her in his arms, holding her close against him and kissing her long and slowly flashed into her mind, causing heat to explode onto her cheeks.

'Nothing. Nothing at all,' she burst out to cover her embarrassment.

'Nothing?'

'It will provide me with a diversion from the tedium of another Season,' she said, her words tumbling over each other. 'Do you know how boring the Season can get, especially when you've attended five, like I have?'

He made no response, but signalled for the coachman to stop at the large gold and black gates, still bearing the Viscount's crest, that led to her family home. 'After your own deception, it might be best if you don't arrive home in my carriage. I suspect that, along with your attire, would be difficult to explain to your parents.'

'Yes, right. It will be our little secret.'

Before he could respond, she climbed out of the carriage and rushed down the pathway, hoping he had not noticed her burning cheeks and had no inkling that a decidedly inappropriate and unwanted image had crashed into her mind completely uninvited.

Chapter Three

Adam watched Miss Georgina dart to the nearest tree in the row of elms lining the long path that led to the house, peek out, then dash to the next one. She continued this bizarre behaviour until she reached the edge of the house. Then she bent low, scuttled around the side of the building and disappeared from view.

She really was an unusual young lady. But she was also right. He was hopelessly ill-prepared for the Season. The ease with which she had fooled him showed just how easy it would be for any young woman with an eye on his title to deceive him. He'd had his suspicions when he'd found her on the side of the road but had never for one moment thought she would be a wealthy heiress in disguise, and that it would be *him* she was fleeing from.

And that wasn't the only worrying aspect of their encounter. Despite her being wholly unsuitable as a wife for him or a mother to his children, he could not deny that there was something about her he found damnably attractive.

But that was not enough. He needed a wife who had a level of maturity—someone quiet, who would unobtrusively fit in with his household and cause him no disruption. Hopefully, he would meet a young lady who genuinely possessed these qualities early in the Season and his search would be a short one.

But how was he going to ensure that he did find such a bride? If he could be attracted by a young lady who was so patently unsuitable, did that mean he was in danger of having his head turned by any pretty young thing with an endearing smile, and of forgetting what he really needed in a wife?

Perhaps it was merely that he had been five long years without a woman in his life. That too, unfortunately, made him vulnerable. Loath as he was to admit it, perhaps her assistance in his quest was not quite so ridiculous.

He waited a few moments longer to ensure she had made it inside safely, then signalled for the coachman to take them up to the house. This was going to be an absurd encounter. Everyone was going to be deceiving each other. The Season hadn't even begun and already he had encountered a disheartening level of what Miss Hayward described as manoeuvring and manipulation.

The three-storey house loomed up before him as he travelled up the driveway. The magnificent ochre stone building dominated the landscape and rivalled the best in England. Mr Hayward might have lied about his daughter, but he had not been deceptive about the extent of his wealth.

The carriage pulled up in front of the house and Mr and Mrs Hayward and a young man in his mid-twenties emerged from the grand entrance and waited under the portico. The parents presented the picture of contented wealth. Mr Hayward's rotund shape and florid complexion suggested a man who liked to indulge, or overindulge, in the finer things in life. His wife's ornate gown and the jewels bedecking her neck, ears and wrists further emphasised this impression.

Unlike most wealthy families, who had accumulated the family jewels over many generations, Mrs Hayward's would have been purchased from the considerable profits of her husband's businesses, which were believed to include shipping lines, railways, mines and manufacturing concerns throughout the land.

Adam drew in a deep, resigned breath and descended from his carriage, determined to get this charade over and done with as quickly as possible.

'Welcome to our humble home, Your Grace,' Mr Hayward said, giving Adam's hand a hearty shake. 'May I present my wife and my son, Thomas?'

Mrs Hayward gave a low curtsey, while Thomas smirked as if enjoying an amusing private joke, before shaking his hand.

'I'm so sorry Georgina is not here to greet you,' Mrs Hayward said as she took his arm and led him into the house. 'She's a bit shy and she really did want to make an extra effort with her appearance. You know what young ladies are like when they are courting.'

Adam merely nodded in response to these outrageous lies.

'Not that she really needs to,' Mrs Hayward said with a small, false laugh. 'My daughter is such a pretty young thing, even if I do say so myself.'

That was something Adam could not dispute. She was indeed pretty.

'And she's so excited to meet you,' she added. 'She had to try on every dress in her wardrobe in an attempt to find the perfect gown.'

Including a maid's uniform, Adam could have added.

'She is so nervous about making a good first impression,' Mrs Hayward continued as they strolled down the entranceway, lined with marble statues the previous owner must have purchased during his grand tour of Europe.

'I don't know what she has to be nervous about,' Thomas said, still smirking. 'Georgina never fails to make a memorable first impression.'

Mrs Hayward frowned briefly at her son, then smiled at Adam as she led him through to the drawing room overlooking the gardens.

'Dorset is lovely at this time of year,' Mrs Hayward said, abruptly changing the subject as she seated herself on the divan with much rustling of skirts.

Adam stifled a sigh. He had forgotten that such social visits required small talk. It was an artform he had never perfected. Rosalie and he had been content to remain in the countryside and take no part in the social whirl the aristocracy enjoyed so much. Now he was going to have to endure an entire Season of commentaries on the weather and endless, mindless gossip.

'Indeed it is,' he responded. Mrs Hayward smiled with delight as if he had just made a witty riposte.

'We visited the Brookshires in Dorset last year,' she said, reminding Adam that name-dropping was another essential aspect of social chit-chat. 'Lord and Lady

Brookshire are such good friends of ours, aren't they, dear?' she added, turning to her husband.

'What? Oh, yes, the Brookshires. They've got some very productive land I was interested in acquiring.'

Mrs Hayward frowned at her husband, then smiled at Adam. 'Oh, let's not talk about business. That's not what this weekend is about.'

Adam could have informed her that business was exactly what this weekend was about. The Haywards were using their daughter to advance their position in Society, and he was in the market for an heiress. It was the depressing truth, but one none of them were going to openly admit to.

The door opened and Miss Hayward entered.

He stood up, surprised by the transformation—and by his reaction. She'd made a pretty maid, but now she was dressed as an elegant, sophisticated young woman, wearing a flowing pale blue lacy dress, with a dark blue sash showing off her slim waist. Her full breasts and rounded hips had been disguised in her shapeless maid's uniform, but they were on display now, as if for his admiration. He knew he shouldn't, but he couldn't help his eyes from sweeping up and down her curvaceous body.

'May I present my daughter, Miss Georgina Hayward?' Mr Hayward said.

She lowered her eyes and performed a low curtsey. 'Your Grace,' she said in a quiet manner.

He wasn't sure why she was indulging in this charade, but if it was to prove her point as to how easily he could be deceived, she was achieving her goal. If he had not already met her, he would have thought her perfect and exactly as her father described—gentle, amiable and content with the idea of such a marriage.

'Now, don't be shy,' Mrs Hayward said to the young woman who Adam suspected had never been shy in her life. 'Come over here and sit beside His Grace.'

Her eyes still lowered, she rose from her curtsey, crossed the room and sat down on the divan. He looked at the Haywards. Both parents were smiling with delight at this performance while Thomas's smile was that of someone watching an amusing play.

'We were just discussing Dorset,' Mrs Hayward said as the men took their seats. 'I believe your family has resided there for many generations.'

'Yes,' Adam responded, somewhat distracted as he watched Georgina's demure performance. 'The Knightly family has lived there since Tudor times, but the sixth Duke of Ravenswood extended the house considerably in the early Georgian period.'

'Did you hear that, Georgina?' Mrs Hayward said. 'A family that can trace its history back to the Tudor period.'

Miss Hayward's eyes remained lowered. 'Yes, Mama,' she said in a barely audible voice.

'Georgian period?' Mr Hayward added. 'I imagine a house built back then would need a lot of upkeep. This house is also Georgian, and when I think about the amount I've spent on it to make it liveable, it would probably have been cheaper to tear it down and build the thing from the ground up.'

Adam merely nodded his assent as Mr Hayward reminded him of yet another reason why he needed to marry an heiress.

'Mama, perhaps I could show His Grace around the estate,' Miss Hayward said, and Adam had to lean forward to hear her quiet words.

'Excellent idea,' Mrs Hayward responded enthusiastically. 'It will give you two a chance to get to know each other better, and His Grace can tell you all about his estate in Dorset.'

Miss Hayward stood up, her eyes still lowered, and glided across the room and out of the door, leaving Adam with no choice but to follow on behind. The moment the door closed behind them, she raced down the hallway and out into the gardens, as if fleeing from armed guards, leaving him following in her wake.

'I believe you can drop this act now,' Adam said when he caught up to her on the gravel pathway.

'Not yet,' she whispered. 'They'll be watching out of the drawing room window. We need to look as if we are complete strangers.'

Adam turned to look over his shoulder to see that all three Haywards were indeed watching them.

'Don't turn around,' she said in a low voice. 'We don't want them to think we're talking about them.'

Adam released an exasperated sigh, but did as she commanded, and followed her down the path and into the formal garden, his irritation at this game-playing continuing to grow.

'There, we're out of sight now,' she said and gave a little laugh. 'These topiaries will hide us from their prying eyes.'

'You don't think you're overdoing the meek and mild act somewhat?' he said as he indicated a stone bench overlooking the garden.

'Nonsense,' she stated in a manner that was neither meek nor mild. 'I was merely following all the instructions I was given at Miss Halliwell's Finishing School for Refined Young Ladies. Miss Halliwell was of the opinion that a young lady could never, ever be too meek or too mild.'

'Miss Halliwell, whoever she might be, never saw *that* performance.'

She laughed as if he had made a joke, rather than stating a fact.

'Surely your parents will know it was all pretence,' he said as he sat down beside her.

'Of course they will. But what do they care, as long as I catch a duke? They'll just be grateful to see that the expense of sending me to Halliwell's to turn me into a proper, refined young lady was money well spent.'

'I'd hate to think what you were like before you were sent off to finishing school and became proper and refined.'

She laughed again as if he had made another joke, which he hadn't.

'You can rest assured that Halliwell's had no effect on me whatsoever, except for teaching me how to *pretend* to be a proper young lady when it suits. But it was worth every penny my father spent as I met my closest friends there, Amelia, Irene and Emily. It was thanks to them that I survived the ordeal.' She looked over at him. 'Irene is the Duchess of Redcliff. That's who I was planning on fleeing to in order to escape…' She shrugged her shoulders and smiled. 'Well, to escape you.'

'I take it the Duchess of Redcliff also failed to become a proper, refined young lady.'

'Yes, she was as hopeless as I was.' She laughed as if this was a great achievement. 'But oh, the four of us had such fun. You can't imagine the things we got up to.'

Adam would rather not.

'We called it Hell's Final Sentence for Rebellious Young Ladies and made a pact that we would continue to rebel, no matter what.'

'A pact that you have obviously managed to adhere to.'

'I have,' she said, not registering Adam's sarcasm.

'So how long do you think we have to remain out here, before we can agree that we are completely mismatched and I can return home?'

'A few minutes more should do it. So, what are you going to tell my father?'

'That we have no wish to marry.'

She turned on the bench and grasped his arm. 'No, don't say that. Then I'll be subjected to a boring lecture about not making enough of an effort, and about how I'm getting old and time is running out, and on and on and on. It's been five Seasons. Five.' The grip on his arm tightened. 'I'm about to start my sixth, and still no marriage prospects. Father will be unbearable if he thinks I let a duke slip through my fingers, and as for Mother, well…' She threw her hands up in the air. 'Please don't get me into any more trouble than I already am.'

'What do you expect me to say?'

She thought for a moment, then gave him a wicked smile. 'Tell him I'm far too passive for your taste. That you want a wife with a bit of pluck. That will teach them.'

'You want me to lie to them?'

She raised her eyebrows and smiled as if she had caught him out in a deliberate deception. 'Don't try and tell me you're incapable of lying. I know you're not because you lied to me!'

'When?'

'When you tricked me into getting back in your carriage. You said you were taking me to the next village, but you were really delivering me back into my parents' clutches and forcing me to endure all this.'

'I was doing it for your own protection. Anything could happen to a young lady alone without a chaperon.'

'Yes, she could get abducted by a duke and held captive in his carriage.'

'I was not... I did not—'

She patted his arm. 'I'm just joking. But just as you meant no harm in lying to me, there will be no harm in lying to my parents. After all, they've been lying to you.'

He nodded slowly. He didn't like it, but she did make a good point. It was not in his nature to tell lies but, given the absurdity of this entire encounter, and the way Mr and Mrs Hayward had contrived to pull the wool over his eyes, there would be a certain satisfaction in letting them think their deception had the opposite to the intended effect.

'So, have you thought about my offer to help you navigate the Season?' she said, obviously assuming the question of what he would say to her father was now settled and he would do exactly as she wanted.

'Yes, and I can see there is some merit in your suggestion.'

'Oh, goodie.' She clapped her hands. 'Let's start

straight away by listing some of the qualities you *do* want in a bride.'

Let's not, Adam wanted to say, but knew that such objections would fall on deaf ears.

'As I said, I need a wife who is happy with the arrangement, and one who will make a kind and loving mother to my children.'

'Right. Kind, loving, happy.' She ticked them off on her fingers. 'What about intelligent?'

'Well, yes, I suppose so.'

She gave him an assessing look. 'Although most men prefer a young lady who agrees with them rather than one who has a mind of her own. When they say a woman is intelligent, that is usually what they mean.'

She gave him a pointed look, and before he could contradict her claim she continued. 'Charming?'

'I don't know what that means.'

'Well, you know, flirtatious, someone who laughs at your jokes, who flatters you, that sort of thing.'

'I do not make jokes.'

'No, you don't, do you?' She laughed as if that in itself was a joke.

'And I have no interest in being flattered or flirted with.'

Her eyebrows drew together and she gave him a shrewd look. 'I suspect you are now the one being deceptive. All men like to be flirted with and flattered.'

'Not this man.'

'Hmm, we'll see. So, a good conversationalist?'

'Again, I don't know what that means.'

'Someone you can talk to.'

'We're talking now. Does that make you a good conversationalist?'

'No. I failed conversation skills when I was at Halliwell's.'

'How could you possibly fail that? You hardly stop talking long enough to catch your breath.'

She smiled at him as if mistakenly believing he had given her another compliment. 'I failed because I'm hopeless at talking to shrubs.'

'Shrubs?'

'Yes, at Halliwell's Hell our lessons in good conversation skills involved walking around the garden, stopping at each shrub and making polite conversation. We had to come up with a different topic with each shrub. That would prove we could circulate at a social occasion and engage every man in interesting conversation.'

He stared at her in disbelief. 'So if a young lady asks me if I get watered frequently enough or enquires as to how much fertiliser the gardener spreads around my roots I'll know she's a graduate of Halliwell's.'

She laughed and leant in towards him. 'I thought you said you didn't make jokes.'

He hadn't lied. He didn't make jokes, but he had to admit it was rather nice to make her laugh. And it *was* a rather pleasant sound. Rosalie was the last woman he had made laugh, and there hadn't been anything worth laughing about since her death.

'I have no idea what sort of woman would make the ideal wife,' he said, bringing all joking to an end. 'As I said, I need an heiress. All that matters is she has no qualms about such a marriage, that she will be kind to my children, and she will be someone with whom I have a sufficient degree of compatibility.'

'Hmm, when it comes to qualities, that is rather vague. Perhaps we should discuss what flaws you want to avoid. We already know you don't want impetuousness or a young woman who takes risks.'

Adam cringed slightly at his bad manners. 'Miss Hayward, I meant no offence in what I said.'

'I know that. You were just being honest and I was just teasing.' She gave another carefree laugh. 'Maybe that's something we should add to the list. You don't want a young lady who teases you.'

Adam had no answer to that claim.

'Although you might have to get used to a bit of teasing during the Season. But don't worry, most young ladies know how to do so in a manner that flatters you, or flatters them, or ideally both of you.'

He huffed out another sigh. 'Once again, I have no idea what you are talking about.'

She gave him an appraising look. 'Perhaps you need a lesson or two. If a young lady ever criticises herself, you have to immediately tell her how wrong she is.'

'So, I should tell you that you're not impetuous, that you don't have a mind of your own and your behaviour is cautious and considered.'

'I can see you need a lot more help than I first thought,' she said, her mock frown showing she was amused rather than disapproving. 'No, if I said, *Oh, the other young ladies at this ball are so much prettier than me,*' she said in a coy voice with much fluttering of eyelashes. 'Then you should say, *No, Miss Hayward, there is none prettier than you,*' she added in a deep, somewhat pompous tone.

'No, Miss Hayward, there is none prettier than you.'

She placed her hand on his arm and laughed. 'It might be better if you said it as if you meant it.'

Adam thought he *had* said it as if he meant it. She was indeed a pretty woman and seemed to be getting prettier the more time he spent in her company. She had a delightful, musical laugh, a vivacious personality, and when she smiled, which was frequently, the dimples that appeared in each cheek were enchanting.

'If that's the best you can do, it might be better to avoid flattery,' she continued. 'And I suspect it won't matter what you say and do. You're an eligible duke. That is all anyone will see.' She gave a small sigh. 'You're a bit like me in that regard. No one ever really sees me, or cares about getting to know me. All they see when they look at me is my marriage settlement.'

'That is surely not true. I'm sure men are attracted to you for many other reasons.'

She gave one of those tinkling laughs. 'That was much better. You are a quick learner. Although perhaps you should have said, *I'm sure men are attracted to you for your beauty and wit,*' she added, once more adopting that rather pompous tone that sounded nothing like him.

'But I mean what I said,' she continued. 'When young ladies talk to you, they'll all be imagining what it will be like to be a duchess. They'll be picturing themselves at the very pinnacle of Society and being able to lord it over their friends and family.'

'That most certainly is not the sort of woman I want.

I do not want a woman with pretensions. I do not want to marry a woman who cares only about becoming a duchess, one who is mercenary.'

Her big blue eyes grew wide. 'If you don't want a woman who is desperate to advance her position in Society then I think you're about to join the wrong game. And as for mercenary…' She tilted her head and raised her eyebrows, as if she needed to say no more on that subject.

Adam huffed out a loud breath. 'Yes, all right. I will no doubt be the most mercenary man present.'

'It's all so wrong, isn't it?' she said with a deep sigh. 'Was your first marriage a love match?'

As if a physical weight had descended on him, Adam's shoulders grew heavy. 'It was,' he said quietly, as if talking to himself. 'I loved her more than life itself, and yet she was taken from me. But before that happened, I vowed to her that I would stay faithful to my love for her till the day I die.'

He closed his eyes, remembering Rosalie's beautiful face, her smile and her laughter.

He felt a hand placed lightly on his arm, reminding him of Georgina's presence. Had he really spoken of Rosalie? He never spoke of the woman he loved to anyone, and yet he had mentioned their love to this flighty young girl who meant nothing to him.

'I'm sorry,' she said quietly.

'I believe we should return to the house now,' he said, standing up and bringing this inappropriate conversation to an abrupt end. 'We have had sufficient time to convince your parents that we have become acquainted.'

'As you wish,' she said, taking his hand and standing up.

They commenced walking arm in arm back to the house in silence. 'So what do you plan to say to my father?' she asked, her voice regaining its usual bubbly sound.

'I will make sure he is left with no illusion that there could ever be a marriage between the two of us, and that it is pointless to try and change my mind. Then I will inform him that I plan to leave immediately.'

'Oh,' she gasped, presumably in response to his stern manner and not his compliance with her plan.

Why was he speaking to her in this manner? It was not this young woman's fault that she was so full of life, joy and vitality. Nor was it her fault that Rosalie's life had been cut short. He had no right to be so terse with her. The fault for Rosalie's death lay with one person and one person only. Him.

'Well, I'd appreciate it if you didn't say anything about the maid's uniform, the drainpipe escape or any of that,' she said.

He nodded. 'I will do everything in my power to convince your father you did your best to capture my heart and you are not to blame.'

'Thank you,' she said, but her gratitude did nothing to assuage his guilt over his terse reaction to the mention of his beloved Rosalie.

They turned the corner, out of the sanctuary of the formal garden and back onto the gravel path.

'Right, no more laughter, no more jokes, no more teasing,' she said. 'We want them to think that we had nothing to talk about and spent the entire time in an uncomfortable silence.'

Adam was indeed feeling uncomfortable, but would have difficulty explaining to Miss Hayward or even to himself, why that should be.

Chapter Four

'Did you have a pleasant walk?' Mrs Hayward asked as they entered the drawing room.

Adam merely bowed his assent and remained standing as Miss Hayward took her seat beside her mother, her eyes lowered in that absurd manner. He knew she was playing a game with her parents, just as she seemed to turn everything into a game. But he was not prepared to remain in this house a moment longer to be part of the entertainment.

'Mr Hayward, may I have a word with you?'

The mother's smile grew wider as she took her daughter's hand, while her husband stood, pulled down his jacket, squared his shoulders self-importantly, then ushered Adam out of the room.

'My study would be the best place for this conversation,' Mr Hayward said, escorting Adam down the hallway. 'I've got a rather nice French brandy I've just bought and suspect now will be the perfect occasion to open it.'

Adam said nothing until they were behind the closed

doors of the book-lined study. Mr Hayward sat in a large leather chair and indicated that Adam should take the other one. He declined the offer and remained standing.

'Regretfully, I will not be courting your daughter.'

Mr Hayward sprang to his feet. 'Why not?' Then he sank back into his chair, his face the picture of despair. 'What did she do now? What did she say?'

'She did nothing wrong.' Adam could say that, under the right circumstances, with the right man, Miss Hayward would make a perfect wife, and perhaps they should let her just be herself so she could find a man compatible with an impetuous imp who loved to enjoy life.

'Then why?' Mr Hayward looked up at him, his eyes beseeching.

'I'm afraid she is somewhat too passive and demure,' he said, inwardly cringing at his lie, even if it was a lie that would save Miss Hayward from a reprimand. 'I have a rumbustious five-year-old son who needs a mother, one who is energetic, even feisty, and two daughters who would easily get the better of such a reserved and docile young lady.'

Mr Hayward flinched as if he had been struck. Adam suspected he was desperately wanting to tell him that few young ladies were more energetic or feisty than his daughter, but that would require admitting he had lied in his initial description of his daughter, and her prim and proper behaviour had been designed to deceive him.

'Perhaps over the weekend you will come to see there is more to my daughter than you first thought,' he said. This was becoming embarrassing. The man was actually pleading. 'I'm sure you'll find that Georgina is more than a match for even the most unruly child.'

Adam did not doubt that, but it was hardly the point. He didn't want to marry her. She didn't want to marry him. That was the end of any discussion. He had stayed long enough. To stay any longer would be a trial for all concerned.

'I believe it will be best if you give my apologies to Miss Hayward and your wife.' Adam knew that was somewhat impolite, but for all concerned, including himself, it would be best to leave immediately.

'Are you sure I can't tempt you to stay?' Mr Hayward said with a note of desperation. 'I still have that French brandy.'

'I thank you, but no.'

He bowed to the older man, who had crumpled in on himself in his large leather chair, then headed out of the house and called for his coachman to take him away from this estate as quickly as the horses would allow.

Georgina's father entered the drawing room and slumped into the nearest chair.

'It didn't take you long to see off another one,' Tommy said with a look of unbridled glee. 'You're getting ever more efficient at this, Georgie. So what did you do or say to send this one packing?'

Her father glared at his son. 'This is no laughing matter, Thomas. She's twenty-three, for goodness' sake. She'll be turning twenty-four during the coming Season. I had hoped by marrying her off to the Duke we'd be saved the humiliation of escorting her to yet another

Season. If she doesn't make a suitable match soon...'
He sighed and placed his head in his hands.

Georgina almost felt sorry for her father. Almost.

'I believe we have different definitions on what makes a suitable match, Father,' she said, stopping herself from feeling pity for a man who continually thrust her in front of men who anyone with any sense could see would make terrible husbands.

Her father looked over at her through his spread fingers, then dropped his hands and sat up straight. 'We have indulged you far too much, my girl. All we ask in return for all that we have given you is for you to make a suitable marriage to a titled man.'

Georgina matched his glaring look and ramrod posture. 'Why can't Tommy be the sacrificial lamb? Why isn't he being forced to marry a titled lady?'

Her father exhaled loudly and shook his head slowly. 'How many times do I have to tell you? Because if he marries a titled lady, nothing will change. He'll just get a wife and it will make no difference whatsoever to this family. If you married the Duke you would become a duchess and your children would all have titles.'

He scowled in Georgina's direction. 'I would have preferred it if he didn't have a son so my grandson would be a duke one day, but at least we'd have a title in the family.' He shook his head and huffed out a loud sigh through flared nostrils. 'After five Seasons and no takers, we're hardly in a position to be fussy, and at least my grandchildren would have titles.' He lifted his nose into the air. 'That would be part of my legacy.'

Georgina pouted. He was right. Not in his assertion that she should marry a titled man, but that she had heard similar lectures many times before, and frankly it was getting boring. But the other part of his argument was completely ridiculous. Surely his legacy was that he had made bundles and bundles of money. And it wasn't as if Society excluded them. Countless aristocrats attended the Hayward balls. Although she had to admit that was probably because they were the most lavish of the Season. But still, she did not see why she had to be sacrificed for her father's ambitions.

He walked over to the sideboard and poured himself a brandy from the crystal decanter. 'I have been very patient with you, Season after Season, but by the end of this Season you will be married, or else.'

She increased her pouting, while Tommy scoffed at the threat that had been made many times before.

'I mean it, my girl. It's humiliating enough having to drag you to your sixth Season. If you are not married to a titled man by the end of this one, we will be a laughing stock. I have never allowed anyone in Society to laugh at me, and I'm not about to start now. Do you hear me?'

Georgina tried not to laugh as Tommy rolled his eyes.

'Well?'

'Yes, Papa,' she said in her little-girl voice that had won him over so many times before.

'You still haven't told us how she managed to see this one off so quickly,' Tommy said, ignoring his father's wrath and smirking in anticipation of a tale of outlandish misbehaviour. 'Did you do that trick of eating a raw onion?' He looked around the room as if their parents would share his amusement. 'Remember when she did that to Lord Snidley, then breathed onion breath all over him until the poor man was fighting back the tears?'

Her father downed his glass of brandy and poured himself another.

'Or did she try the method she used with the Earl of Granston—?'

'He said she was too passive, too docile, too reserved,' her father interrupted and knocked back another brandy.

Tommy and her mother turned fully in their chairs to look at her with matching expressions of wide-eyed surprise, then Tommy burst out laughing.

'That's a new one, Georgie,' he said, wiping away tears of mirth.

'I behaved in exactly the manner you told me to, Father,' Georgina said, trying to stop herself from smiling and ruining her look of self-righteous indignation. It wasn't entirely a lie. She *had* behaved in that manner in front of her parents.

Her father puffed out his cheeks and released a loud sigh of exasperation. 'Well, it seems this time I was wrong. You should have just been yourself. The Duke doesn't want someone quiet and demure. He wants… well, he wants someone more like the way you usually are.'

Georgina knew that was not the truth either, but if that was what her father thought, who was she to disagree with him?

'You mean he wants someone who is rude and impertinent,' Tommy added.

'Don't be ridiculous,' her father said, glaring at his son. 'He wants a wife who will be a good mother to his young son, and that means someone with a bit of a spark.'

'Georgie has certainly got that,' Tommy said. 'Remember how she continued to box my ears until I got too tall for her to reach. And I've never seen anyone climb a tree the way she can.' He sent her a sly look. 'And I suspect she could still climb down a drainpipe or two if she had to.'

'I doubt if those are the qualities the Duke is looking for in a bride,' her father said, slumping back down in his chair and gripping the crystal glass in his plump hand. 'But it hardly matters what he wants. He's gone and has said she is not the one for him.'

'I wouldn't be so hasty, dear,' Georgina's mother said, smiling and looking strangely like the family's cat, Puffy, after he'd consumed a large bowl of cream. 'I don't believe the Duke is a lost cause.'

'He said he didn't want to marry me,' Georgina stated. 'He left the house. Didn't stay for the weekend. I think that is conclusive evidence that he has no interest in me whatsoever.'

'Nonsense,' her mother said, sweeping her hand in the air as if brushing away all Georgina's statements of fact. 'I saw the way he looked at you when you entered the room. Mothers do not miss such things. Cupid's dart went straight to his heart. The man is smitten.'

Everyone in the room stared at Georgina's mother as if she had lost her senses, while she continued to do her impression of Puffy at his most self-satisfied.

Georgina had not seen the look her mother was alluding to as she had kept her eyes demurely lowered, but nothing about the Duke's behaviour suggested an attraction. Quite the opposite. He had given every impression of being irritated with her, especially when she'd ventured to ask about his wife. He had shuffled her back inside as quickly as he could. Then he was gone.

It was tempting to inform her mother of all this, and that when they'd met in the drawing room they had only been pretending they had never seen each other before. In the unlikely event that her mother was right and he had looked at her as if he found her attractive, that would explain it. He'd been pretending, and obviously doing it rather well. That was something else she needed to thank him for, along with expressing her gratitude for telling her father she was too docile.

No, the Duke was not attracted to her. He most certainly would not have had fantasies of kissing her. Unlike her, he would not have wondered what it was like to be taken in his arms, to taste his sensuous lips. No, he would have had no such thoughts.

'The only thing that put off the Duke was your silly act, Georgina,' her mother continued.

'I behaved exactly as you always said I should,' she said, rekindling her mock outrage while trying to dampen a peculiar, irrational hope that her mother was right. 'I followed all the lessons I learnt at Halliwell's, to the letter.'

'Well, yes, and your father and I appreciate the effort you made, but in this instance I believe it would have been better if you had just been yourself. If you had, I suspect the Duke would have found you irresistible.'

The foolish hope deep within her was further inflamed, before Georgina remembered that she had already been herself in front of the Duke, and that was the person he didn't want to marry, not the meek and mild Georgina.

'When you next meet the Duke just be yourself,' her mother said, while her father and Tommy looked on in disbelief.

'Are you sure that's a good idea, my dear?' her father said quietly, as if being gentle with a person who had lost their reason.

'Well, perhaps don't be completely yourself. Maybe a slightly muted version, but definitely not meek and mild.'

Her mother stood up and began pacing the room, while the three seated Haywards' heads moved as one, following her progress.

'This could all work to our advantage,' she said, pausing and tapping her chin. 'We know he doesn't want meek and mild. If I tell all the other mothers that he rejected Georgina because she's too feisty and he prefers a more docile young woman, then they'll all make their daughters act in an exaggeratedly demure manner. You'll have no competition.'

Georgina decided now was not the time to point out the Duke did not want a feisty young woman. Not when keeping silent meant she would be given permission to act exactly as she wished. Not that she really needed permission. She would do so regardless, but at least if she misbehaved this Season she would not be subjected to endless, boring lectures on how a young lady should behave if she wished to find a husband. This was all working out rather splendidly and boded well for an entertaining Season.

Well done, Your Grace.

'If Georgie suddenly turns from Miss Meekness into Miss Mischievous, don't you think the Duke will notice?' Tommy asked, still smiling as if he found this all to be an entirely amusing diversion.

'Nonsense,' her mother stated. 'Men turn into imbeciles when they're attracted to a young woman. He won't notice a thing.'

It sounded unlikely, but what would Georgina know? No man had ever been attracted to her, including the Duke, although she had had many a man attracted to her dowry, including, unfortunately, the Duke.

'But he has already said he doesn't want to marry her,' Tommy added.

Her mother shook her head, then looked at Georgina, her eyes growing wide, as if to say, *See? Men, they really are imbeciles, including your brother.*

'I saw how he looked at her, even if neither of you men did. He wants Georgina. He just doesn't want a meek and mild Georgina. We just have to show him he wants the real Georgina.'

Except he's already met the real Georgina and he definitely doesn't want her, Georgina could have said. Instead, she sighed.

'Don't sigh like that,' her mother said, frowning. 'And sit up straight.'

'I thought you wanted me to be myself.'

'Yes, but don't be too much like yourself. Just enough to prove that you're perfect for the Duke.'

'What?' Georgina glared at her mother, shocked by her lack of logic.

'And don't let your eyes bulge either. You need to be feisty and strong, but also genteel and agreeable.'

'Isn't that a bit of a contradiction?' Georgina asked rhetorically.

'And don't question everything, in that way that you do. Agree with the Duke, but not so much that he thinks you are overly submissive. And please, keep your more peculiar habits to yourself.'

'You mean like my habit of talking to shrubs?'

All three Haywards looked at her, her parents frowning, Tommy grinning.

'So, let's see if I've got this right,' Georgina said, adopting a mock serious expression. 'You want me to be feisty and strong-minded, but genteel and agreeable. I need to question everything, but not ask too many questions. Be myself, but under no circumstances be peculiar.'

'Exactly,' her mother said. 'And very soon we'll have a duchess in the family.'

Tommy and Georgina both rolled their eyes, while her parents adopted contented grins, as if in competition over who looked more like Puffy the cat at his most self-satisfied.

Chapter Five

Adam missed his children. He missed being in Dorset. And, of course, he missed Rosalie with every fibre of his being. He would give anything for life to return to the time when they were together, deeply in love and believing that they had many happy years ahead of them.

Instead, he was forced to spend the next six months at his London town house, suffering through the social Season, making idle chit-chat with debutantes, one with whom he would hopefully be able to come to a satisfactory arrangement and take home to Dorset as his wife.

He closed his eyes and tried to ready himself for the task ahead. While Rosalie had been alive he had shunned Society, not wanting to subject his lovely, gentle wife to the snobbery and disapproval their marriage had caused.

'How could you be so stupid as to marry a woman of such low birth?' his father had said at the time, his face red with anger. *'You're the eldest son of a duke, for God's sake. You were supposed to marry someone with money.'*

On Rosalie's death, instead of offering condolences, he had once again informed Adam of his duty to marry for money.

'This time, get it right. Lord knows, if your mother would do the decent thing and die instead of gallivanting around the Americas with heaven knows who, then I'd waste no time marrying a sweet young thing with an even sweeter marriage settlement.'

And now his father's death and the revelation of just how many debts he had accrued had left Adam with no choice but to do exactly what his father had always expected of him.

As his valet brushed down his swallow-tailed evening jacket, Adam stared at the forlorn man reflected back at him in the looking glass. It was not the look of a man in search of a wife. It was more that of a man standing in the dock awaiting sentencing.

'May I offer some advice, Your Grace?' his valet said, standing back and assessing Adam's appearance.

'By all means, Wilson.'

'Perhaps a little colour. It is a ball you are attending. It is supposed to be a joyous occasion. Maybe a more colourful waistcoat.'

They both looked at his black suit and dark grey waistcoat.

'I think not,' Adam responded. There was nothing joyous in what he was about to do. He could only hope that by the end of this first ball an arrangement would be made and this ordeal would have come to a quick and relatively painless end.

He exhaled a loud, despondent breath.

Not for the first time, he wondered if there was another way in which to dig the estate out of the enormous financial hole his father had left. Perhaps he could ask Mr Hayward for a loan. A very large loan. One that would no doubt take many, many years to pay back. He quashed that idea as soon as it surfaced. He knew what that man would expect in return—that Adam marry Miss Hayward. And that was something he would not do.

The memory of Miss Hayward's laughter resurfaced in his mind, and he was reminded of why they were so badly suited. She was so energetic and joyful. She needed to marry a man who could offer her a life full of fun and enjoyment, a man who could love her, and that was not him.

He did not need or want Miss Hayward. The woman he married would be content with a quiet life and would accept being married to a man incapable of loving again. She would not object to having a husband who missed his first wife, his true wife, so much her absence was a constant ache he carried in his heart. She would accept that he was a man who had not wanted to marry again but had no choice.

He drew in another deep breath. He had to stop feeling sorry for himself and dedicate himself to the task ahead.

He thanked his valet, picked up his gloves and hat and headed out of the house towards his waiting carriage. While his children had found it difficult to understand why their father would be spending such a long time away from them in London, Rosalie's mother had understood and made it clear that she did not approve.

But then, Mrs Wainwright had never approved of anything he had done, especially marrying her daughter. It was the one thing she had in common with Adam's father. She too had wanted her daughter to marry a man from the same class and had taken no pride in the thought that her daughter would one day become a duchess.

And she continued to disapprove of Adam. When he'd thanked her for caring for the children while he was in London, she had merely sniffed and said it was never a chore for her to care for her grandchildren. Then she had added a comment that had cut him to the quick.

'I've looked after my daughter's children for the last five years and am happy to continue doing so. You just go off and enjoy yourself with all those other aristocrats and don't give any of us another thought.'

She had then looked at the portrait of her daughter sitting on the sideboard.

He had wanted to tell her that no one would ever replace Rosalie in his affections, that he would never forget her, and he was only going to London and attending the Season because he did care about his children, their future and the future of everyone on the estate. Enjoyment did not factor into it. But he didn't say any of that. Instead, he had kissed the children goodbye and left.

Adam's carriage joined the parade of carriages pulling to a halt in front of the Belgravia house where the ball was being hosted. The other guests were chattering excitedly as they walked up the well-lit steps and gave their cloaks to the servants waiting at the entranceway. The babble of voices assaulted his ears as he passed through the heaving crowd and entered the ballroom.

He looked around the large, brightly lit room, at the debutantes chatting in small groups, all dressed in pretty pastel gowns. They were all so damn young. Far too young to marry, surely. But then, when he had met Rosalie she had been eighteen, he only nineteen. They had not thought themselves too young to fall instantly, hopelessly in love and to run off and marry, despite their parents' objections. But now he was a man of thirty, and was expected to select one of these sweet, innocent young ladies to be his bride. But which one?

Miss Hayward was right. He was hopelessly out of his depth and he needed her guidance. He spotted her standing at the end of the ballroom with her parents and brother, talking animatedly, with much gesturing of her hands. Her parents were looking abashed, but Thomas was amused. The siblings suddenly laughed uproariously, drawing disapproving glances from several nearby matrons.

Still laughing, she looked around the room, caught his eye, excused herself from her now preening parents and crossed the room towards him. The tension he hadn't known he was holding in his shoulders released.

'Miss Hayward, you look lovely tonight,' he said with a small bow when she joined him.

'Well done, Your Grace. Flattery is always a good way to start,' she said with a light laugh.

It was not idle flattery. She did look lovely, as she always did, even when dressed in a sack-like maid's uniform. But tonight she was more appropriately dressed in a pale mauve gown that brought out the myriad shades of blue in her sparkling eyes. A single strand of pearls adorned her neck and matching pearl earrings hung from her pretty ears.

'So, have you had a chance to identify the heiresses

you will be targeting tonight?' she said, looking round the room.

Adam cringed, not just because of her bold statement, but because it was true. He *had* taken the time before he'd arrived to scrutinise the guest list and assess who were the heiresses with the largest marriage settlements, and the ones most likely to being amenable to trading that marriage settlement for the chance of becoming a duchess.

'I believe Miss Arabella Bateman and Lady Cecelia Greville are two of the young ladies deemed to be the most eligible this Season,' he said, reminding himself that he had no need to feel ashamed. He was here to find an heiress and there was no point pretending otherwise.

Miss Hayward snorted and turned back to face him. 'Really? Well, if all you want is an enormous marriage settlement, then yes, they are the most eligible young women on the market this Season.'

'You have objections to the two young ladies in question?'

'No, not at all,' she said with a disapproving sniff.

He waited for further explanation. None came. 'In that case, perhaps you can point them out to me.'

'They're the two staring at you with the most interest. The ones standing beside the mothers who are all but salivating at the thought of marrying their daughter off to a duke.'

His gaze swept the room. Almost every young lady seemed to be staring in their direction, along with their mothers.

'You're going to have to be a bit more precise.'

'Miss Bateman is the one dripping with diamonds,

as if she's carrying an advertising sign that says she is the daughter of one of the richest men in America. Lady Cecelia Greville is the one dressed in an understated beige gown, as if to say, *I have so much money and come from such an impeccable background I do not need to display my wealth in front of all you peasants.*'

A note of pique had entered her voice as if he had caused her great offence. He turned from scrutinising the young women in the ballroom to the one standing beside him. Was she angry with him for some reason?

'I hope your father did not blame you for my decision not to court you.'

'No, not at all.' She smiled up at him and lightly tapped his arm with her fan. 'In fact, I believe I should thank you. Your rejection of me could not have worked out better.'

'How so?'

Her smile grew wider. 'Mother is under the mistaken impression that you are attracted to me. She thinks all I have to do is act more like myself and you'll be mine for the taking.' She clapped her hands together in pleasure before he could respond to this peculiar statement.

'That means I can do whatever I like this Season and they won't be able to object. I can laugh loudly, disagree with whomever I choose. I can be rude to all those horrid fortune-hunters. I can even dance on the tables if I want to.'

The music started for the first dance and she looked towards the tables in the corner, bearing punch bowls and glasses, her expression wickedly joyous.

'Miss Hayward, may I have the pleasure of the first dance?' he said before she made good on her threat.

'Excellent idea,' she said with a wink. 'My parents will think it's working and that you are attracted to the real me.'

He led her into the centre of the dancefloor and placed his hand on her waist. She looked up at him, a cheeky smile curving her lips.

'Oh, and do some more of that,' she said as she placed her hand on his shoulder.

'More of what?'

'More looking at me like that. It's very good. If Mother sees it, she'll think I'm doing something right, maybe being agreeable or witty or flattering you or something.'

Adam was unaware that he had looked at her in any manner worthy of comment. However, he had to admit he *had* registered how slim her waist was when he'd placed his hand on her, and how her rounded hips flared out in a becoming feminine manner, but that was all. And yes, he had noticed the tendrils of hair that had escaped from her ornate hairstyle, and how they drew the eye down her creamy neck to where they curled on her naked shoulders. And yes, perhaps he had noticed the plunging cut of her gown exposed rather a lot of her cleavage to his view. But he was merely making a few observations about her appearance. They meant nothing. And nothing could be read into the manner in which he looked at her.

And even if he *had* been somewhat distracted by Miss Hayward's appearance, that was not why he was here. He was here to find a wife. That was what he needed to focus on, and not on Miss Hayward's hairstyle, her silky skin, nor her shapely figure.

* * *

This was perfect. Georgina could imagine her parents smiling benignly at her from the edge of the dancefloor, delighted to see their daughter in the arms of the Duke.

That was why she was so happy, because she was fooling her parents. It had nothing to do with actually being in the arms of the Duke. It was not because the touch of his hand was like a warm caress on her skin. Nor was it because she was so close to him she could feel the heat of his body and smell his cologne of bergamot, sage and something else. She sniffed as discreetly as she could. It was something rich and musky, something that filled her senses and caused a strange tingling sensation to shimmer through her.

She moved closer towards him and briefly closed her eyes, drawing in that masculine scent. Oh, yes, she was very happy. This Season she would be free to do whatever she wanted and it was all unintentionally thanks to him.

For the first time since that first naïve Season when she had actually thought balls were magical, romantic events—and had had her delusions cruelly ended by the Duke of Cromley's honest but hurtful comments—Georgina had actually looked forward to attending this ball.

She glanced around and decided that no ballroom had ever been grander. No crystal chandelier had ever sparkled more brightly. No parquet dancefloor had looked more inviting. And no band had played more divinely. It just made one want to dance the night away.

And what could be better than to have the first dance with the man who had changed everything? The man who had inadvertently given her the freedom to be exactly who she was.

She looked up at him and wondered if placing her head on his shoulder would be pushing her newfound freedom to be herself just a tad too far. She suspected it would be. While her parents might not object to such boldness, the Duke would not welcome it. After all, he was not here to court her, but to find a bride.

The tingling that had possessed her from the moment she had seen him standing at the side of the ballroom, looking so masculine and so…well, aristocratic, disappeared, overwhelmed by a tight gripping in her stomach and a flare of anger that chased away her happiness.

The unwanted feeling suddenly possessing her was something suspiciously like jealousy, but she could not be jealous. That would be ridiculous. He was a man in search of a loveless, mercenary marriage. She was a woman who was doing everything she could to avoid a loveless, mercenary marriage. Two people could not be more wrong for each other.

No, she was definitely not jealous. She pushed those feelings down and forced herself to smile. What she needed to do was just enjoy this moment. And this moment *was* rather pleasant. She moved slightly closer to his warm, hard body.

No doubt other young ladies watching them dance would think that she had a chance with the Duke. None would realise she had already been assessed and dismissed. And none would realise just how happy she was with this arrangement. It suited her perfectly. It did. It really did. And she wished the Duke all the best in his search. Why else would she have offered to assist him? A jealous woman certainly wouldn't do that.

'So, have you taken some time to practise your flirting skills?' she said, annoyed that she sounded peevish when she was merely trying to be helpful.

'I have not,' came his brief reply.

She forced herself to give a little laugh. 'No, I suppose you don't need to. You're a duke. You can be as boorish and boring as you like and no one is going to care.'

He raised both eyebrows.

'Not that you are boorish or boring,' she added, wishing she could stop talking and just enjoy the dance. It was the first time she was in his arms and it quite possibly would be the last. And that was as it should be. Once he met the young lady he wished to marry he would be dedicating all his time to courting her.

'And will the new, liberated Miss Hayward be flirting tonight?' he asked.

She snorted in a manner that no flirtatious young lady ever would. 'I too have no need to resort to such tactics. The men at this ball fall into two distinct categories. The men who are not the slightest bit interested in me because I am not of their class, and the men who overlook my appalling background because they need my father's money. The first group would look down their raised noses at me if I deemed to try and flirt with them. The second group are falling over themselves to impress me, so I too could be the most boring, boorish woman in the room and they'd still tell me I was an absolute delight.'

She could add there was a third category. Men who

needed her father's money but did not want her. That was a category that included only one person. Him.

'I can assure you, Miss Hayward, you are certainly not boring.'

She laughed at the guarded compliment. 'Are you saying I'm boorish?' She waited with some pleasure for him to look embarrassed, and to rush to assure her that this was not what he meant.

'I believe you take pleasure in being bad-mannered. Isn't that what you said to me before we started to dance? That you were looking forward to misbehaving this Season.'

'Oh, yes, I suppose so,' she said, not sure whether to be disappointed or pleased by his assessment of her character.

'I also believe you were doing what you said all young ladies do. Making a critical statement about yourself so the gentleman will rush to assure you that no, you are not boorish but the most refined, sophisticated young lady in the room.'

Georgina snorted again, with embarrassment at being caught out as much as by amusement. 'And you failed the flirtation test by being far too honest.'

'Is that what you are doing with me, flirting?'

Heat rushed to Georgina's cheeks. Was she?

'Well, if I was indulging in a bit of harmless flirting, it was only to help you,' she quickly responded, willing her cheeks to stop burning. It would be too awful if the Duke did think she was flirting, especially when such behaviour would be so unwelcome.

'So, which heiress do you plan to charm tonight?' she

added, determined to move the conversation away from the flirting she most certainly was not doing.

He huffed out a sigh. 'Miss Bateman and Lady Cecelia are the most likely candidates. I believe Miss Bateman's mother has made no secret of the fact that they are in this country to secure a title for their daughter, and there are few families more socially ambitious than the Grevilles.'

That tightening sensation returned to Georgina's stomach, but she forced herself to keep smiling.

'And there is Lady Gwendolyn Smithers,' he continued. 'Although her fortune is not as vast as the other two ladies, it would suffice and she is reputed to be a pleasant young lady.'

Georgina released a puff of disapproval. 'Lady Gwendolyn? Pleasant? I suppose you do know she is a frightful gossip.' Georgina knew she was not being entirely dishonest. Lady Gwendolyn *was* known to gossip, although no more than practically any other young lady present, including Georgina.

'And as for her family, well, the stories I could tell you.'

He looked down at her, his eyebrows raised in question.

'Yes, all right. I suppose that would be gossiping, but I would be doing so simply to prevent you from making a terrible mistake and marrying the wrong woman.'

'So I shouldn't marry Lady Gwendolyn because she gossips and there are rumours about her family?'

'I'm just saying.' Georgina wasn't entirely sure what she *was* saying, especially as Lady Gwendolyn probably would make an ideal wife. She had attended Halliwell's a few years behind Georgina and had never once got caught sneaking out after hours and was reputed to be able to make fascinating conversation with even the dullest of shrubs.

'And what of Miss Bateman? Is she a gossip? Are there rumours about her family?'

Georgina shrugged. 'Well, her father is an absolute fright. They say he's quite the tyrant.'

'I'm not intending to marry the father.'

'No, but still.' Georgina was unsure of her argument, she just knew that Miss Bateman would not be suitable for the Duke, despite her wealth, her beauty and her grace.

'And Lady Cecelia? Is she a gossip? Are there rumours? Is her father a tyrant? Her mother a shrew?'

'No, but…' Georgina knew there had to be a *but*. Unfortunately, when placed on the spot, she couldn't think of one.

Those annoying, judgemental eyebrows rose up his forehead yet again.

'Well, you did agree for me to help you navigate this Season,' she added, painfully aware she was sounding petulant. 'I'm just trying to give you some good advice.'

He nodded slowly. 'You are right. I am sorry,' he said as the music came to an end. 'I value your insightful comments.'

Was he being sarcastic? It was hard to tell.

He took her arm, led her off the dancefloor and bowed. 'Thank you, Miss Hayward. I shall heed your advice and I wish you well in your Season of misbehaving.'

With that, he turned and walked across the room towards Miss Bateman, quite obviously neither heeding nor valuing her good advice one little bit.

Chapter Six

Adam escorted Miss Bateman onto the dancefloor for the quadrille. Allowing Miss Hayward to guide him through the treacherous waters of the Season was obviously not such a good idea after all. Why would she mention that the young lady's father was a tyrant? If anything, that was surely a good reason to marry her, to rescue her from an unpleasant situation. And as for Lady Cecelia, while he did not particularly approve of gossiping, if that was a young lady's only flaw then it was one he could easily overlook.

He should have known that Miss Hayward would be of no help whatsoever in his quest. All he'd had to do was remember how they'd met. No one would expect good counsel from a young woman who'd escaped from her parents' home on a bicycle dressed as a maid.

He looked across the ballroom to the lady in question. She was talking to Lord Fernley. No, revise that. She was talking *at* Lord Fernley, apparently giving him instructions, but he did not appear to mind. The man had an obviously false smile fixed to his face, as if trying to convince Miss Hayward that everything she said and did was fascinating. Fernley apparently fell into the category of men after her money. Men like himself, but unlike himself—men who did not care whether the arrangement suited the young lady or not.

Fernley opened his mouth to talk, but Miss Hayward took his arm, led him across the dancefloor and joined their group, making up the last of the four couples in the quadrille.

He should be annoyed. He was supposed to be focusing all his attention on Miss Bateman, but Miss Hayward's presence was oddly reassuring, like seeing a lifeboat appear in a turbulent sea. But he was more than capable of rescuing himself. He did not need a lifeboat and he must not get distracted again.

He turned from watching Miss Hayward to his partner. 'Are you enjoying your time in England, Miss Bateman?'

She kept her eyes lowered in a demure manner that could challenge Miss Hayward's act of meekness. 'Yes, Your Grace,' she whispered. This was a surprise. He had been told that American women were confident and effusive, not shy and retiring.

He hadn't meant to, but he looked over at Miss Hayward. The smile she sent him could almost be called victorious. That too was most peculiar. He really was out of his depth, and the sooner he found his bride and escaped the horror of the Season the better.

He turned back to Miss Bateman and racked his brain for a suitable topic of conversation. Perhaps he should have practised on the shrubs before he arrived. Once again, he glanced in Miss Hayward's direction.

Being in her company might be somewhat disconcerting but he never felt this awkwardness, nor did he struggle to find anything to talk about.

The music started. At least there would be little time to make uncomfortable conversation while they moved through the formal steps of the dance. And yet, when Miss Bateman and Miss Hayward approached each other in the centre of the group, there was no ignoring the quick exchange that took place between the two young ladies. For one brief moment, Miss Bateman ceased to keep her eyes lowered. She looked straight at Miss Hayward and said something to cause her to gasp and shoot a quick look towards him.

When she took his hand again, Miss Bateman raised her eyes and gave him the sweetest smile imaginable. Something had just happened and it did not take a man well versed in the machinations of the Season to know it involved him. Nor did he need to be a genius to know he was being played by Miss Bateman, but then, wasn't that exactly what Miss Hayward had warned him about?

This duplicity was far too baffling and the sooner he found a wife and escaped this confusing world the better.

Georgina smiled triumphantly to herself. Mother's plan was working. Miss Bateman, who Georgina knew could talk the hind legs off a donkey, was acting like a spineless ninny without a word to say for herself. Not that it really mattered. That was her mother's plan, not Georgina's. And if it hadn't been for that quick exchange in the middle of the quadrille there would be no reason for Georgina to take pleasure in Miss Bateman ruining her chances with the Duke.

But there *had* been that furious, rather harsh exchange. Mr Bateman was reputed to be a tyrannical businessman and it looked as if the daughter was no different.

'*Back off! This one is mine,*' she had hissed at Georgina. '*Try and get in my way and I will crush you like an ant.*'

Georgina could have told Miss Bateman she had nothing to fear, that the Duke was not interested in her, but instead she had been left uncharacteristically speechless.

She continued dancing, her determination to ensure that Miss Bateman did not win the Duke intensifying every time she looked at them. Georgina had not, and would not, reassure Miss Bateman that she had nothing to fear from Georgina. Quite the contrary. Anything she could do to unnerve that frightful young lady she would take enormous pleasure in doing.

Not for her own sake, of course, but for the Duke's.

As Lord Fernley led her around the square of dances, she continued to watch the Duke and Miss Bateman. She still had her eyes lowered, her long dark lashes sweeping her high cheekbones in what she obviously thought was an enchanting manner. She was rather pretty, Georgina had to admit, but she could see the boredom and frustration on the Duke's face, even if Miss Bateman couldn't.

She smiled with satisfaction. The Duke might not be interested in a woman as boisterous as Georgina, but Mother was right. It was now obvious he really did not want meek and mild either.

That horrid Miss Bateman might think she was enchanting the Duke with this submissive act, but she was doing exactly the opposite.

The dance came to an end and, still feeling surprisingly pleased with herself, she allowed Lord Fernley to lead her off the dancefloor. As he chatted on and on, repeatedly telling her what an elegant dancer she was, she watched the Duke escort Miss Bateman back to her mother, bow, exchange a few polite words then depart, without a backward glance.

He looked over at her and she smiled at him in anticipation. He was going to ask her to dance again.

Perhaps this next dance would be another waltz. Her pulse raced. Not because she wanted to be held by the Duke. Not because she wanted to feel his arms around her or his strong, oh, so manly chest close to hers, but because it would give them a chance to talk without anyone overhearing. If he needed further convincing, she would be able to tell him why Miss Bateman was certainly, categorically, not the woman he was looking for.

The Earl of Cranford stood in front of her, blocking her view of the Duke. 'Miss Hayward, would you do me the honour of this dance?' he said with a low bow and a supercilious smile. The Earl had lost his wealth at the gaming tables and could see no better way of recouping his losses than marrying an heiress. Georgina had been fending him off for five Seasons and yet he still persisted, like a gambler unable to leave the gaming table despite being on a losing streak.

'I'm sorry, I...' Georgina said, leaning to the side so she could see around the Earl. The Duke was not heading in her direction, but had crossed the floor towards Lady Cecelia.

Had that been his intention all along? Was he under the impression that he was not in need of her advice after all? Well, he was wrong. He definitely did need her and it would be remiss of Georgina to stand by and watch him make mistake after mistake with the wrong young ladies.

'Oh, yes, all right,' she said, taking the Earl's arm and leading him onto the dancefloor, as close to the Duke and Lady Cecelia as the crowded ballroom floor would allow.

The music began and it was a galop. As the Earl dragged her around the floor, she moved her head, looking over and between the swirling dancers so she could keep an eye on the Duke and his partner. She would have preferred another quadrille—that way, he would not have Lady Cecelia in his arms. Not that it should really matter but, strangely, it did.

The Earl tried to lead her in a different direction to the one she needed to go, but she put a stop to that. While it might be considered ungainly for the lady to lead the man, needs must. With much tangling of legs and treading of toes she steered Cranford closer to the Duke and his partner.

To her horror, she could see Lady Cecelia was making polite conversation with the Duke, and he was listening to her as if he actually found her interesting.

Had she not got the message? Had her mother's word not got through to Lady Cecelia? The Duke liked meek and mild young women, not ones who made conversation, who smiled at him, who held his attention. Well, perhaps he did. She didn't really know what sort of woman attracted him. All she knew was, she wasn't it. And she also knew she had no reason to object if Lady Cecelia was exactly what he was looking for in a bride.

Hadn't she said she would help him? And surely that didn't just mean preventing him from making a mistake but also assisting him to find the right woman.

Georgina didn't know. All she knew was that she was not enjoying herself any more. And the more the Duke and Lady Cecelia conversed, the less pleasure she was taking in this entire enterprise.

The dance over, the Earl led her to the edge of the dancefloor but did not leave. Instead, he continued to attempt to make conversation with her—conversation she did not hear, her entire focus taken by what was happening on the other side of the ballroom.

The Duke bowed to Lady Cecelia and exchanged a few words with her mother, then departed. Georgina's breath caught in her throat. Maybe this time the Duke would ask her to dance. Yes, that would make more sense. Then they could discuss both young ladies.

But no. Instead, he crossed the room and bowed in front of Lady Gwendolyn.

'Excuse me, I'm afraid I need to go to the ladies' retiring room,' she said, interrupting whatever it was the Earl was saying.

The Earl bowed and left, but her exit was halted by the obsequious Viscount Smarley. Another man drawn like a moth to the flame that was her marriage settlement.

'I'm sorry, my lord. I need to sit this dance out. I must retire to the ladies' room to fix my hair.'

'But your hair is magnificent, like sunlight on a wheatfield in the morning, like—'

'Yes, yes,' she said absentmindedly as she walked away. She skirted around the edge of the dancefloor, her gaze firmly fixed on the Duke and Lady Gwendolyn. She was smiling up at him in a decidedly pretty manner and chatting politely. Georgina stifled a curse that would have shocked the nearby matrons. Lady Gwendolyn had won top honours in conversation at Halliwell's and it seemed she was putting those skills to good use with the Duke.

Georgina knew she should not be objecting. There was nothing actually wrong with Lady Gwendolyn. She was sweet, polite, well-versed in all the skills that a young lady was supposed to possess. And she was nothing like Georgina. That probably made her perfect for the Duke.

Smarley once more blocked her way. The man really was insufferable. Even Georgina knew he kept a mistress, one he was in danger of losing if he did not restore his family fortune in the immediate future so he could keep her in the level of comfort she demanded.

'Miss Hayward, I can assure you, no young lady in the room has more beautiful hair. Would you do me the honour—?'

'I'm not dancing. Go away.' She was not usually quite so blunt but he was being even more insufferable than usual.

'Well, really,' he said, that insincere smile disappearing. 'I don't know why you're acting so high and mighty. You're not the only heiress here tonight and you're far from the prettiest,' he added before striding across the room, his long nose high in the air.

Georgina was tempted to call out to him that he wasn't

telling her anything she didn't already know. Instead, she watched Lady Gwendolyn giggle as the Duke spun her round the room in the polka.

This was definitely not the fun Season full of mayhem and mischief she had been looking forward to. It had hardly even begun and it was turning out to be her worst Season ever, and there was a lot of competition for that title.

Chapter Seven

The polka came to an end and Adam led Lady Gwendolyn back to her waiting mother. After the obligatory exchange of pleasantries, he looked around the room to select the next young woman with whom he would dance. He scanned the crowd. He wasn't deliberately looking for Miss Hayward, but he couldn't help but notice that she was nowhere in sight.

During the polka he had seen her have a terse exchange with Viscount Smarley, then he had lost sight of her.

Had something happened to her? Had Smarley upset her? The man was a buffoon, so that would not surprise him. What did surprise him was that Miss Hayward would care about anything that man could say to her. She appeared to be made of much sterner stuff. But then, did he really know her?

Mr Hayward strode across the ballroom towards the exit and he did not look happy. Something *had* happened to Miss Hayward and, whatever it was, he wanted to know. It might not be any of his business but he could not continue to dance if that young lady was in any distress.

At what he hoped was a discreet distance, he followed Mr Hayward towards the exit and into an adjoining drawing room that had been cleared so that supper could later be served. Mr Hayward then disappeared through French windows that led to the terrace.

Adam walked towards them, then paused. Was he intruding on a private exchange between a father and daughter? Would his presence be welcomed or not?

'Your mother said I might find you here,' Mr Hayward said, sounding happy rather than concerned. 'So, my dear, how long will it be before we are posting the banns?'

That drew Adam closer and he leant against a marble pillar, anxious to hear her answer. Was Miss Hayward courting? She gave no impression that was the case. Quite the opposite. If anything, she had asserted she had no interest in marriage, to anyone, including himself.

'I believe you are getting ahead of yourself, Father. The Season has only just begun. You said I had until the end of the Season to find a husband.'

So she *was* in search of a husband, although, again, not him.

'That's as may be,' her father said. 'But your mother has been paying close attention and she is confident that the Duke is on the hook. All you have to do is reel him in. And that's not going to happen if you hide away out here and allow him to dance with other young women.'

Adam closed his mouth, which had inexplicably fallen open. Had he heard correctly? Mr Hayward had said '*the Duke*' and there was only one duke present tonight. Himself.

What was going on? Was Miss Hayward involved in some scheme to marry him herself? If she was, it was an extremely convoluted and confusing scheme. Surely if she was planning on marrying a man she wouldn't run away from him, then inform him that she did not wish to marry him, but would help him find another, more suitable, wife.

And as for being on the hook, well, that was ridiculous. Yes, he had enjoyed his dance with Miss Hayward. Yes, she was a decidedly attractive, shapely young woman who would appeal to any man, and he did enjoy her company, plus she was a delightful conversationalist, despite what those idiots at Halliwell's might think. But she was not for him. Was she? Adam tried to remind himself of what his objections to marrying Miss Hayward actually were. Although he did remember that foremost amongst his reasons was *her* objection to marrying *him*.

'Oh, Papa,' Miss Hayward said with a light laugh. 'You and Mama have got it all wrong. I'm not going to marry the Duke. All I'm doing is helping him find his perfect bride. He's so naïve when it comes to women.'

Naïve? Adam wanted to disagree, but the longer he stayed at this ball, the more he had to admit that women were a complete mystery to him, and this bizarre exchange was not disabusing him of that belief.

'He thinks the way a young lady pretends to be is exactly what they are,' she added.

That was a conclusion he too was starting to arrive at.

'I'm just setting him right, so he doesn't make the wrong choice.'

Adam nodded and ignored the peculiar crushing sensation inside his chest. She had merely repeated what he already knew. She did not wish to marry him. Just as he did not wish to marry her. But he was pleased that Miss Hayward was not, like so many other young women seemingly were, a game player.

None of this would be news to the father either, and Adam waited for his reply. A reply that was taking a long time to come, as the protracted silence stretched on and on.

'You're doing what?' he finally said in a low tone as if he was fighting to control his anger.

Adam braced himself, suddenly on alert. He suspected that Miss Hayward was more than capable of fighting her own battles, and this was not really any of his concern, but he wanted to be on hand in case she needed him. Although what he could do to help her, he had no idea.

'I'm merely assisting him to navigate the Season so he doesn't make a terrible mistake. The marriage mart can be so perilous.'

Adam was relieved that her voice was still light and musical, her father's wrath having no apparent effect on her.

There was another long silence.

'So what about Cranford, Fernley or Smarley?' he said, his voice barely controlled. 'Despite your appalling behaviour towards them, they're still showing their interest.'

Miss Hayward laughed dismissively but made no comment.

There was yet another long silence that appeared to hang in the air.

'I've had it up to my back teeth with you, my girl,' Mr Hayward said, his voice so controlled Adam could tell he was barely holding onto his rage. 'You seem incapable of understanding your situation. You'll soon be twenty-four. You can't possibly attend another Season after this one. You have to marry this Season or it will be a total humiliation for the entire family.'

'Don't be so silly, Papa,' Miss Hayward said dismissively, either oblivious to or unaffected by the controlled rage in her father's tone.

'No, do not act as if this is a joke,' Mr Hayward said, his voice rising. 'This is not a joking matter. And as for helping men find a wife, rather than finding a husband for yourself, well, that is…that is…' He spluttered to a halt.

'I'm not helping *men*. I'm just helping the Duke.'

'My God, girl, are you simple-minded? If you want to help find a wife for the Duke then marry him yourself. And if he still doesn't want you, then marry Lord Fernley, the Earl of Cranford or Viscount Smarley. They're all eminently suitable.'

'You mean they've all got titles,' Miss Hayward mumbled.

'Exactly. So, which is it to be?'

Adam leaned closer and waited for her answer, he suspected with as much anticipation as Mr Hayward.

'I don't know why you're even bothering to ask. I won't be marrying any of them.'

Relief washed through Adam. He could tell himself that it was relief that she still did not wish to marry him but, strangely, it was relief that she was not interested in the other three men either. None of whom seemed at all suitable for a woman with Miss Hayward's spirit.

'You will,' her father said in a low growl. 'You will be married by the end of this Season…or else.'

'Or else what?'

Adam smiled at her defiance. He could imagine how she looked, her eyes blazing, hands on hips, chin raised.

'Or else I will cut you off without a penny.'

Adam's smile died as the implication of Mr Hayward's words hit him. A young woman cut off from her family was placed in a perilous position. With no money of her own, and no means of earning a living, Miss Hayward was completely dependent on her family for support. If that was taken away, she would be set adrift in a world that could be cruel and heartless for a woman.

'You will not,' Miss Hayward said, her voice no longer quite so defiant.

'I will. I've indulged you for far too long, my girl. Your mother has warned me repeatedly that I let you get your own way far too much. Well, that stops right now. You will find a husband with a title this Season or you will no longer be my daughter.'

'Is that all I am to you? Someone who you can use to secure a title for the family?' The strained sound in her words suggested she was holding back tears. Adam felt a strong compulsion to go to her, to comfort her, but what could he say? And he was sure neither father nor daughter would appreciate that he had been eaves-dropping.

'Yes, finally, it is getting through that thick skull of

yours. You need to grow up and start doing your duty by the family. You have been given so much, and there is only one thing I expect from you in return and, so far, you haven't even done that. If you don't marry and raise the social standing of the Hayward family, then I can see no point having a daughter.'

'You can't make me marry someone I don't want to.' She still sounded defiant, but the tremulous note in her voice suggested it was pretence.

'No, but I can let you know what the options are. You either marry or you will have to make your own way in the world. Without my support, you would have to find employment and earn your own money. Do you have any skills?'

There was silence.

'No, you don't,' he answered his own question. 'Do you know how to do anything other than cause trouble?'

Again, there was silence.

'No, you don't. The best you can hope for is to become a governess for some family desperate enough to take on a young woman who actually failed at finishing school, something I would not have thought possible. Or you could become a companion to an elderly lady. Although what elderly lady would want the companionship of such a disobedient girl I do not know. And those are by far the best options available to a girl such as yourself. Believe me, there are many more options that are far, far worse than having to marry a titled man and live a comfortable life.'

Miss Hayward still made no reply. All Adam heard was the rustle of silk crumpling as she sat down.

'Do I make myself clear?'

Again, there was no reply.

'Good. Then I'll leave you to contemplate everything I've said, but before the end of this night I expect to see you back on the dancefloor, smiling and flirting with as many titled men as you possibly can.'

Adam moved quickly behind the pillar to avoid being caught in such an inappropriate position, as a red-faced Mr Hayward strode through the terrace doors, across the room and back into the ballroom.

This was not a problem of his creation, and yet it felt like it. He should return to the ballroom and continue his search for his heiress. That was the only reason he was here. But he had to do something. He could not leave Miss Hayward in such a state of distress. Unfortunately, the question was, what on earth *could* he do? And that was a question to which he had no answer.

This was terrible. Georgina rocked slowly to and fro, her head in her hands. She had never felt so miserable. Her father had made threats before, but never any so vile. He'd often alluded to cutting off her dress allowance or confining her to home until she behaved, but she had always managed to get around him and make him see reason.

But tonight he'd looked so fierce, so intractable, as if no argument would move him from his outrageous position of expecting her to marry one of those men. Lord Fernley, Viscount Smarley or the Earl of Cranford. Georgina gripped her head tighter and rocked faster. How could her father possibly condemn her to marriage to one of those men? And as for the Duke—well, despite what her irrational parents thought, that was not an option.

It looked as if she would have to find a way of supporting herself. She looked out at the dark garden through the net of her fingers, the light from the room barely stretching past the dimly lit terrace.

If she did have to support herself, how on earth would she do so? Her father was right. No one in their right mind would hire her as a governess, and she would make a hopeless companion for an elderly lady. If she undertook such work, it would not be long before she was dismissed and tossed out onto the street, and then what would she do?

A shadow passed across her. She released the fingers covering her eyes, looked up and gasped. What was the Duke doing here? She sat up straighter, brushed down her crumpled gown and tried to smile.

'Did you feel the need to take the air as well, Your Grace?' she asked, hoping she sounded lively and did not betray any of her inner anguish. 'It's rather delightful out here, isn't it? Just smell that fresh air.' She sniffed, and unfortunately caught the fragrance of bergamot and sage, sending shivers through her as if the air was not just fresh but decidedly chilly. She did not need the Duke unsettling her and adding to her anguish and yet, at the same time, she did want his company. Wanted it too much.

'Are you tired of dancing?' she burbled on. 'Tired of chasing heiresses?' She gave a little laugh that sounded false to her ears.

'I heard what your father said.'

'Oh,' she said on a gasp. 'All of it?' She hoped he had missed the part when her father had discussed him.

'All of it.'

'I can explain,' she said, turning towards him on the wooden bench. 'I thought it best to let my parents continue thinking that you were interested in me, then they would leave me alone. It was all so silly really. Mother seems to think that you really are interested in marrying me. I suppose she's a bit desperate and sees what she wants to see.' Georgina knew she was gabbling but seemed incapable of stopping. 'I did nothing to encourage her in this misguided idea, but yes, I'm sorry, I also did nothing to discourage my parents from their delusion that you might actually want to court me. It was a bit selfish, but I thought they would stop constantly pestering me about marriage this Season and I could just enjoy myself.'

Her shoulders slumped and she crumpled down on the seat. 'I couldn't have got it more wrong if I tried. Could I?' she added, finally running out of words.

'Is it really such a bad idea?' he said, looking out at the garden.

'What?'

'Marriage. If we did marry, it would solve both our problems.'

'What?'

'It would satisfy your father's need to have a title in the family. It would save you from a terrible fate and, as we both know, I'm in need of an heiress.'

She stared at him, sure that he had gone slightly mad. 'Was that a proposal?'

He shrugged one shoulder. 'Yes, I suppose it was.'

She stared out at the garden, looked at him, then back at the garden, shrouded in darkness. 'It's not a very romantic one.'

'This is not a very romantic situation in which we find ourselves. Neither of us wants to marry, but neither of us has any choice. But, as I said, it would solve both our problems if we did marry.' He turned on the seat to face her. 'You know my situation. You know that I have to marry an heiress. You are an heiress. Your father has given you no real option. You have to marry a titled man. I am a titled man. And, unlike those other men who are trying to court you, I am not lying to you. This will simply be an arrangement that suits both of us.'

'Yes, all right.' The words were out before Georgina could think of the full ramifications of what she was saying.

She looked up at him to gauge his reaction, but could barely see his face in the dim light. Was he looking pleased, surprised, horrified? Had he expected her to say no? Had he hoped she would say no? Was he merely being polite or gallant in making an offer he expected to be rejected?

His silence did not suggest happiness nor any enthusiasm for making her his wife. Should Georgina retract her acceptance?

'Good,' he finally said. 'I am sorry about this, Miss Georgina. It is not an ideal situation for either of us, but I promise I will do everything in my power to make this arrangement agreeable for you.'

Everything except love me, Georgina could say, but

she knew that love had nothing to do with what she had just consented to. As he said, it was merely an arrangement which would save them both from a worse fate.

Chapter Eight

Everything moved so quickly. The day after the ball the Duke visited Georgina's parents and officially asked for her hand in marriage. It came as no surprise to anyone that her father gave his immediate consent. What did surprise Georgina was the way her mother sprang into action. The banns were read, a date was set, invitations were sent out and the wedding gown made all before Georgina had time to fully digest that she was soon to be a bride.

Her parents seemed to care nothing for what rumours such unseemly haste might generate. Obviously, their fear that the Duke might withdraw his offer, or Georgina might try and run off before they got her up the aisle, was greater than their fear of what the twittering gossipmongers might say about such a rushed wedding.

Despite being engaged, Georgina saw little of the Duke leading up to their wedding day, and she was never alone with him. She suspected that too was a deliberate ploy by her mother. She did not want to risk Georgina doing anything to cause the Duke to change his mind, and the best way to achieve that was to ensure they saw as little of each other as humanly possible until they were at the altar. Then there would be no going back.

That meant they had no time to discuss what their marriage would be like. Georgina knew it was an arrangement, but exactly what sort of arrangement she had no idea.

She did, however, have time to discuss the entire disaster with her good friends from her time at Halliwell's. They consoled, they advised, suggested ways in which she could get out of the situation in which she'd found herself, but no one would hazard a guess on what her marriage would be like.

Irene and Amelia also offered her a home, to counter her father's threat to make her homeless, and both said they would be more than happy to support her financially. They had even said they could probably find her employment if she wished, although the tone of their voices when they discussed her prospects suggested that, like her father, they were struggling to think of any job which would use Georgina's skills, or lack thereof.

As she had no desire to take charity, she thanked her friends, and told them she would just have to accept her fate. She was to wed. It would mean doing the one thing she had been determined not to, marrying a man her father had chosen for her. A man who did not love her and was only marrying her for her money. Well, that, and to save her from a life of penury.

If the Duke had not come out to the terrace to take some air. If he had not accidentally overheard her father's threat. If he was not prone to helping damsels in distress, then he would probably have chosen Lady Gwendolyn, Lady Cecelia or Miss Bateman to be his bride.

Instead, their fates were sealed, and within a short month of that hasty, unromantic proposal, Georgina was walking up the aisle of the flower-bedecked local church to the sound of the Wedding March, on her proud father's arm, followed by her closest friends as her bridesmaids, towards her husband-to-be.

Her husband-to-be.

She would soon be his wife. She paused briefly, overawed by that realisation. It would soon be a reality. The handsome, formidable man standing at the altar, dressed in a black morning suit, a red rose in his buttonhole the only splash of colour, would be her husband. Georgina could hardly believe that it was actually happening. And tonight would be their wedding night. She almost stumbled over her feet and came to a halt.

What was their marriage night to entail? They both knew this was an arrangement, not something either was entering into willingly, but what would that mean when they became man and wife? Georgina would discover that tonight, when they were alone in his bedchamber. A tingle of anticipation radiated through her as her eyes quickly scanned the Duke, his broad shoulders, strong arms and those long slim legs.

Alone. In his bedchamber.

'None of your tricks, Georgina,' her father whispered, pulling slightly on her arm to encourage her to continue moving up the aisle. 'You agreed to this, you cannot back out now.'

Her father's words reminded her of what this was.

It was not a love match, but something that suited her father's ambitions. The man standing at the altar was not waiting for the love of his life, he was waiting for his promised dowry.

She commenced her slow walk towards the Duke as the organ music swirled around her. Everyone in the church was smiling as if this was the happiest of days. No one suspected she was a mere pawn in other people's games, or if they did, they did not care. This marriage would mean the Duke would save his estate, her mother could boast connections to the highest echelons of Society and her father would have an aristocrat in the family and grandchildren who went by the titles lord and lady.

She bit her lip. *Children.*

She would be expected to produce children. Another shiver of excitement fluttered through her and her toes curled inside her white satin shoes as an image of being in her future husband's arms crashed into her mind. She looked at the breathtakingly handsome man watching her slow progress. Would he soon be kissing her? Tonight, would he take her by the hand and lead her to his bed? And what would that be like?

As yet, he had not even kissed her. She still did not know what his lips felt like, what they tasted like, what his body felt like pressed up against hers. Warmth enveloped her. Tonight, she would find out.

She reached the altar. Her father handed her over to the Duke and they stood facing the vicar.

Georgina knew she should be paying attention to the service, but her awareness was too focused on the man standing beside her. The man who she would soon be married to, *till death us do part.*

This might not be what she wanted, but it certainly could have been a lot worse. She could have been forced to marry Lord Fernley, the Earl of Cranford or Viscount Smarley.

But she was not marrying any of those appalling men. She was marrying Adam Knightly, the Duke of Ravenswood, a man so handsome that every time she looked at him she had decidedly unacceptable thoughts. Thoughts that would soon be entirely acceptable when she became his wife.

While this marriage had been forced on her, it definitely had some compensations. She smiled up at her husband-to-be and realised the vicar had stopped speaking.

Like the engagement, the wedding service had gone by in a whirl, and she hadn't heard a word spoken. She heard her father cough and she looked at the vicar.

'Wilt thou have this man to thy wedded husband?' he repeated with a note of impatience.

'Oh, yes, I will,' she said.

The vicar prattled on for a bit longer, until finally the church bells rang out joyously as her husband—*her husband*—led her out of the church on his arm, followed by the happy congregation.

On the doorstep, while everyone cheered, he took her in his arms and kissed her lightly on the lips. Like their courtship and their wedding service, it was over before she had barely registered what was happening.

It was their first kiss, and it had been a quick peck in front of her family, friends, relatives, other invited guests and curious locals who had gathered on the lawn outside to watch the bride and groom emerging from the church.

She smiled up at him, willing him to kiss her again, really kiss her, and ignore all who were watching.

But he didn't, nor did he smile at her or say any words of reassurance. Georgina's hopes plummeted. This coldness could not be an omen of what their marriage was to be like, could it? No, it would not be. He just didn't want to kiss her properly in front of the milling crowd. He would save that for when they were alone.

Alone. Alone and married, with no restrictions on what they did and what they shared. Then he would kiss her the way a man kissed a woman, the way a husband kissed his wife.

While the congregation threw rose petals over the heads of the supposedly happy couple, he took her hand and helped her into the open carriage, festooned with white flowers, that would take her back to her family home for the wedding breakfast.

'So, husband,' Georgina said and gave a small giggle as if she had said something rather ridiculous, 'we're now married.'

She looked at him in expectation, waiting for him to laugh, to smile, to say something joyous and encouraging.

'Indeed we are,' he replied in a tone that was neither joyous nor encouraging. 'After the wedding breakfast we shall return to my estate. I believe it would be best if you met the children as soon as possible and I have been away from them for far too long.'

'It's such a shame they couldn't attend the wedding ceremony. The girls could have been bridesmaids, your son a pageboy.'

'I discussed this with the children's grandmother and

she decided that, as it is not long since the children lost their mother, it would be difficult watching their father taking another bride.'

'Would it not have been better for them to have met me before the wedding day? I was surprised you did not insist on that with Father before the engagement was announced.'

'Why?'

'Well, in case they didn't like me. After all, I'm now their stepmother. They might worry that I'm going to be one of those evil stepmothers, like in the fairy tales.' She bared her teeth in her best impression of a witch.

His expression remained impassive, showing he could see no humour in this situation. 'The children are cared for by their grandmother and a nanny. Your duties as my wife will not entail being their mother.'

Her duties as his wife

She was to have duties and he was to decide what they entailed. Georgina thought not. She might be his wife now, but that did not give him the right to tell her what she could or could not do, what was or was not expected of her.

'Anyway, I am looking forward to meeting them and if I'm not going to be their evil stepmother, I hope we can all become good friends.'

He raised his eyebrows as if he was unsure what to make of the idea of his children becoming friends with Georgina, but made no reply.

The carriage came to a halt in front of the house, and they were soon surrounded by happy guests, so there was no time to further discuss these so-called wifely duties.

Nor did they have time to converse during the wedding breakfast, the whirl of the event making this all but impossible. On the few occasions Georgina did try to converse with her husband, her voice was drowned by the noise of the celebrating guests, the clatter of dishes, the rushing here and there of servants and the toasts and speeches.

When the dancing commenced, the Duke held out his hand and led her onto the dancefloor. She placed her hand on his broad shoulder as he took her other hand, and felt his strong hand move to her waist. She was now in the arms of her husband, a man who was all hers.

Her wifely duties.

Georgina sighed gently. There was one wifely duty she was certainly not going to object to.

Last night, her mother had entered Georgina's bedchamber, her lips pursed tightly, her body held rigidly, and had proceeded to tell Georgina what her wifely duties on her wedding night would entail. Her mother had looked so embarrassed as she'd stumbled over her words, and Georgina had to stop herself from giggling. It was as if her mother was providing her with an instruction manual on what went where, when and why it had to occur.

Her mother's talk would have dismayed Georgina and filled her with qualms if she had not already had a similar conversation with her married friends, Amelia and Irene. Their description of what Georgina was to expect had less to do with what went where, as to what it would feel like, and if it was half as glorious as they described it was going to feel simply wonderful.

She moved closer to her husband and breathed in that

intoxicating scent of bergamot, sage and masculinity. What was expected of her on her wedding night, and throughout her married life, was one wifely duty he would get no dispute over. Whatever he wanted from her, whenever he wanted it and wherever, she would be in full agreement.

Her hand moved slowly along his shoulder, feeling the coiled strength under her fingers, and the fire that had been smouldering deep within her since he'd led her onto the floor ignited further, making her entire body warm and deliciously tingly.

She could stay in his arms, dancing to this music, for the rest of her life and know that she would be content. But the inevitable happened and all too soon the music came to an end. The Duke placed his hand on the small of her back and led her off the dancefloor. They had exchanged hardly a word as he had held her in his arms, and she hoped that it was because he too was contemplating what was to come.

Before they reached the edge of the dancefloor, her brother intervened.

'May I dance with the Duchess?' he said with a wry smile.

Her husband bowed to Tommy, then, surprisingly, gave an equally formal bow to her, before departing.

'Well, you've got what you wanted, haven't you, Duchess?' Tommy said, while Georgina continued to contemplate the Duke's formality towards her.

Surely they should be more relaxed with each other now. And he was yet to ask her to call him by his given name. Did he expect her to keep calling him 'Your Grace'? Well, that wouldn't be happening. From now on he would be Adam, whether he liked it or not. And she would only respond to Georgina, or perhaps Georgie, or maybe even darling or sweetheart. She smiled at the thought.

'I said, you must be pleased to have got what you wanted,' Tommy repeated.

'What?' she said as she looked from the Duke—Adam—and commenced dancing with her brother.

'You got the man you wanted, just as you always get everything you ever want.'

'No, you know that is not the case. Father gave me an ultimatum. Marry a titled man or be thrown out of the house. It was either this—' she lifted her hand off his shoulder to indicate the wedding '—or I would have to become a governess or paid companion, or something equally horrific.'

Tommy gave a small dismissive laugh. 'We both know that isn't true. Father has been threatening you with dire consequences if you don't change your ways since you were a little girl. If you'd wanted to get out of this marriage you would have found a way.'

'Nonsense. I… He… I…' she stumbled, baffled by Tommy's assertion. 'No, you're wrong. Father does make good on his threats. Remember when he threatened to send me to Halliwell's if I didn't change my ways. I didn't change and he did.' She sent her brother a satisfied look to underline the fact that she had proven him wrong.

'You know that if you hadn't actually enjoyed your time at Halliwell's you would have come home, full of tears and tantrums, and Father would have surrendered, as he always did. But you did have fun there, didn't you? You made friends. You enjoyed yourself. So you stayed.'

'Well, yes, I suppose, but it was still a threat Father went through with, so you're wrong.'

'Do you really think Father would have seen his little Georgie thrown out into the street?' Tommy's smile was decidedly smug. 'You've had Father wrapped around your little finger from the first time you smiled up at him from your crib with those little dimples in your cheeks. You're married to the Duke because you want to be married to the Duke.'

'That's not true,' she said, aghast that he should think her capable of doing something so underhand.

Tommy merely raised his eyebrows, that smile becoming even more smug.

She continued to stare at her brother in shock. Was he right? Had she been merely trying to convince herself that this was all against her will? Had she, deep down, intended to marry the Duke from the moment she'd met him?

If that was true, what sort of woman did that make her? One who played games with men in order to get what they wanted? That would make her no better than all those women she had warned the Duke about. Worse, because she had pretended that she was different.

She looked over at the Duke—Adam—her husband, who was talking to her father. Tommy was right. She was attracted to him, and had been from the moment she'd first seen him when he'd stopped to help her at the side of the road. How could she not be attracted to a man with his sublime good looks? But that did not mean she had intended to marry him. And yes, she would admit she had been somewhat jealous when he had shown an interest in Miss Bateman, Lady Cecelia and Lady Gwendolyn, but again, that did not mean she'd intended to marry him herself. And yes, Tommy was perhaps correct in his claim that she had made no effort to change her father's mind and had simply accepted Adam's proposal. But that was because she could think of no alternative, or at least an alternative that wasn't simply horrid.

She shrugged a shoulder dismissively as Tommy led her back to her husband. While her brother was right that she was attracted to the Duke, he was wrong about everything else. Circumstances beyond her control had led to them becoming man and wife. She had no reason to feel the slightest bit of guilt. And, anyway, there was no going back now. All she could do was make the best of the situation in which she now found herself, and that was exactly what she intended to do.

Chapter Nine

It was done. Adam was now married. Again. One moment he was looking at the account books and coming to the daunting conclusion that the only way to save the estate was to marry again, and this time for money, the next moment he was seated beside his new wife and travelling back to his Dorset estate to start their life together.

It was hard to believe it was just over a month ago when he had met Georgina on the side of the road while she was trying to escape from him. Now she was his wife. If this was daunting for him, it must be frightening for her. Although frightened did not describe the chirpy woman sitting beside him in his carriage. Despite her apparent ease, it was still up to him to reassure her she had no need to be anxious concerning their future life together.

'Miss Georgina.' He paused. She was no longer Miss Georgina but the Duchess of Ravenswood.

'Ah-ah-ah,' she said, waggling her finger at him. 'Now that we are married you *must* call me Georgina. And I shall call you Adam.'

'Georgina,' he said, surprised that a softness had crept into his voice. He coughed lightly. 'Georgina,' he repeated. 'Now that we are man and wife, we need to discuss what that will mean.'

'You mean what my wifely duties will be,' she said with a little laugh and a slight colouring to her cheeks.

'Yes, well, no. Your duties, such as they are, will be limited. I have already said I do not expect you to act as mother to my three children. I will expect nothing of you. We both know that this is a marriage of convenience, one that saved both of us from an undesirable future. I believe you should be free to continue to live exactly as you did before you married.'

'Oh, I see.'

He had expected her to smile, to make one of her silly jokes, to do something, anything, to show that she was in agreement with this arrangement. Instead, she looked strangely disappointed.

'Does that not meet with your approval?'

'Yes, I suppose it does.' She looked out at the passing scenery then back at him. 'But I don't really know what that means. Before I married, all I was expected to do was find a husband. Now I have a husband so I'm not sure what will be expected of me.'

Adam too was at a loss. What did young women like her do with their time? Embroider? Paint watercolours? Somehow, he could see neither of those activities occupying a woman such as her.

'You seem to be very good at enjoying yourself. Perhaps you could continue to do that.'

She smiled as if he had given her a compliment, causing Adam to wonder if that was a wise suggestion.

'There's no point climbing down drainpipes now that I'm married, and as for being rude to suitors, well, that's all over and done with now, isn't it?' She shrugged. 'Mother said that once I was married I would have to run the household, but that doesn't sound like much fun for me or anyone else who lives in the house.'

'My former mother-in-law has run the household since my wife's passing. I doubt if she would welcome another woman taking over that task.' Mrs Wainwright had stepped into her daughter's role as soon as Rosalie had become sick and had done so with daunting efficiency. Despite being a somewhat difficult woman, one who never missed an opportunity to let Adam know what she thought of him for marrying outside his class, he owed her an enormous debt of gratitude for managing his household and caring for his children, especially in the early days when he was so stricken with grief he could barely look after himself. He would do nothing to upset her, including challenging her position in the household now that he had a new wife.

'Mrs Wainwright also cares for the children,' he continued. 'I believe that situation should remain, as you have no experience with children.' That had been one of his main objections to marrying Georgina. He could not imagine her caring for children, especially as at times she acted like a child herself.

'Well, she doesn't perform all the wifely duties, surely.' She giggled nervously, then her pink cheeks turned a deep red, making it obvious to what she was referring.

This was the conversation Adam was dreading, but

one he knew he had to have, and the sooner they got it over and done with the better.

'Miss Hay… Georgina, I know this marriage is against your wishes. I am not such a cad that I would expect you to share my bed.'

He turned and looked out of the window, seeing nothing. He might not be such a cad that he would insist that the marriage be consummated, but by God he was enough of a cad that he wanted to.

From the moment he had seen her standing in the doorway of the church on her father's arm he had been powerless to think of anything else, despite spending an inordinate amount of mental energy attempting to ferociously crush it throughout the day.

'I am aware that young ladies are informed by their mothers about what is expected of them in the bedchamber,' he said, still staring out of the window and unable to look at his wife. 'But this marriage is different, and I will not be expecting such duties from you.' He winced at how priggish he sounded. 'And I already have an heir, so…' He came to a halt, uncomfortable that he was suggesting the only reason a man and woman made love was to produce children. But it was essential that Miss Hayward—Georgina—knew she was safe.

'I see,' she said quietly. 'So we are not really going to be man and wife?'

'Yes. Is that not what you wanted?' He turned to face her, and a small flicker of hope sparked within him.

'Oh, yes, yes. I was just making sure.'

The flicker died immediately, as it should. Now that was out of the way he could gratefully move onto other less disconcerting matters.

'I have already discussed your allowance with your father and made provisions with my estate manager. It will be much more generous than the one your father gave you, allowing you complete freedom.'

'That's nice, thank you,' she said, almost dismissively. Was she drawing his attention to the fact that her allowance would come out of her own marriage settlement? If she was, she had every right to do so. It was her money, and his debt to her was enormous.

He turned in the seat to fully face her. 'I am sorry about this, Georgina. I know a marriage such as this is exactly what you were trying to avoid and I understand completely why you would be upset.'

'Do you?'

'Yes, I think so. You have been used by your father and, I'm ashamed to say, used by me. You deserve so much more than this forced marriage. But I promise I will do everything I can to make sure this marriage is tolerable for you. If there is anything you want, please just ask. If there is any way in which you want me to change my behaviour towards you, tell me. Will you promise me that?'

For the first time since they'd started this uncomfortable discussion she smiled. 'Oh, yes, I promise.'

It really was a beautiful smile. But then she *was* beautiful. Radiant, vivacious and so full of life. And he had trapped this spirited young woman in a life she did not want. She should be free to live life to the full, to dance, laugh and fall in love. He had lied to himself and that was unforgivable. He had tried to tell himself he was marrying her to save her from her father's threats, but he knew that was not entirely true. He wanted her.

Even when she'd been dressed as a lowly maid and he knew she was forbidden to him, he had wanted her. When he'd seen her dancing in the arms of other men, he had wanted her. Now he had her, but he had no right to her.

At least now he was being honest with himself. That was something, he supposed. When he'd heard her father threatening her, he had tried to pretend he was acting as her white knight, but his thoughts had been entirely selfish. He had wanted her, in his arms, in his bed. It was almost more shameful than Adam could bear to admit, but it was the truth. And it was wrong, so wrong.

But he would not act on his lustful thoughts. That would be his punishment for his selfishness. That would be his punishment for marrying a spirited young woman for her money. He would have to see this beautiful woman every day, and know that she could never really be his.

'Good,' he responded, to both his thoughts and her agreement. 'I do not want you to feel trapped.'

She shrugged one shoulder. 'I never feel trapped. And if I did, I could always climb out of a window. As you know, I'm very good at shimmying down drainpipes.' She gave a little laugh to show that it was a joke, but that didn't stop Adam from wincing at the memory of how she had tried to escape from him.

'Anyway,' she continued, 'if you knew anything about me, you'd know that I always make the best of any situation and I always get what I want.' The colour that was still tinging her cheeks unaccountably flared again.

'That is good. I too will endeavour to make the best of this unfortunate situation.'

The coach came to a halt in front of her new home, and Adam helped her down from the carriage. It was certainly a house suitable for a duke and rivalled her family home in its grandeur. Three wings surrounded the courtyard, adorned with statuary of what Georgina assumed were Greek or Roman gods, or something like that. While most of the building was in a similar style to her family's home, and built from soft yellow stone, an older section of red Tudor brick could also be seen.

She could imagine her father looking at it with approval, particularly as it had been in the family for countless generations rather than something newly bought.

They entered the house and walked down the long hallway to the drawing room, where they found the revered Mrs Wainwright waiting for them, along with the children.

'I've kept the children up late,' Mrs Wainwright said to Adam, not even looking at Georgina. 'I hope that is all right. They were anxious to meet your new wife.'

Unfortunately, the children did look rather anxious, and not from excitement. Georgina gave her sunniest smile. No one smiled back. Did no one in this household know how to smile, including her new husband?

Well, Adam had given her permission to be herself, to ask for anything she wanted or any changes she wanted made. And the first change she wanted was for these children to smile at her.

'Let me guess,' she said, approaching the children.

'You must be Charlotte. Your father said you were a rare and exquisite beauty. And you must be Dorothea, because you're as pretty as a peach, just as he described you. And you have to be the handsome, indomitable Edwin. Am I right?'

They all turned towards their father with matching looks of trepidation. He had said no such thing, but Georgina was sure that if she had asked that was exactly how he would have described his children.

'Children, greet the Duchess properly,' their grandmother instructed, as if trying to make this occasion as formal and as uncomfortable as possible.

The two girls curtsied while Edwin gave a bow and all three muttered, 'Your Grace...'

'Georgina. That's my name, so please don't call me Your Grace.' She looked to Mrs Wainwright so she would know she was included in that as well. 'And I do hope we can all be the best of friends.'

'May I present Mrs Wainwright?' Adam said, indicating his former mother-in-law.

Mrs Wainwright gave a small curtsey and also muttered, 'Your Grace...' She scowled as if the words were unpleasant in her mouth, but apparently not as unpleasant as calling Georgina by her given name.

'Please, I would really prefer to be called Georgina. Adam says you are simply marvellous with the children and do a splendid job running the household. I do hope you will allow me to assist you in any way I can.'

Mrs Wainwright sent Adam a sideways look, then turned the full force of her glare onto Georgina. 'It's your household now, Your Grace.'

'Nonsense. And please call me Georgina. After all, we're all family now.'

Everyone looked at everyone else, as if needing some clarification of this statement.

'Well, I believe it is past your bedtime,' Mrs Wainwright said to the children. 'I'm sure your father would like to be alone with his new bride.' She glowered at Adam before bustling the children out of the room.

'Well, at least it's not just me she disapproves of,' Georgina said once the door had closed and they were alone. 'Did you see the way she looked at you?'

'Hmm,' was all her husband said.

'And I'm sure the children will warm to me once we've spent a bit of time together. This must be very confusing for them.'

'Hmm,' he repeated. 'It has been a long day. I am sure you would like to retire early.' He crossed the room and pushed the bell to summon a servant. 'I believe your lady's maid arrived earlier today so your bedchamber will be ready and your trunks unpacked.'

Georgina wondered if now would be an appropriate time to mention that he had said if she wanted him to change his behaviour in any way all she had to do was ask. For a start, he could treat her like his wife and not with the polite formality of a guest.

'I have been away from the estate for far too long and there is much that needs to be seen to,' he continued, still standing on the other side of the room. 'Mrs Wainwright will introduce you to the servants tomorrow and show you around the estate.'

No, she was wrong. It seemed she was to be treated like a guest who could be all but ignored. Was this what their married life was to be like? Georgina hoped not. And if it was, that too would be something she would be changing.

A maid entered and gave a quick curtsey, while keeping her eyes lowered.

'Molly, will you show the Duchess to her room, please?'

Georgina turned to face him and waited. Was he going to at least kiss her goodnight? After all, she was his wife.

He bowed. 'Until tomorrow.'

No, there would be no kisses.

'Goodnight then,' she said, and waited for a few more seconds to see if he changed his mind, then departed and stomped down the hallway and up the stairs to her bedchamber.

This was certainly not how she'd imagined spending her wedding night. And certainly not how she wanted her marriage to be. He did not expect her to run the household, thank goodness, as she'd be hopeless at that. He did not expect her to care for his children, which, all things considered, was probably for the best, and now he did not expect her to be a real wife to him either. And that was something she could actually do, was expected to do, indeed, wanted to do.

Her mother had informed her it was the duty of both bride and groom to consummate the marriage as soon as possible, whether they wanted to or not. Until that happened, it was not a real marriage and could be annulled by either party.

She had made consummation sound like an arduous task for the bride, but Amelia and Irene had explained it did not have to be like that and could be glorious. That was what Georgina wanted. Glorious. And she wanted it with Adam, so she could be his real wife.

She came to a halt at the top of the stairs. Somehow, she was going to have to make him realise it was what he wanted as well. If he wasn't going to consummate this marriage out of duty, then she was going to have to convince him he was doing it because it was what he desired.

All she had to do now was work out how one went about making a man desire you so much he just couldn't keep his hands off you. Otherwise, despite being a married woman, she was going to spend the rest of her life living like a lonely spinster, and that simply would not do.

She entered her bedchamber and gave a little giggle over her new plan. When Adam had told her she would be free to do what she pleased, Georgina had been confused, unsure what she actually would do with her time. Now she knew. She would be dedicating her time to making her husband desire her, to convincing him that he simply must make her his real wife.

Smiling to herself, she pulled back the covers and climbed into bed, for the first, and what she intended would be the last, night in which she slept alone.

Chapter Ten

Georgina rose the next morning and dressed with care, in line with her new decision to change her husband's attitude to her, but when she entered the breakfast room he was nowhere in sight. The children and Mrs Wainwright were seated around the table and all stared at her, as if still unsure how to behave in her company.

This uncomfortable situation had to change, and the sooner the better.

'I believe we are all going to have to get to know each other a lot better,' she said, looking from one child to the next. 'After breakfast, shall we go for a nice long walk? You can show me around the estate, tell me all about yourselves, and I can tell you all about me.'

The children all stared at her, then looked to their grandmother as if for approval.

'With your grandmother's permission, of course.'

'It's not my place, I'm sure, to tell you what you can and can't do,' Mrs Wainwright said, her lips pinched.

'Good, that's settled. We'll have a lovely walk and a nice long chat and then we'll all be the best of friends.'

Georgina continued to chatter as they ate their breakfast, with the children giving quiet answers to her questions in as few words as possible, while the formidable Mrs Wainwright barely said a word. It was as if there was a dusty shroud hanging over this house, one that Georgina was determined to whip away and expose everyone to the glorious sunshine. If she was to spend the rest of her life in this house, she wanted there to be fun and laughter. There had to be fun and laughter or she was sure she would be forced to climb out of the window and make her escape to stop herself from going quite insane.

Once they had finished eating, Mrs Wainwright took the children upstairs to dress for their outing. It was a lovely day, and if it had been up to Georgina she would have just taken the children and immediately burst out of the house and freed them from the confines under which they were living. But she was sensible enough to know that it would not be a good idea to antagonise Mrs Wainwright. Not yet.

The children arrived at the entranceway dressed in sensible plain clothing and sturdy boots, a sharp contrast to Georgina, who was still wearing her pretty blue and white striped day dress. One she had chosen because it flattered her figure and colouring and had been intended to tempt her husband. She had to admit it was more suitable for a gentle stroll in Hyde Park than a trek across the countryside. But she had no intention of changing now, and no intention of being sensible.

'Right, let's have some fun,' she said, which elicited no smiles from the children.

'So, I want you to show me everything,' Georgina

went on as they walked down the gravel path. 'I want to know the best trees for climbing, the best lakes for catching frogs, the best places to hide when playing hide and seek or escaping from your grandmother. All the important things.'

The children exchanged curious glances. 'There's a river on the other side of those trees,' Charlotte said, pointing to the woodland. 'And I believe one can find frogs there.'

It was the longest speech she had heard from any of the children.

'Good. Then that will be our first stop. Lead the way, Charlotte.'

While Charlotte walked ahead, Georgina followed with the other two children and was heartened when Edwin put his little hand in hers. She looked down and smiled at him, but he merely gave her a shy look from under his lowered eyelashes.

The estate was magnificent and a perfect place for children. Their stroll took them through extensive areas of grassland, wooded groves, and to a winding river with lovely old arched stone bridges. Georgina could imagine her and Tommy climbing trees, staging mock battles, running around and generally causing mayhem. But these children looked as if they had never run amok or created mayhem in their lives. That would have to change.

'So,' she called out to draw the children's attention. 'What am I supposed to call you?'

Charlotte turned around and all three frowned at her. 'Charlotte, Dorothea and Edwin,' Charlotte said tentatively, as if speaking to an imbecile.

'I know that is what your names are, but what do you call each other? What do your friends call you?'

'Charlotte, Dorothea and Edwin,' Charlotte repeated.

'Hmm, my name is Georgina, but my brother always called me either George or Georgie, never Georgina, and I called him Tommy, and occasionally "you little beast".'

This at least got a small smile from the children.

'I know. I'll call you Lotte,' she said, pointing to Charlotte. 'You can be Dora,' she said to Dorothea. 'And you will be Eddie. I'm surprised no one has called you that before.'

Charlotte looked down at her boots. 'Mother called us by those names. Except Edwin, because they hadn't yet chosen a name for him when...'

The two sisters exchanged pained looks. Georgina knew that Edwin's mother had died only a few days after his birth and regretted having said anything that reminded them of that tragic event.

Charlotte put her arm around her little brother, whose lips had turned down and was blinking rapidly. 'But when she held you in her arms when you were first born she called you her little duke,' Charlotte said, causing her brother to smile.

'Little Duke,' Edwin repeated, looking as pleased as punch.

Georgina's heart clenched for the children. As much as her own mother annoyed her at times, she could not imagine life without her, particularly when she had been young. These children had experienced so much loss, so much unhappiness in their short lives, they deserved, more than anyone, to have some fun, to see that life could be full of wonder and excitement. And she was just the person to provide them with that fun and excitement.

'So, we have Lotte, Dora, Eddie, also known as Little Duke, and Georgie, and we're a band of jolly buccaneers off on an adventure.' Georgina adopted a hearty tone, determined to put an end to this sombre mood.

Eddie's smile grew wider, but the girls did not look quite so convinced and certainly did not look jolly, but they obediently followed Georgina until they reached the edge of the pretty stream, where weeping willows dipped their branches into the gently moving water.

The children came to a halt as if unsure what to do now that they had reached their destination. Georgina picked up a stone and threw it into the water. Eddie followed her example but the two girls stood staring at the water, their arms hanging limply at their sides. Did these children not know how to play?

'Let's see who can throw their stone the furthest.' She picked up a stone and tossed it so it spun across the water and nearly made it to the other bank.

Eddie copied her, his stone plopping a few inches from where he was standing. But this did not deter him and he quickly picked up another and repeated his action. The two girls obediently picked up stones and weighed them in their hands uncertainly, still wearing those confused expressions.

Georgina threw another, which unfortunately did not reach the same impressive distance. Lotte copied her movements and sent her stone skimming across the water almost to the other side. 'Mine went further than yours,' she cried out, picking up another stone to repeat that performance.

Not to be outdone by her sister, Dora picked up a stone, and almost reached the spot her sister's stone had sunk. Soon the girls were competing and arguing good-naturedly, in much the way Georgina and her brother had spent their childhood, while Eddie was content with throwing more and more stones over the edge of the riverbank.

'That almost made it to the bank,' Lotte called out. 'I'm winning.'

'No, it didn't,' Dora said, turning to Georgina. 'She's not winning, is she?'

Georgina stifled a smile at their newfound exuberance and acted as if she was seriously considering the question. 'I believe Lotte's went the longest distance,' she said, causing Lotte to give a look of smug satisfaction. 'But Dora does have an excellent technique so deserves points for style.'

'Exactly,' Dora said.

'So, buccaneers, do you think we should make a raft and sail away on the high seas?' Georgina announced, looking up and down the river as if this was a serious proposition.

'Yes, let's do that,' Dora said, scouring the banks for suitable pieces of wood.

It was something that Georgina and her brother had often attempted when they were children. They'd never actually succeeded in making a raft capable of floating, their enthusiasm being greater than their ship-building skills, but it had provided them with hours of entertainment.

Lotte and Dora began piling up branches, while Edwin added a few twigs.

'Once we've got all the wood we need, we'll have to go back to the house for twine so we can bind it all together,' Lotte announced.

'No, our ribbons will be perfect, and they'll look pretty as well,' Dora said, pulling the carefully tied ribbons out of her plaits.

Georgina was unsure whether Mrs Wainwright would be happy with their silk ribbons being used for such a purpose, but that was a discussion that could be held at a later date. In the meantime, the children were having fun, and that was the one and only point of today.

'We need some bigger pieces,' Dora said, looking at their pile and around the river. 'Some bits like that.' She pointed to a fallen branch that had become wedged in an overhanging tree.

'Perfect,' Lotte agreed as she hitched up her skirts and climbed out on the tree to retrieve the branch. Georgina looked on with proud amazement. Only a short while ago these children were reserved and overly cautious but, thanks to her, they were now having fun and being adventurous. It was the one skill Adam acknowledged that she had and she hoped he would appreciate all her good work.

Her excitement waned as she watched the little girl move out further on the branch. 'Um… Lotte, perhaps you shouldn't go quite so far out—'

Georgina's pride at the girl's adventurous spirit came crashing down, along with Lotte, as she toppled off the branch and, with a large splash, tumbled into the middle of the river. A shriek went up from Dora, who instantly waded into the water, followed by her little brother.

'Eddie, get back here immediately!' Georgina called out, causing the little boy to burst into tears, but at least he returned to the bank. 'Dora, you come back as well. I'll save Lotte. You look after your brother.'

Georgina lifted up her skirts and waded into the brown water, feeling the mud squelch over the top of her shoes. Perhaps sensible walking boots would have been a good idea after all.

Dora fortunately did as she was instructed, returned to the bank and put her arms around the sobbing and hiccupping Eddie.

Before Georgina reached her, Lotte stood up and it became apparent there was no danger. The water was barely at her mid-thigh, and despite the weight of her sodden dress she was able to wade over to Georgina.

'Are you all right, Lotte?' Georgina asked.

Lotte wiped at the mud on her face, but only managed to smear it further. 'Yes, I'm fine. But look, Georgie, your lovely dress is ruined.' She pointed at Georgina's sodden, muddy skirt.

Georgina smiled at the girl. She had called her Georgie. Despite her obvious inability to supervise young children, and despite putting them in apparent danger, the girl had called her Georgie. They were now friends, just as she had hoped.

'I think we'd better return to the house and get you cleaned up,' she said, taking Lotte's hand so they could wade back to the river's edge.

Lotte looked down at her own now filthy dress. 'Buccaneers don't care about such things.'

'No, but grandmothers do, and so do servants,' Georgina said, surprised that for once she was being the sensible one.

They made it back to the shore, where Eddie and Dora were waiting for them, wide-eyed, with an apparent mix of admiration and awe.

'That really was an adventure, wasn't it?' she said, hoping that Eddie would not start crying again. He gave a small hiccup, then smiled.

'But I think that's enough adventuring for today. Let's go home and have some nice hot chocolate.'

This got a cheer of approval from all three, and the dirty buccaneers began their squelching progress back to the house.

As they made their muddy way up the gravel path, Mrs Wainwright and Adam emerged from the house. Georgina was unsure what she was going to say or how she was going to explain the three children returning in this state, not to mention her own filthy appearance.

The closer she got, the easier it was to see the expressions on their faces. The Duke did not look pleased but, to her surprise, Mrs Wainwright was smiling. Could that be right? That dour woman, the one Georgina was sure would tear strips off her, possibly even ban her from having anything more to do with her grandchildren, was actually smiling.

'Well, it looks like you've all had a grand time,' she said. 'But it might be best if you go in through the servants' entrance and not tread mud all over the entranceway.'

'Yes, Grandmother,' the three children said, turning and walking around the edge of the building.

'I can explain,' Georgina said, not entirely sure how she would do that.

'I think it best if you join the children,' Mrs Wainwright said, saving Georgina from doing the impossible.

'I'll ask the maids to prepare a bath for you, but I don't think your lady's maid is going to be too happy about the state of your clothing.'

This was all so unexpected. Mrs Wainwright was not angry with her. If anything, she seemed to approve of Georgina's wayward behaviour. The same could not be said for Adam. He was looking at her as if she was one of his children and he was thoroughly disappointed with her bad behaviour.

'Well, I suppose I'd better get cleaned up,' she said. 'Oh, and I promised the children there would be hot chocolate.'

He made no response, leaving Georgina with no choice but to squelch round the side of the house and join the children, where they were being washed down with buckets of water by one of the stable hands.

Georgina tried to take solace in achieving one aim for today. The children had had fun, albeit dirty and perhaps rather reckless fun, but she was no closer to achieving her second goal. It was now obvious that if one was trying to get one's husband to see you as a desirable woman, appearing in front of him, caked in mud and smelling like a stagnant river was not the way to go about it.

'Well, I'll be…' Mrs Wainwright said after Georgina departed.

'I am so sorry,' Adam said. 'I will have a word with

her and tell her she has to be more careful with the children.'

This was a disaster. He knew Georgina could be
impetuous and somewhat childish, but he had not expected that on her first day at the estate she would cause
such disruption.

'Nonsense. You'll do no such thing.'

He turned to look at Mrs Wainwright. She was smiling, something he had not seen for a long time.

'Those children need to get out and enjoy themselves.
Lord knows I'm too old to play with them, and, well,
since Rosalie's passing, I haven't had the energy to do
much more than make sure they are cared for.'

'But they were covered in mud,' Adam said, stating
what he would have thought was obvious.

'Mud washes off and no harm was done. And the
children looked as if they had enjoyed themselves. That
matters more than a few muddy clothes ever will.'

He continued to stare at her in disbelief. Mrs Wainwright approved of nothing he did. Was she now ap-
proving of his bride's misbehaviour?

'But I can't stand here talking all day. I've got baths
and hot chocolates to organise, and clothing to be repaired,' she added in her more familiar brisk tone as if
it was Adam who was holding her up from her work.

He watched as she went back into the house. This
was not what he had expected when he had looked out
of the study window and seen the muddy Georgina
and the even muddier children walking up the path.
He'd rushed down, certain that he was going to have to
mediate a confrontation between Mrs Wainwright and
Georgina. Instead, the two women appeared to be on

the same side. While he was pleased there had been no disagreement, he was unsure whether having those two women collaborating was going to prove to be a good thing or a bad thing when it came to his own well-being, but that was something only time would tell.

Chapter Eleven

After a warm bath and a change of clothes Georgina was starting to feel like a woman again, and not a mud-lark who had spent the day scouring for treasures in the Thames. She had apologised profusely to her lady's maid about the state of her dress, but Betsy was unperturbed, as usual, reminding Georgina that it was not the first time she had had to repair damaged clothing or had to clean mud off her dress and shoes. Although her raised nose did suggest Betsy had not expected to be still doing so now that Georgina was a married woman.

Wearing a clean salmon-pink dress, her hair free of mud, pieces of twig and other flotsam from the river she'd rather not think about, Georgina inspected herself in the full-length looking glass. She wasn't sure if she now looked like a duchess, but her appearance was certainly much more feminine. If she behaved really, really well at luncheon, perhaps she would redeem herself in Adam's eyes for this morning's unfortunate incident and prove to him she was a woman worthy of his attentions.

But all her preparations were for nothing. She joined

the children and Mrs Wainwright in the dining room only to discover that, yet again, Adam was absent. Was she ever going to see him again? Seducing him was going to be difficult enough, but it would be impossible if he never put in an appearance. And even more difficult if the only time he *did* see her was when she was dripping wet and smelling rather unpleasant.

'This morning was such fun,' Dora declared as Georgina took her place at the table. 'When will the buccaneers have their next adventure?'

The other two children looked at her in expectation. It was as if she were in the presence of completely different children than the ones who had looked at her tentatively across the breakfast table just this morning. Even Mrs Wainwright was still unaccountably smiling at her.

'Nothing can stop buccaneers when they are in a mood to rampage across the countryside.' Georgina's comment caused the smiles to grow brighter.

'Will Adam be joining us, Mrs Wainwright?' she asked quietly as the children continued to discuss their future adventures and tried to come up with suitable piratical names for themselves.

The older lady shrugged and frowned disapprovingly. 'No, he has much more important things to do than to spend time with his family.' Her look softened and she smiled at Georgina. 'And if I'm to call you Georgina then I believe it is only proper that you call me Agatha.'

Georgina beamed in delight. She might be failing in seducing Adam, but at least she was winning over the children and Mrs Wainwright.

'Agatha,' Edwin said, looking decidedly pleased with himself, while his sisters giggled.

'You, young man, will continue to call me Grandmother,' Mrs Wainwright said in mock reprimand.

'Yes, Gammie,' he said, then commenced chewing on a piece of bread.

'Thank you, Agatha,' Georgina said, sending a quick wink in Eddie's direction, which caused him to give her a cheeky grin. 'I thought you'd be angry with me after this morning's escapade. I really, really am sorry for letting the children get so dirty.'

Agatha brushed her hand in front of her face as if swatting away Georgina's apology. 'You're a breath of fresh air, my dear, and that is what the children need. I was worried when His Grace said that he planned to marry again. I imagined some snooty young thing coming in here and acting all superior, but that's not you at all, is it?'

'No, you can rest assured I am superior to no one.'

Agatha stared at her for a moment, then gave a small chuckle. 'You are a card, aren't you? My Rosalie would want the children to be cared for by someone who knows how to laugh and play games.'

'Playing games and having fun are my specialities, and I'm afraid I'm not much good at anything else,' Georgina announced proudly, causing Agatha to raise her eyebrows.

'But I have to admit, I am so pleased you are here to help with the running of the house as I'm afraid no one would describe me as a particularly responsible adult.'

'But you will be able to prepare the girls for their entry into Society. That is something I am completely ignorant of,' Agatha said with a sniff, as if her ignorance was something she was rather proud of. 'It is a role a woman from your background should have no problem with.'

Georgina grimaced as the two girls stopped eating and listened with extra concentration. 'If that is something Adam expects of his wife, then I'm not sure if he married the right woman,' she mumbled.

'But you married Father,' Lotte exclaimed. 'You must have been the belle of the ball to capture the heart of a man as handsome as my father.'

'Yes, tell us how you did it,' Dora added, leaning forward in expectation.

Georgina flinched slightly. She did not want to ruin the girls' romantic illusions, and certainly did not want them to know that this marriage was little more than an arrangement for the betterment of both families, as was the case with most Society marriages.

'I don't know what I did,' she said instead. 'I think I was just very lucky.'

'But you will help us be lucky in love as well, won't you,' Lotte said, while Dora nodded.

Georgina forced herself to keep her face straight and not grimace again. 'I promise I will help you negotiate the highs and pitfalls of the Season so you have a thoroughly enjoyable time.'

'And find love, just like you and Father,' Dora added as if this was a statement of fact.

'Hmm,' was the only response Georgina could give. She looked at Agatha, who was eating her meal, seemingly intending to detach herself entirely from this conversation.

'So what shall we do this afternoon?' she said, desperate to change the subject.

'We have lessons,' Lotte said with a sigh.

'Oh.' She looked to Agatha, hoping her horror at this prospect was not written on her face. Georgina had never paid attention to anything her despairing tutors had tried to drum into her and had little interest in anything that could be learnt from books.

'A retired professor who lives in the village visits the house three afternoons a week to give the children instruction,' Agatha said, much to Georgina's relief. 'I help the girls with their needlework, but you might have to instruct them in watercolours as I have never held a paintbrush in my life.'

'Oh,' Georgina repeated. Painting in watercolours was another skill she had never quite mastered. No one could tell what it was she was trying to depict, and the paints tended to run into each other until everything became a strange shade of muddy brown. 'I shall invite my friend Irene Huntington, the Duchess of Redcliff, to visit. She's a renowned artist, you know, which means the girls will be taught by the very best.'

'The Duchess of Redcliff?' Mrs Wainwright said with a frown.

'She's not snooty either. She's really lovely and a famous artist, and I'm sure she would love to give the girls instructions because, believe me, you don't want me anywhere near an open tube of paint.'

Agatha looked unconvinced.

'None of my friends are snooty. Snooty people don't like me because my grandfather started life as a baker and Mother's mother was a seamstress.' She gave a little shudder, remembering all those men who'd shunned her throughout the Season, and all those girls at Halliwell's who'd thought they were oh, so much better than her.

'A baker? A seamstress?' Agatha said as if these were impressive occupations. 'My husband and I were tenant farmers, still are, really.' She looked over at the children, who had gone back to finding more and more outlandish pirate names for themselves and had lost interest in the adults' conversation.

'I still can't forgive the Duke for taking my daughter out of the life she knew and away from the people she loved,' she said quietly. 'But one thing I will say about the Duke, at least he's no snob, although it might be better for everyone if he was.'

Georgina thought it best not to ruin this new cordiality between herself and Agatha by pointing out that Agatha was indulging in a bit of snobbery of her own. It seemed the only reason she was so mean to Adam was because the man had the misfortune of being born a duke and falling in love with a woman outside his class.

'Anyway, that will take care of all the children's lessons, which is good,' she said instead. 'Because, when it comes to children, I have absolutely no experience, apart from having been one myself, and some people, including my father, would say I still am a child.'

'No one has experience with children. I'm afraid it's one of those jobs you learn by doing.'

Despite Agatha's attempt at reassurance, Georgina suspected it was yet another skill she would never acquire. But as long as Agatha was present to do the serious parenting and all that was expected of Georgina was to have fun with the children, then this would all work out rather splendidly.

After lunch, while the children rushed off to prepare for their lessons, Agatha informed Georgina that now would be the perfect time to introduce her to the household staff and discuss what was required in the running of the house.

In Georgina's opinion, it was all rather a waste of time. After all, Adam had told her that managing the household was Agatha's role, one she would be reluctant to surrender to the new Duchess, but she obediently followed Agatha around the house, greeted each servant, listened to all Agatha said, tried to ask questions that weren't too silly, and acted as if she was taking in everything she needed to know.

And so her first day passed, without seeing any more of her husband. When she dressed for dinner, she again took inordinate care in the selection of a lovely pale green satin gown with lace trim, and instructed Betsy to take extra care with her hair.

She entered the drawing room and finally her husband was present, sitting in a wing chair and looking handsome, as always. She paused at the door. He looked up from his newspaper, stood up and bowed.

Was that an assessing look he gave her? Was it one of approval? Had all her efforts been to good effect? She was sure it was. But what did it mean? Was he just pleased that his wife was not dripping mud all over the Oriental carpet? Whatever it was, whatever it meant, as his eyes held hers a tantalising little shiver vibrated within her.

Delightfully aware that his eyes were on her, she

crossed the room with as much feminine grace as she possessed and sat down on the settee. Then she smiled, but before her smile had reached its full beam, he sat down and went back to reading his newspaper.

Oh, well, at least he had looked at her. That was some progress.

Agatha entered with the children and signalled for them to stand in a nice straight line, as if part of some regimental guard, with Agatha standing behind them like their commanding officer.

'Right, children, say goodnight to your father and Georgina.'

'Oh, won't the children be having dinner with us?' Georgina asked.

'No, the children will be taking their dinner in the nursery with their nanny.'

'Oh.' Georgina found that an odd arrangement. She and Tommy had always dined with their parents unless they were entertaining. Even then, they were sometimes included in the dinner party, as long as they promised to be on their best behaviour. Something they did try to do, mostly.

The children performed their well-practised formal curtseys and bow, although, unlike last night, they also gave her small smiles. Georgina stood up and did her own extremely low curtsey with much circling of her hands in response, which caused the children to giggle. Then they turned towards their father and repeated the performance, but he merely wished them goodnight.

Georgina was unfamiliar with a duke's household, but such formality really was a terrible bore, and yet another thing that she intended to change at the earliest opportunity.

'I'll say goodnight then, Georgina,' Agatha said, while Adam looked in their direction and frowned at the informality, causing both women to smile. 'Goodnight, Your Grace,' she added and bobbed a quick curtsey in Adam's direction.

'Aren't you joining us for dinner?' Georgina asked. 'Surely you don't intend to have your dinner in the nursery as well.'

'No, I intend to dine with the servants.' Agatha smiled at Georgina's reaction. 'There's much I wish to discuss with Mrs Browne, the housekeeper.' Then she did something that almost caused Georgina to choke. She winked. Agatha actually winked, before heading out of the door.

Georgina watched the door shut behind her, then closed her mouth, which had unaccountably fallen open, and turned to Adam.

'It looks like it will just be the two of us tonight,' she said in the now quiet room.

'Yes,' he responded, looking up from his paper.

Georgina sent him what she hoped was her most endearing smile. They would be alone. This would be her opportunity to seduce her husband. But there was one rather insurmountable problem. She didn't know how. She had never had to entice a man before, nor had she ever *wanted* to entice a man before and was not sure how to go about it.

Still smiling, she thought back to the lessons she had been taught at Halliwell's. Why hadn't she paid more attention? By the time most of the other girls had left finishing school they knew how to flirt, how to be coquettish, how to converse with a man using one's fan and the fluttering of eyelashes. All Georgina had learnt at Halliwell's was the best way to escape out through the top window, how to sneak back into the dormitory without the staff seeing and how to encourage Cook to give her extra servings of pudding. None of these skills were going to help her now.

One of Miss Halliwell's instructions popped into her head. *Ask them questions about themselves and always look interested in anything they have to say.* That was it. That was one of the lessons she had been particularly dismissive of at the time, but it might just work.

'Did you have a pleasant day, Adam?' she asked and added a small flutter of her eyelashes for effect.

'Yes, thank you,' he responded, his eyebrows drawing together as he looked at her over the top of his newspaper.

'I'd love to hear all about it.'

His frown deepened and she forced herself to maintain her interested smile.

He folded the newspaper and placed it on the arm of the chair. 'I spent the day with the estate manager, going over the books. Do you really want to hear about the expected yield from the farms this season, or the new agricultural machinery we are intending to purchase, or perhaps you want me to discuss the repairs that need to be made to the roof in the west wing?'

Georgina's smile became strained. 'That all sounds fascinating. Yes, I would simply love to hear all about it.'

'Really?'

'Yes, really.' Georgina made herself keep smiling,

despite finding nothing to be amused by. Would another flutter of her eyelashes be a bit too much?

'I doubt that very much,' he said.

He continued to frown at her as Georgina tried desperately to think of something else, anything else, to say.

Nothing came to mind. She needed to try another approach. But what? Flattery. That was another lesson they attempted to drum into her at Halliwell's. *All men respond well to flattery*, according to Miss Halliwell.

'You're right, it will all be far too complex for me to understand, but I'm sure a man as intelligent as you will sort out all those problems and will know exactly what to do.' She gave what she hoped was a coquettish smile.

He did not smile in appreciation as she hoped. Instead, his brows drew even closer together and the creases in his forehead grew deeper. 'Are you quite well, Georgina? Did you bump your head when you fell in the river this morning? Did you catch a chill? Are you perhaps feverish? Should I call for a doctor?'

'What? No, certainly not. I'm perfectly fine.' Then she remembered herself and resumed smiling. Snapping at a man was definitely not something advised by Miss Halliwell. 'I'm just interested in what you did today.'

'Why?'

Because I want you to be attracted to me. I want you to ask me to do my wifely duty. I want you to take me by the hand and lead me up to your bedchamber and do all those wonderful things I've been told that a man does to his wife.

'That is what a wife should do,' she said, in response to her own thoughts, not to his question.

He stared at her, as if she were a curiosity on display

at a fairground sideshow. She suspected this was not how a man looked at his wife prior to expecting her to perform those wifely duties.

'So why are you doing it?'

'Because I'm your wife.'

'I know, but why are *you* doing it?'

'Oh, all right. I don't give a fig about agricultural machinery, the west wing's roof can collapse for all I care, and I have no idea what yields even mean, never mind caring about them.' Georgina knew she sounded like a sullen child, but he really was infuriating.

'That's as I thought.'

'So what are we going to do now? Sit here in silence and glare at each other?'

'You could tell me about *your* day. Falling into the river sounds somewhat more interesting than my discussion with the estate manager.'

'Oh, yes, well, sorry about that. I don't suppose I've made a very good impression, have I?'

'You've made a surprisingly good impression on Mrs Wainwright,' he said, slightly raising one eyebrow. 'And the children do appear to have responded to you warmly.'

'They're delightful, the children, that is,' Georgina said with a genuine smile. 'And Agatha is a surprise. I thought she'd be all gruff and disapproving but she's really rather lovely.'

'Is she? I've known her for more than ten years and have never known her to be anything but gruff and disapproving.'

'Perhaps you need to throw yourself in the river on occasion. That seemed to do the trick.'

He did not smile. Did he ever smile?

'But I am sorry about what happened. Lotte was climbing out onto an overhanging tree to fetch a piece of wood caught in its branches to use for our raft. She lost her grip and slipped. Then, before I had a chance to stop them, Dora and Eddie waded in, thinking they could save her, which was rather sweet of them, even if it was ill-advised. Then I had to rescue the two of them before I could get to Lotte to help her out. It was all really rather silly as the river is little more than knee-deep, but it all happened so fast and I was worried that... Well, that's what happened.'

She shrugged her shoulders, hoping he would see that it was all just bad luck really, and had nothing to do with her lack of skills as a mother.

'It seems no real harm was done,' was all he said but his look was still that of someone trying to hide his disappointment.

My goodness, he could be judgemental.

'No, no harm *was* done. In fact, lots of good was done, as the children enjoyed themselves. Even Agatha could see that.'

He nodded slowly. 'Yes, you are right. I am sorry.'

That almost sounded as if he was pleased with her. His agreement didn't come with a smile, and there was certainly no fluttering of eyelashes, or anything that could be considered flirting, but it was something. And something, as they said, was much better than nothing.

To make up for his lack of smiling, Georgina beamed one back at him, then lowered her eyes. 'Thank you for that,' she said, trying for humility. Humility was another lesson Miss Halliwell tried to teach, and yet another one Georgina had failed to learn.

But her attempt at humility worked as well as her flirting and flattery. She looked up to find those dark eyebrows once again drawn together, a reaction that was, unfortunately, becoming familiar to her.

'Agatha said the strangest thing to me over luncheon,' she continued, determined to ignore his stern expression. 'It seems she's expecting me to help Lotte and Dora prepare for their debut.'

He moved slightly in his chair. It was obviously a sign of discomfort, but it did draw her eyes to his long legs, and those muscles delineated under the fabric of his trousers. Perhaps she should compliment him on them. No, she doubted that would be approved of by Miss Halliwell. In fact, she suspected that noticing a man's body, his muscles, or even thinking about what he looked like under his clothes would have resulted in her having to write pages and pages of lines.

I will not look at a man's legs and will not think about his naked body.

She swallowed and forced her eyes back up to his face.

'I'm afraid, before I left for London, I told the girls that it would be the role of my new wife to help them prepare for the Season.'

'I suppose that was before you and I were engaged.'

'It was.'

'Will that be a role you still expect of me?' She gave a little laugh. 'Do you really want me in charge of turning them into proper young ladies who know how to behave in Society?'

He looked at her under raised eyebrows. 'Perhaps we could send them to Halliwell's.'

She laughed, then stopped. 'That is a joke, isn't it?'

'I'm not in the habit of making jokes, but if you feel incapable of providing them with the guidance they need, then perhaps we should consider a finishing school when the time is right.'

'And have them talk to shrubs like ninnies?'

'It would not have to be Halliwell's.'

'They're all as bad as each other. You do not want to turn your daughters into simpering idiots just so they can get a husband.'

He gave her a long, considered look. 'Then it will be up to you to prepare them for their debuts and what will be expected of their first Season.'

'Yes, right. I will.' She crossed her arms defiantly even though she suspected this was another mothering task that would be beyond her.

'I wish for my daughters to find suitable husbands and to learn how to behave in Society without causing a scene, without upsetting anyone and without embarrassing themselves. Are you capable of that?'

'Agatha can help.'

'Agatha… Mrs Wainwright…is not a member of the aristocracy, as I'm sure she will inform you at every available opportunity. She did not have a coming out and does not know what is expected.' He paused. 'And neither did Rosalie.'

He looked to the sideboard, towards a miniature portrait of a young lady in a silver frame, and his face became wistful. It had to be Rosalie, the woman he had loved, the woman he still loved. A lump formed in Georgina's throat. She was trying to seduce Adam under the gaze of his former wife. No wonder she was failing so dismally.

'I'm sorry,' she said quietly, unsure whether she was apologising to Adam or to the woman staring out at her from the sideboard.

'For what?'

'For everything. For all of this.' She waved her hands around the room to encompass the two of them and the woman on the sideboard as if to say, *For you no longer being married to the woman you love, for your children not having their mother, for Agatha not having her daughter. For you being forced to marry me. For me being me.*

To her surprise, he stood up, crossed the room, joined her on the settee and took her hand. 'You have nothing to be sorry for. None of this is your fault. This was an arrangement forced on you even more than it was forced on me.'

Tommy's words rang in her ear. '*You've got what you wanted.*' She mentally swatted them away. She moved slightly closer to Adam and clasped his hand in return. If he really wanted to reassure her, now would be the perfect time for their first proper kiss.

His gaze *was* on her lips. Yes, he was going to kiss her. Then he would ask her to perform her wifely duties. This was it. Her heart pounding out a frantic beat, her body aching with anticipation, she parted her lips, ever so slightly.

He did not move closer, but he still had her hand in his, his gaze was still fixed on her lips. Would it be too obvious if she ran her tongue along the bottom lip? No, it would be perfectly acceptable. After all, they were rather dry.

A knock on the door and the entry of a servant drew Adam's attention away.

'Dinner is served, Your Grace,' the annoying footman said.

The tip of her tongue retracted as quickly as it had emerged. Damn it all. Did they really need to eat? Georgina certainly wasn't hungry. Well, she was, but not for food.

He stood up and offered her his hand. It seemed, for now, she had no choice but to accompany him into the dining room and eat a meal she did not want.

Chapter Twelve

Adam knew Georgina was an unusual woman, so he should not be surprised by tonight's peculiar behaviour. As they walked the short distance from the drawing room to the dining room, he reminded himself that he hardly knew the young lady who was now his wife. All he really knew about her was that she behaved badly and had not wanted to marry. If he thought she was acting in a surprising manner tonight, all he had to do was remind himself of how they'd met. She had been sitting on the side of a country road dressed as a maid. No behaviour could be more peculiar than that.

But this odd coquettishness was new and difficult to understand. Had she been instructed by her mother that she needed to flirt with her husband? And, if so, why? They were already man and wife. Her mother had done her job and secured a titled husband for her daughter. Any flirting would have been done before the marriage service, and there had been none of that. And if Georgina had been told to flirt with her husband, she was just as likely to do the opposite.

He looked down at her, hoping to glean some understanding. She smiled up at him and did that odd thing with her eyelashes once more. Perhaps she *had* hit her head during this morning's escapade. To be on the safe side, perhaps he should call the doctor in the morning.

They entered the dining room, and he held out her chair. Her smile grew wider, as if a man holding out a chair for a lady was an act of great chivalry, then made a small performance of seating herself, with much rustling of silk and tossing of hair.

'Do the children usually take their evening meal in the nursery?' she asked as he took his seat.

'No, we usually dine together,' he said as he indicated to the footman that he could serve the soup.

'I think Agatha is trying to encourage us.'

He frowned in confusion. 'Encourage us to what?'

'You know. Get to know each other better, become more like man and wife.'

'I find it hard to work out anything that Mrs Wainwright is thinking,' he said. 'But she seems to have accepted you, which is good, and somewhat unexpected.'

'Yes, isn't it?' She smiled and looked decidedly pleased with herself. 'She was so grumpy to me on that first night I thought she was going to try and make my life a misery, but she's not grumpy at all. She's rather lovely.'

Lovely? Mrs Wainwright had never shown a lovely side of her nature in the many years he had known her.

'She is very good with the children, and I don't know what I would have done without her since…' He stopped. He would not mention Rosalie's name so casually in front of his new wife. That would be too much of a betrayal of the woman he loved. 'And the children also seem to have warmed to you.'

'Oh, they're lovely too. Little Eddie is such a treat, and the girls are a delight, I can see we are going to have a lot of fun together.'

He raised his eyebrows. 'There is more to parenting than just having fun.'

She sent him an assessing look. 'It seems to me that it's been a long time since anyone in this family had fun. I might not know much about parenting, but I do know that children need to laugh, to have adventures, to even be naughty occasionally.'

Her words hit him like a blow to the chest. She was right. Before Rosalie's death, Charlotte and Dorothea had been light-hearted and joyful children, and poor Edwin had been born into a house in mourning and knew no other way to live.

'You are right,' he said. 'There has not been enough laughter in this house for some time.' He looked down at the soup in front of him. Had there been any laughter since Rosalie's death? He suspected not.

'And what about you?' she asked quietly.

'I am not a child. I do not need to laugh or have adventures and I certainly do not need to be naughty on occasion.'

To his surprise, she laughed loudly at his response. 'I'm not a child either, but I think it essential to laugh, have adventures, and I hope I continue to be naughty on the odd occasion for a very long time.'

'It seems this is one area in which we differ,' he said, aware that he sounded somewhat priggish and judgemental.

'Oh, come on. Surely you occasionally want to be just a little bit naughty.'

An image of stripping Georgina of her clothing, of his hands and lips exploring her naked beauty, of him burying himself deep within her exploded, uninvited and unwanted, into his mind. He moved uncomfortably in his seat and attempted to rein in his fervid thoughts.

'I can see you are thinking of something naughty you'd like to do right now, aren't you?' she said in a teasing tone.

Guilt ripped through Adam, chasing away that unforgivable image. She was so innocent. If she had known where her talk of being naughty had taken him she would not be smiling at him, or teasing him, she would be outraged.

This marriage was merely an arrangement forced on them, he reminded himself. She deserved to be treated with respect, not to be thought of as an object, the subject of his lustful longings.

And he did not want her or any other woman. He loved Rosalie and would be true to her. He would not lust after another woman, no matter how attractive she was, no matter how beautiful she looked in that green gown. He would not notice how the low cut of the neckline revealed a tempting hint of her cleavage, or how the pearls around her neck drew his eyes to those soft mounds. No, he would not think of such things.

He coughed to clear the restriction in his throat. 'I am not,' he stated, sounding even more priggish.

'Come on,' she said, her tone still teasing. 'Forget about being so sensible and responsible. If you could do one naughty thing, what would it be?'

I would take you right here, on this table. I would wrap your long legs around my waist and enter you hard and deep. I'd make you writhe beneath me until you were begging me for more and crying out my name in ecstasy. I would feel the pleasure of being with a woman...a pleasure that has been denied me for so long.

Adam took a long quaff of his wine. 'I believe this is a pointless conversation and if it is all you wish to discuss, perhaps we should dine in silence.' *And perhaps you could stop torturing me.*

'Come on. Just one little naughty thought,' she said, as if oblivious to the torment to which she was subjecting him.

'I said enough,' he barked, louder than he intended. 'Stop this now.'

Her blue eyes grew enormous, and her hand covered her heart as if he had wounded her.

'I'm sorry, so sorry,' he said, reaching across the table for her hand, then withdrawing it just as quickly. If he wanted to avoid reigniting those inappropriate images, and he most certainly did, then touching her skin was one thing he must not do. 'I'm sorry. I did not mean to be so harsh.'

'And I assume you did not intend to tell me off either,' she said, lowering her hand from her heart and glaring at him. 'I am not one of your children. You will not reprimand me.'

'I said I am sorry.' And he could point out that she was now reprimanding him but, given his own behaviour, he had no right to point that out to her.

'Good,' she said, sending him one more look of reprimand before continuing to eat her soup. 'So, if we can't talk about being naughty, what are we going to talk about? Because I, for one, do not intend to spend every evening sitting in silence.'

He drew in a long breath and exhaled slowly. It seemed once again he had been told off, and by a young lady whose behaviour could never be called exemplary.

'What are your plans, now that you are a married woman?'

'My plans?' she asked, the soup spoon halfway to her mouth.

'As I said yesterday, as this is an arrangement rather than a marriage, you are completely free to do as you please. So, do you have any plans for this freedom?'

She placed the soup spoon back in the bowl and indicated to the footman that she was finished. 'I haven't really thought about it.'

'Do you think you might return to London? I have a townhouse that will be at your disposal.'

'Are you trying to get rid of me already?' She gave a little laugh to indicate this was a joke, but there was no laughter in her eyes.

Yes, he could answer. *I, for one, would be more comfortable if we put some distance between us. If you remain in this house, if I continue having to spend time with you, seeing your womanly body, breathing in your feminine scent, listening to the sound of silk whispering to me every time you move, it is going to be torture.*

'I merely wish for you to feel free to do as you wish. I am aware that this marriage was not what you wanted and I do not want it to be any more of a burden for you than it has to be.'

She shrugged one slim shoulder, drawing his eyes

to her creamy skin. He quickly looked back up at her blue eyes.

'But if I went back to London, I'd miss... I'd miss the children.'

'And I believe they would miss you too.' That he knew to be the truth. After one day she had managed to make the children happy, something neither he nor their grandmother had been capable of doing since their mother's death. It would be cruel of him to encourage her to leave, even though, for the sake of his sanity, he wished she'd go back to London.

'Then it's agreed,' she said. 'I will stay here and we will both make the best of this marriage.' With that, she began eating the dish of salmon the footman had placed in front of her, as if all problems had been solved.

Adam stared down at his plate. It was all so easy for her. She thought they could continue as they were, playing at being a married couple like two innocent children, never knowing the effect her presence was having on him.

Chapter Thirteen

Georgina had tried everything, and failed at everything, and now he wanted her to leave. There was no point trying any of those dimly remembered Halliwell lessons again. They had been a complete waste of time and effort and had resulted in him looking at her as if she had lost her senses.

And now he was trying to drive her away. When it came to seduction, she really was dismal. Perhaps she did deserve all those low grades at Halliwell's. Despite her determination to marry a man who wanted to marry her for herself, she had ended up married to a man who wanted her only for her dowry and, despite her best efforts at seduction, he now would prefer it if she moved out so he could have nothing more to do with her.

And he wanted her to move out before she'd performed her wifely duty even once. She looked at him across the expanse of the dining room table. And, by God, she did want to perform it. Every time she looked at him, her body was aching to do its duty. She only had to look into those brown eyes for heat to engulf her and a persistent pounding to start deep in her body. It seemed no matter what part of him she looked at she reacted in the same way. His hands only made her imagine what it would be like to feel them stroke and caress her, his arms made her remember being in his arms when they'd danced. She could almost feel his strength surrounding her, holding her, leading her where he wanted her to go. And as for his eyes, when she looked into them it was as if she was surrendering herself to those brown depths.

She released a quiet sigh. And then there were his lips. How could she possibly look at his lips without imagining what it would be like to feel them on her own? All she had experienced was that one quick, very public kiss on the steps of the church. But, even then, it had been a glorious hint of what was to come. Except it didn't come, and she'd now been married two whole days.

Perhaps it would have been better if Irene and Amelia had not explained to her what to expect in the bedchamber in such exquisite detail, then she would not be so desperate to experience it.

She sent him a defiant look but he continued eating, oblivious to her torment. If he didn't demand that she perform her wifely duties soon she would do what he wanted. She would move back to London and to teach him a lesson she would take herself a lover.

Her defiant look crumpled. Of course she would not be doing that. All she was doing was trying to fool herself, and it wasn't working. She only wanted one lover. And it was him. A man who had married her for her dowry. A man who hadn't wanted her and still didn't want her.

The meal wore on, course after course, while they made small talk, about what, Georgina hardly knew. Once it was over, he led her back to the drawing room and made a formal bow as she seated herself on the settee.

'I'm afraid I still have much work to do, which I neglected while I was in London. If you will excuse me, I will leave you to…' he looked around the room '…your needlework or something.'

Georgina scoffed. He really didn't know anything about her, did he, if he thought she would want to occupy her time making samplers or putting little flowers on the edges of lace handkerchiefs.

'I don't do needlework.'

'I'm sure you will find something to occupy your time.'

'But—'

'Goodnight,' he rudely interrupted before she could insist that he keep her company, and departed as if he couldn't get away from her fast enough.

Georgina released a deep sigh and looked around the room. It was still so early, and somehow she needed to find a means of occupying herself until it was time to go to bed, alone, yet again.

She walked over to the sideboard and picked up the miniature of Rosalie, his wife. The woman he really did love. The woman he really wanted in his life.

'I'd wager he never suggested you go and live in London,' she said to the pretty young woman staring back up at her.

Georgina had to admit she was extremely attractive, with kind eyes and a gentle smile. If her expression was a true reflection of her nature, she would have made a lovely mother for Lotte, Dora and Eddie. And no doubt the perfect wife for Adam.

They'd all loved her, as, of course, had Agatha, and they had lost her. It was no surprise that there was so much sadness in this house.

'And instead of you, they've now got me,' she told the miniature. 'Someone who has no idea how to be a mother and is proving to be useless as a wife. So useless my husband doesn't even want to stay in the same room as me and is trying to pack me off to London a mere two days after our wedding.'

She sighed loudly into the empty room. 'So do you have any advice for me?'

The pretty woman said nothing, merely smiled her gentle smile.

'Yes, you're probably right. I'm fighting a lost cause.' She placed the miniature back on the sideboard. 'Your husband is still your husband and he's never going to see me as his wife.'

She looked around the room. 'Well, I suppose I'd better try and find a good book to read. It's either that or massacre some innocent handkerchiefs with my embroidery.' She went over to the bookshelf, ran her hand along the boring tomes, then spotted a section full of gothic romances.

'Well, I never.' Georgina looked over at the miniature and smiled. It seemed she and Rosalie did have one thing in common. They both liked tales set in creepy castles where brooding men ravished innocent young damsels. She took the book over to the settee and curled up for a good read. If she couldn't have the real thing, it seemed she would have to settle for the next best thing.

* * *

After a fitful night's sleep, Adam again avoided dining with the family at breakfast time. This would have to stop soon. He could not continue avoiding his wife for the rest of their married life, and he was seeing even less of the children than he had before he'd left for London. That simply would not do.

Despite that command, he retreated to his study, telling himself there was work that simply could not wait. He buried himself in his ledgers, but it wasn't long before a sound he hadn't heard for a long time drew his attention from the account books.

Children's squealing and laughter. He moved to the sash windows and looked out over the estate. On the large lawn at the front of the house, Charlotte, Dorothea, Edwin and Georgina were playing a game. From this distance, it was hard to know what the game entailed. Sword-fighting with imaginary swords seemed to play a major part, but, unlike the controlled, almost balletic movements of a swordfighter, this conflict involved much shrieking and jumping up and down, more akin to the behaviour of screaming banshees. And in the middle of it all was Georgina, making as much noise as the children and flailing her arms with as little coordination as Edwin.

Adam shook his head slowly in amazement. When he'd met Georgina, he had been convinced that she was wholly unsuitable to be his bride. He had wanted someone with the maturity required to take on the care of three young children. And maturity was one quality he could not attribute to Georgina.

But he had to admit the childlike pleasure she took in

everything she did was just what the children needed. Mrs Wainwright was correct. His children had mourned their mother for too long. And Georgina was right. Children needed to play and to laugh, to be naughty on occasion, and that was just what she could offer them.

On the day they had met he had told her father that he could not marry such a passive young woman because he had three young children. He had inadvertently told the truth. His children needed someone with Georgina's spirit, energy and enjoyment of life.

He sighed deeply. That was something he had been unable to offer them since Rosalie's death. He watched as the children continued their progress across the lawn and disappeared into the woodland, then continued standing at the window.

His own enjoyment of life had died the same day as Rosalie. His beautiful, lovely, gentle Rosalie. It should be Rosalie, their mother, who was playing with the children, who was making them laugh. While she hadn't been as rumbustious as Georgina, she'd had a kind, loving manner with the children. He was pleased they were now happy, but he hoped they would never forget their real mother, just as he knew he would never forget his real wife.

But was that entirely true? He clenched his hands tightly behind his back. Only a short while ago, Rosalie had been foremost in his thoughts at all times. But she had not been in his thoughts when he had been lusting after Georgina during dinner last night. She had not been in his thoughts when he'd retired to his bedchamber and spent the night tossing and turning, thinking about Georgina's full lips and that tempting, curvaceous body.

What sort of man was he, who could bring a woman into his life, supposedly to save her from being cast out of her home, and to save his own estate, and then start fantasising about all the different ways he wanted to take her?

He returned to his ledger books, hoping the dull figures would drive out any thoughts of Georgina's hourglass figure, of her parted lips, of her soft skin.

He threw his pen down, sending ink spattering across the page. What on earth was wrong with him? Yes, she was beautiful, but he had never wanted her as his wife. She was simply not the sort of woman he was attracted to. She was silly, impetuous, and thought only of enjoying herself.

He looked back towards the window as he reminded himself of the first time he had met her, dressed in that silly maid's costume. Then of her appearance on her first day in this house, standing at the entranceway covered in mud. How could he possibly be attracted to such an irresponsible, childish, totally unsuitable young woman?

Although at least she was not a vain woman. That was something, he supposed. A vain woman would never have dressed in that sack of a maid's uniform, nor allowed her clothing, face and hair to become soaked in slimy river water. And yet she had every reason to be vain. That thick strawberry blonde hair must be the envy of many a young woman, and those blue eyes that sparkled like cut gems were seemingly created to capture a man's attention. And her lips... Men must have been tempted to write poems about the effect of those full red lips. There was no denying she was a beauty, damn it all. His life would be so much easier if it were not so.

He picked up his blotter and attempted to undo the damage he had done to the columns of figures in the ledger.

The arrival of his estate manager was a welcome reprieve, and he provided Adam with some distraction, saving him from looking out of the window as he heard the boisterous children returning from their morning romp in time for luncheon. It didn't, however, stop him from wondering what state she had got herself into this time.

The estate manager left but Adam still did not feel up to joining his wife. He summoned a servant and informed him he would be taking his meal in his study as he had much work to do. He was unsure why he felt the need to justify his absence from the dining room to his servant but, strangely, he did.

And he remained there for the rest of the day. As the evening approached, he tried to think of further reasons that would keep him away from the dining room. He was unsure whether he could endure another evening in Georgina's company, looking at her and fighting his desire for her. But then, he was the master of the house. He had no need to explain his actions to anyone, including himself. So he summoned a servant who would inform Cook that a small plate of cold meat, cheese and bread was all he required and it could be served in his rooms.

When the knock came on the door he reminded himself he did not need to justify his actions to anyone and he would not repeat that foolish, unnecessary explanation he had given his footman at lunchtime.

The door opened. It was not a servant who entered but Mrs Wainwright.

'I thought this was where I'd find you, hiding yourself away,' she said, getting bluntly to the point as she always did.

'I'm not hiding away. I'm…' He indicated the books opened in front of him on his desk. Hadn't he just told himself he did not need to justify his behaviour to anyone? Although that did not appear to include Mrs Wainwright. In fact, when it came to that woman, he always felt he needed to justify everything, including his very existence.

'I'm sure that can wait. After all, it waited all that time you were up in London, galivanting around in search of a replacement wife.'

Adam winced. He had not been trying to replace Rosalie. That was something he would never do. She would always be in his heart, but that was one thing he did not intend to explain to Mrs Wainwright. And, yes, he had danced at that one ball he'd attended, but he would hardly describe that unwanted ordeal as gallivanting.

'And now that you have brought home a wife, you should at least have the decency to spend some time with her.'

'I dined with her last night,' he said, sounding annoyingly like a child trying to justify his bad behaviour.

'Yes, and ignored her all day today.'

'I had…' Once again, he indicated his books and, once again, he reminded himself that *he* was master of this house, not Mrs Wainwright.

'Well, you can dine with her again tonight. You brought her into this house because you needed her money. The decent thing to do would be to make her feel welcome, not spend all your time working out how best to spend *her* money.' It was Mrs Wainwright's turn to indicate the ledgers spread out in front of him.

He quickly shut the books, shame washing through him. He had indeed taken her money. He was indeed trying to work out the best use that money could be put to, to ensure the estate not only got out of debt but started to turn a profit as soon as possible. But that was not the reason why he was avoiding Georgina, although he could hardly explain the real reason to Mrs Wainwright.

'All right. I shall dine with my wife tonight, but I want you and the children present.'

For protection.

'It would be good if we dine as a family from now onwards.'

You coward. You liar.

As much as he wanted to, and knew he should, spend more time with his children, he also did not trust himself to be alone with his wife.

Chapter Fourteen

Adam knew he was being foolish. Dinner with the family was hardly an event that should disconcert him in any way. After dressing, he entered the drawing room, where the children and Agatha had gathered and were chatting amiably. Perhaps Georgina had decided to take her dinner in her room. He relaxed slightly and sat down in the wing chair.

Charlotte and Dorothea were both talking at once, describing to their grandmother the day's adventures, which included the climbing of trees, the storming of castles and the tracking of wild beasts through the jungle.

'I was the wild beast,' Edwin proudly announced and gave a loud growl. 'And no one caught me.'

'Yes, we did,' Charlotte and Dorothea announced as one.

'Only because I let you!'

This caused the girls' voices to rise louder in dispute.

The door opened and Georgina entered, causing the squabbling to come to a halt as they all looked in her direction, including Adam. The children stood up and rushed towards her, and immediately resumed their chatter. She smiled at them and appeared to listen to their stories with surprising tolerance, given that the volume had risen to an almost unbearable level, and led them over to the settee, where all three children tried to squeeze onto the seat along with her.

Adam realised he was still standing and staring at her, so he took his seat. She looked breathtaking tonight. It must have been the time in the outdoors that had brought such colour to her cheeks and caused her to take on an almost radiant glow. Despite knowing absolutely nothing about female fashions, he had to admit that her pale blue gown suited her admirably, bringing out the various hues of blue in her eyes and seemingly making them sparkle.

The gown was cut low, presenting him with a view of her naked shoulders, tantalisingly covered with sheer lace, and the hint of tempting décolletage. She really was a stunningly attractive woman, and she was his wife.

No, she was not his wife. He looked over at the portrait of Rosalie. Georgina was merely the woman he had married. Composing himself, he turned back to the family. The children were still talking excitedly, discussing what they would do tomorrow, while Mrs Wainwright looked on with pleasure.

His former mother-in-law turned to look at him, still smiling, and there was a wealth of meaning written in that smile. He nodded his agreement. She was right. Georgina had fitted into the household remarkably well, much better than he would ever have imagined possible, and the children were actually happy. You would never suspect that these were children who only a few days ago were still in mourning.

He looked over at Rosalie's portrait, wanting to send her an apology, to let her know that Georgina would never really replace her in the children's hearts, and most certainly would not replace her in his. He coughed and crossed his legs. That was an apology he had no need to make. Of course she would not replace Rosalie in his heart. To even think there might be a possibility was an absurdity.

The footman announced dinner, and the children sprang to their feet and all grabbed at Georgina's hands to pull her up from the settee, causing her to laugh loudly. She looked over at him, still smiling with pure delight, and he smiled back at the happy scene. She raised her eyebrows, her pretty head tilted slightly, and he realised what he had done. He had smiled. It felt like a long time since anything had made him smile. He looked over at Rosalie and sent her another quick apology. It was not Georgina he was smiling at, he informed his wife, it was the joy she was bringing the children— our children. Rosalie smiled back at him, that gentle, loving smile he had once known so well.

When he turned back to the family, the children had already led Georgina out of the door and they were dragging her down the hallway, so he offered his arm to Mrs Wainwright.

'Isn't it lovely to hear the sound of laughter in this house again?' she said.

'Yes, it is.'

'You made a good choice there. Her family is wealthy, and she has friends who are also duchesses, so, unlike your last marriage, this marriage won't result in your wife being alienated from her family, nor will she be forced to move in circles different from the one she grew up in.'

Adam went rigid at the familiar criticism. Mrs Wainwright had never forgiven him for marrying Rosalie and moving her into this house, a place where her parents, siblings and friends had always felt uncomfortable visiting. The wedding had been a trial for all of Rosalie's guests. They had stood in small clusters on the outside of the wedding breakfast, looking uncomfortable and awkward despite Adam and Rosalie's best efforts to include them, and after she'd moved into his house, her friends had turned down every invitation Rosalie had sent for them to visit. And Adam's father had not made things any easier, treating Rosalie and her family as if they were little more than servants. Fortunately, the old Duke had been away in London most of the time, losing the family fortune at the gambling tables, but even his absence had not lured any of Rosalie's friends to what they insisted on calling 'the big house'.

It was not until Rosalie had become pregnant with Charlotte that her mother had started to visit regularly, and even then she had avoided spending time in Adam's company, and never acknowledged the old Duke's presence. A situation that had suited both parents.

And then Rosalie had fallen ill and her mother had moved in to care for her. That had continued with Rosalie's death, when she had taken over care of her grandchildren. There might now be an uncomfortable truce between the two of them, but Adam was still eternally grateful to her for the help she had given him, and that gratitude was something he would never forget. But he did wish she would stop this infernal criticism of him for falling in love with her daughter.

'And you managed to pick another wife who is a born mother,' she added as they headed towards the dining room.

Adam stared at Mrs Wainwright in disbelief. Nothing about Georgina's behaviour would suggest she had the qualities that would make her a born mother. She was impulsive, irresponsible and at times little more than a child herself.

'Don't look at me like that,' Mrs Wainwright said. 'Yes, she's a bit of a flibbertigibbet, but I suspect that's because no one has ever expected her to take responsibility for anything or anyone.' She frowned at him and he knew a reprimand was coming. 'And it wouldn't hurt if you told the poor girl on occasion how much you value the effort she is making, and how good she is with the children.'

Adam hmphed his agreement.

'Now she has the responsibility of three children and has risen to the task admirably. I suspect she would also run this house with equal efficiency.'

Adam stopped walking. 'You're not planning on leaving us, are you?' That would be a disaster, and he wasn't just thinking about the danger of leaving Georgina in sole charge of the house and children. Mrs Wainwright provided a chaperon. While it was ridiculous that a married woman needed a chaperon, it was yet another role played by his former mother-in-law that he deeply appreciated.

'I'm going to have to leave some time. I do have another family as well, you know.' She sent Adam a consoling smile. 'But don't worry. I'll wait until Georgina is completely settled in and has learnt the ropes.'

Adam looked down the hallway, where the children were pulling Georgina into the dining room while she pretended to resist, and hoped it would be a long time before she did indeed settle in.

Georgina looked over her shoulder at Agatha and Adam, who had halted in the hallway, deep in conversation, then gave a whoop of delight as the children pulled her through the door and into the dining room.

It was always fun to play with the children, but she was hoping that some time, later tonight, playtime would be over and she would once more see *that look* in Adam's eyes. The one he had given her when she had entered the drawing room.

That look was just as Amelia and Irene had described it. It was the way a man looked at the woman he wanted with unbridled desire. It was a look that made your body come alive, to cause it to pulsate with longing. It was a look that caused you to forget everything, everyone and made you want him more than anything else in this world.

She had seen that look in his eyes. It might have been fleeting but it had definitely been there. Adam wanted her and tonight he would take her. She could hardly sit still as she took her place at the dining table, and hardly heard a word the children said. Not that it mattered. All they required from her was to smile and nod as they chatted on about what they had done today and what they planned to do tomorrow.

Adam took his seat across from her. She gazed in his direction and saw it again. He was staring at her. His gaze moved slowly over her, from her eyes to her lips, then down lower. She drew in a deeper breath, as if her breasts were arching towards him, wanting him to look, to touch, to caress. His gaze lingered, then slowly moved back to her face, before he flicked open his napkin and signalled to the footman to begin serving the first course.

She smiled, a delighted smile of victory. He wanted her. He might be trying to hide it, but he wanted her as much as she wanted him. And soon he would have her.

Georgina had never possessed a great deal of willpower, and even less patience, and was not in the habit of having to wait for what she wanted, but for now she was going to have to exercise some self-control, act like an adult and wait until she was alone with Adam—alone with her husband. Then she would finally get what she wanted. She bit her top lip to stop herself from smiling brightly like a demented Cheshire cat, and turned her full attention to the children, safe in the knowledge that tonight would be the night. After all, she had seen *that look*.

'After dinner, will you read to us?' Lotte said.

'Oh, yes, I suppose so.' Georgina had never read a story book to a child before, but yes, she could see that would be fun. 'What books are your favourites?'

'*Black Beauty*,' Lotte and Dora said together and gave little shudders of pleasure.

'No, read *Tom Sawyer*,' Eddie called out. 'It's got a really naughty boy on the cover so that's bound to be good.'

'Yes, naughty boys are fun, and horses are lovely, but shall we compromise? Do you have a copy of *Alice's Adventures in Wonderland*?' She looked over at Agatha, who nodded. 'That's got naughtiness, adventures, lots of animals—' she leant down to Eddie '—and a queen who likes to chop off the head of anyone she doesn't like.'

She made a chopping motion to the back of her head, causing Eddie to give a wicked laugh.

The children continued to chatter throughout the meal, with Georgina, Adam and Agatha adding very little to the conversation. Whenever she could, Georgina took a quick glance in Adam's direction to see if he would give her *that look* again. Every time she caught his eye a little shiver of anticipation rippled up and down her spine, and she sent him what she hoped was a knowing smile.

The meal over, they all paraded back to the drawing room and Mrs Wainwright departed briefly to the nursery to find the copy of *Alice's Adventures*. When she returned, she handed it to Georgina and said goodnight.

'I'm sure the children will be ready for bed very soon,' she said. 'Just call for their nanny and she will put them to bed.'

Georgina smiled in gratitude, sure that Agatha was deliberately making it easier for her and Adam to be alone together.

She settled onto the settee with the children and opened the book. Slowly, her awareness of Adam faded as she lost herself in the story of Alice and the White Rabbit. Eddie snuggled up onto her lap, his thumb in his mouth as he looked at the book and gazed in rapture at the drawings of the funny animals. Lotte and Dora leant against her, also enraptured by the story.

This was not what Georgina had expected of married life, but it was decidedly pleasant. These children wanted her, maybe even needed her, and that felt wonderful. She wrapped an arm around Eddie, and gently stroked his hair.

'I think he's starting to fall asleep,' she said quietly to Lotte and Dora.

The two girls nodded, looking rather tired themselves. Adam stood up, quietly moved over towards them and lifted the sleeping boy into his arms.

'I shall put him to bed, while you see to the girls,' he said quietly.

Taking the two girls' hands, they followed their father up the stairs to the nursery. *We're just like a proper family*, Georgina thought as warm contentment washed through her. *And soon I'll be a proper wife.*

The nanny was waiting to help put the children to bed, and once Georgina had kissed them goodnight she joined Adam in the hallway.

This was it. Now he would act on that look.

Georgina paused outside the children's bedrooms. Would he take her hand and lead her to his bedchamber? Yes, that would be lovely. Or would he scoop her up in his arms and carry her to his bed? Even better.

He did neither, merely commenced walking. It was not as romantic as she would have hoped, but she walked beside him, her anticipation mounting with every step that took them closer to his bedchamber.

They reached the door.

He kept walking. Georgina's confidence that tonight

was the night faltered slightly, but then they approached the door of her bedchamber. Yes. That would make more sense. He would want her to be in familiar surroundings for her first time, in a place she felt comfortable.

They passed her bedchamber door. She flicked a look up at him. Could she have been wrong? Had she not actually seen *the look*? No, she most certainly had. So why was he not acting on it? They walked down the stairs and retraced their steps back into the drawing room.

So, this was all going to happen in a formal manner. That was to be expected, she supposed. Adam, unfortunately, was an extremely formal man. And, even more unfortunately, he was not the sort of man who would drag her into his bedchamber and ravish her.

He indicated the wing chair across from the one in which he normally sat. The settee would be preferable for what she had in mind but, wherever it happened, she would be willing and eager. As she sat, she ensured she did so in her most gracious, most feminine manner, while at the same time leaning forward so he could glance down the front of her gown, if he had a mind to do so.

She looked up, and bit her top lip to stop herself from smiling. He most certainly had a mind to. Good, there was no point wearing your gown with the lowest cut top if your husband wasn't going to appreciate your effort.

'Georgina,' he said, coughing lightly as he took his seat.

'Yes,' she said, once again leaning forward as if anxious to hear what he had to say, and once again having the pleasure of his straying eyes.

His eyes flicked up to her face and he coughed again.

'Georgina, I have not yet expressed my gratitude to you, and that has been remiss of me.'

'Gratitude?'

'Yes, I appreciate the effort you have made with the children.'

'Effort? It's no effort. I enjoy spending time with the children.'

'Good. And I can see they have developed an affection for you.'

'And I for them.'

'When we agreed to this arrangement, I have to confess I had some misgivings, but you have fitted into this household admirably.'

'That almost sounds like a compliment. If I didn't know better, I'd think you were flirting with me.' It *was* a compliment, although the matter-of-fact way he said it was far from flirtatious, but what was the harm in pushing him in the direction she knew he wanted to go?

'I am not flirting with you,' he said, as if outraged by such an accusation. 'But yes, I am complimenting you and thanking you.' Georgina was gratified to hear his formality slip, even if just slightly. Now, all she had to do was force it to slip completely, get him to look at her in *that way* again, and she would have him.

She leant forward as far as her corset allowed. 'I am so pleased you appreciate me,' she said, her words dripping with innuendo.

'Yes, indeed,' he said, his eyes straying to where she wanted them to be.

Perhaps you'd like to show your appreciation by taking me in your arms and kissing me senseless.

Georgina always prided herself on being brave, but even she wasn't brave enough to actually say that.

His eyes flicked from her and over to the portrait of Rosalie and he quickly stood up.

'That was all I wish to say to you, so I shall wish you goodnight.'

'Oh, so early.' She looked at the clock ticking on the marble mantelpiece.

'I have much to do tomorrow and wish to rise early.'

'Oh, yes, well, I suppose it is getting late. Perhaps I'll retire now as well.'

He sent her a confused look, seemingly registering her contradictions, then walked to the door and opened it for her. They retraced their steps back up the stairs and along the hallway. When they reached the door of her bedchamber Georgina told herself to be brave, braver than she had ever been before.

She turned to face him, smiling in what she hoped was an enticing manner. 'It's not really that late, and I'm not really tired,' she said, hoping that he would understand the meaning of her words.

He said nothing, but he was looking at her. It wasn't *that look*, but it *was* something. She smiled again, leaned against the door and placed her hand lightly on the door handle. All he had to do was kiss her, she could turn the handle and they would be in her bedchamber.

He picked up her other hand and lightly kissed the back. Georgina swallowed, loving the feel of his lips on her skin.

'Goodnight, Georgina, sleep well,' he said, releasing her hand, giving a formal bow and walking off down the hallway to his own bedchamber.

His door shut, leaving Georgina standing in the empty hallway, unsure whether to feel insulted, outraged or so deflated she could crumple up on the floor.

After several infuriated sighs, she opened her door and, rather than calling for her lady's maid, ripped at her clothing, venting her fury on the hooks and laces.

She climbed into bed and picked up the open book lying on the bedside table. Last night she had left the heroine trembling alone in the medieval castle, fearful that the handsome rake who had taken her captive was going to have his wicked way with her and take her cherished innocence.

She read a few lines then threw the book across the room. That heroine didn't know just how lucky she was.

The book skidded across the wooden floor and landed in front of the door linking her bedchamber with his. Unlike the rake in the book, Adam did not have to scale a castle wall. All he had to do was turn the door handle, enter her room and she would be his. And he couldn't even do that.

Well, she was no trembling maiden. Nor was she going to passively wait for him to do what was expected of him. She would be the one to storm the castle, figuratively speaking, of course. She would be the one to take what she wanted. And she would have her victory.

She slumped back onto the bed. Yes, that was what she would do. But first, she had to somehow find the courage to put those brave words into action.

Chapter Fifteen

Adam didn't go straight to bed after he said goodnight to Georgina. How could he possibly go to bed? How could he even think of sleep when thoughts of her were rampaging through his mind and pulsating through his body?

Instead, he walked out of his bedchamber, strode briskly back down the stairs, out through the entrance-way and into the garden, hoping the night air would cool his ardour.

His rapid steps took him down the path, the gravel crunching under his boots. When he reached the country road he stopped. What was he going to do now? Walk all the way to London? He wasn't sure if even that much activity would drive away the circling thoughts of Georgina, of the way she looked, of that tantalising scent of lily of the valley, of the temptation of her soft skin and her full lips.

This was impossible. He had brought Georgina into his house as his wife in name only, and now, every time he looked at her, all he could think of was what she would look like naked, lying on his bed, and what it would feel like to take her, to satisfy a craving for her that was becoming increasingly unbearable.

He was a despicable man. This was an arrangement that suited them both, and that arrangement did not and never had included him satisfying his lustful desires with a woman who had been forced into a marriage she didn't want.

He paced up and down the dark country lane. If only she would go back to London, as he'd suggested. That would give her freedom, but, more than that, it would free him from this torment. But if she did go the children would be devastated. They had already lost their mother, and now that they were getting close to another woman it would break their hearts if she left. It was a level of unconscionable selfishness to even think of separating the children from Georgina. He was just going to have to suffer, and hope that at some time these feelings would pass, or at the very least become more tolerable.

He turned and looked back at the house, which was now almost in darkness. Even the servants had retired for the night. Light shone from only one room, his own. Georgina had presumably gone to sleep.

This was ridiculous. He could not spend the night pacing outside his estate. With a deep, resigned sigh he retraced his path back to the house and fought not to think of what she wore when she slept, or what that long blonde hair looked like when it was released and curling down around her shoulders.

No, he must not think of that. It was hard enough to control himself when he thought of her dressed in the blue gown she'd worn tonight. Throughout din-

ner it had been impossible to concentrate on anything
that was said. All he could think of was pushing down
those lacy straps and kissing that creamy white skin.
And, to his intense shame, he could not stop his eyes
from continually straying where they shouldn't when
he was supposed to be doing as Mrs Wainwright commanded and expressing his appreciation. His behaviour
was appalling. He was expressing his appreciation for
her care of his children, all the while wishing he could
fully appreciate those soft, enticing mounds with his
hands and his lips.

At a slow pace he walked back up the gravel path,
into the house and up the stairs to his bedchamber, trying to drive those torturous images out of his mind.

He passed her door and his pace slowed.

Keep walking. Stop thinking.

He opened the door of his room, knowing that sleep
was not going to come easy tonight.

He stopped, his hand still gripping the door handle.

'Georgina?' he said, wondering whether unsatisfied
lust could actually drive a man insane and make his
fantasies appear to come to life.

'I am here to do my wifely duty,' she said, taking a
step towards him.

A low groan escaped his lips as the frantic throbbing
of his heart rushed to his groin, making thought all but
impossible. She had given him permission to take her,
to do what he had been wanting to do from the moment
he'd met her. And, by God, he wanted to, with every
inch of his pulsating body.

'You don't have to do this,' he said, forcing out the

words he knew he had to say. 'We agreed that I would be content for you to be my wife in name only.'

'No, you don't understand. *I* want to do my wifely duty. *I* want you to show me what happens between a man and wife.'

As if his body had taken over his mind, he was immediately across the room and had her in his arms. He was kissing her like a starving man who had been offered a banquet. Still kissing her, he lifted her into his arms and carried her to the bed, desperate to relieve his hard, pounding need deep within her.

He placed her on the bed and, with frantic fingers, ripped at the buttons of his trousers, all the while staring down at the beautiful woman laid out before him, her long hair curling around her shoulders just as he had fantasised, her white nightdress showing off the curves of her breasts.

She smiled tentatively and lightly bit her bottom lip. His hands dropped to his sides. What was he doing? She was a virgin and he was thinking only of taking her hard and fast, and relieving his own desperate, pulsating need.

'I'm sorry,' he said.

She shook her head and lifted herself up onto her elbows. 'No. What? Why are you sorry? The only thing you should be sorry about is that you've stopped.' She climbed off the bed and reached out her hands towards him. 'Kiss me again, please.'

He released a long, slow breath. It was what he wanted, what he had to have, and she wanted it too, but he had to be gentle.

Taking her chin in his hand, he tilted her head and

lightly kissed her lips, fighting every rampaging impulse raging through his body, an impulse urging him to take what he wanted so desperately. Now, without thought, without control.

Her lips pressed against his more firmly, then her lips parted and her hands wound themselves through his hair.

Go slowly. Be gentle, he reminded himself as his tongue moved along her bottom lip, parting them further and allowing him entry.

Kissing her lush lips was even better than he could possibly have imagined. Her soft, plump lips were designed to be kissed and she tasted wonderful. Honey was never as sweet. He entered her mouth slowly. She gave a small moan of encouragement and moved her body hard up against him, her full breasts pressing into his chest, the nipples hard and tight, making his command to go slowly, to be gentle almost impossible to follow.

She was so beautiful. He had to see her naked. He had to see those breasts, to touch them, to caress them, to kiss them. Reluctantly, he withdrew from her kisses. Her head was tilted back, her lips parted as she waited for more, but instead, he reached down and bundled up the bottom of her nightdress.

'Lift your arms so I can undress you,' he whispered in her ear. 'I want you naked.'

She opened her eyes and looked at him, uncertainty in her gaze. He dropped the nightdress. He was a fool. He had pushed her too far, too fast.

She smiled and lifted up her arms. Before he could question himself again, he grabbed the bottom of her nightdress, pulled it over her head in one quick movement and tossed it to the side of the room.

'You're perfect,' he said on a soft moan as he took in her glorious body—the full breasts, the tight nipples pointing expectantly at him, the curve of her waist, her rounded hips and the dark hair of her mound.

Taking her in his arms again, he kissed her hard, with a desperation that was becoming harder and harder to control, as his hands explored her beauty. Unable to wait another second, he lifted her up in his arms and carried her back to his bed, placing her gently in the middle.

With as much control as he possessed, he undressed, his eyes fixed on the beautiful sight before him, waiting for him. She was breathing quickly, almost panting, those magnificent breasts rising and falling and her legs were parted, as if sending him an invitation—an invitation he was incapable of refusing.

He paused at the foot of the bed, completely naked. Her eyes grew wider as her gaze moved up and down his body, pausing at his groin. 'I will be gentle with you, I promise, Georgina. You have nothing to fear.'

She shook her head. 'I'm not afraid.'

He joined her on the bed, telling himself that it could not be an empty promise. Despite how much he wanted her, he *would* be gentle, he *would* go slowly. He kissed her lips again, and she arched into him. The feel of her silky skin against his naked body was almost more than he could bear. But bear it he must.

Slowly. Gently.

He left her luscious lips and trailed a line of kisses down her neck, savouring the taste and touch of her skin.

Her head tilted, exposing the pale white skin of her neck to his kisses. Cupping her breast, his thumb rubbed over her nipple and she all but purred in response. Slowly, his kisses moved lower, to the soft mounds of her breasts, and he took one hard bud in his mouth, while tormenting the other with his hand.

Her purring grew louder, turning to gasps, matching the rhythm of his caressing tongue. Desperate to explore her body further, his hand moved down to the curve of her waist, over the soft roundness of her stomach and the flare of her hips, to the mound at the cleft of her legs.

A deep moan escaped from him as she parted her legs, knowing instinctively what he wanted. His lips returned to her panting mouth as his hand moved between her legs. His fingers moved along the soft folds, parting them gently, then entered her wet sheath. Hunger for her ripped through him as the soft skin closed around his fingers and he made a deep primal growl of pleasure.

Slowly, gently.

The words emerged through the fog of desire, reminding him that she was a virgin. With a level of control he would not have thought himself capable of, he slowly, gently pushed his fingers deeper inside her, while stroking her engorged nub.

His restraint was rewarded when she gave a loud sigh of pleasure. Lifting himself up onto one elbow, he watched her face as he increased the rhythm of his caresses, his fingers entering her deeper and faster. This was what he had fantasised about. Watching her become more beautiful as her arousal increased. Encouraged by her moans, coming louder and faster as he increased the tempo, he kissed her panting mouth, and she arched up against him, her hard nipples rubbing against his chest.

Her breath caught in her throat. She cried out as the tight walls shuddered against his fingers. She was now ready for him. Kissing her again, he blanketed her body, placing himself between her legs. When her long legs wrapped around his waist he almost forgot himself but, forcing himself to use restraint, he placed himself at the tip of her entrance.

'I don't want to hurt you,' he murmured in her ear.

'You won't,' she whispered back.

'Tell me if it hurts and I'll stop.'

Her hands cupped his buttocks, pulling him towards her.

'Don't you dare stop,' she said, her voice husky.

As slowly as he was capable, he pushed inside her and felt the walls of her sheath clench around him.

'Georgina, my love,' he murmured as ecstasy swamped his mind and senses. 'You are so beautiful.'

Exercising more control than he would have thought possible, he withdrew from her and entered her again, slightly deeper, watching her face, telling himself he would stop if he saw any sign that she was in pain, although not sure if that really was something he was capable of. How could he possibly stop something that felt so right, how could he withdraw from somewhere that was exactly where he had to be?

Her eyes opened and she looked up at him. 'Yes,' she murmured, gripping his buttocks tighter, as if aware that he was holding back.

He pushed into her, harder, deeper, still watching her beautiful face. She closed her eyes and murmured, 'Yes,' once more. With each thrust that word came again, encouraging him to go faster, harder, deeper, until he had forgotten all commands to be gentle.

Gripping her buttocks, he lifted her off the bed and entered her fully, her slick wetness telling him as loudly as her words that this was what she wanted. Her moans matching his rhythm, growing louder and faster, he entered her even deeper, harder. Just when he was sure he could hold back no longer, she released a loud cry, her tight walls convulsing around him, and he released himself deep inside her.

His heart still pounding hard as if trying to escape his chest, he wrapped his arms around her, rolled over on the bed and pulled her on top of him and held her closely.

Her heartbeat thumping against his chest, her breathing as laboured as his own, they lay together. They now really were man and wife. This was not what they had agreed to, but by God it felt good.

Chapter Sixteen

Georgina buried her face against Adam's neck and smiled as total contentment wrapped itself around her as tightly as his arms.

She had done it. She had seduced her husband. She suppressed the little giggle bubbling up inside her. And she had done so without following any of the rules taught to her at Halliwell's. If Miss Halliwell had instructed her to enter a man's bedchamber, dressed only in her nightgown, and ask him to make love to her, Georgina was fairly certain she would have paid attention to that particular lesson.

She stretched luxuriously, rubbing herself against him, loving the touch of his naked skin against every part of her body. When she had been lying in her own bed, facing yet another night alone, the obvious solution to her problem had presented itself. Before she'd had time to think it through completely, to question herself or to find reasons to halt her behaviour, she had grabbed the handle on the door linking their bedchambers, given it a decisive turn and boldly entered his room.

Finding him absent had briefly undermined her confidence, but she had forced herself to not flee back to her room. She *would* be bold. As the minutes had ticked by, her courage had started to fray at the edges. Questions had invaded her mind. How would she cope if he said no? What would she do if he turned her away and sent her back to her room? How would she face him the next day? How would they continue to live together when she had exposed her need for him so blatantly?

But she had pushed those questions to the back of her mind and told herself there would be no turning back. She had seen *that look* numerous times throughout the evening. That look that caused expectation to surge through her. That look that told her he *did* want her. That look she could not and would not ignore.

When he'd finally returned to his room, opened his door and seen her standing beside his bed, his first look had been surprise, then she had seen it again. That look, but this time it was a look that burned through her, sending her temperature soaring. It was the look of a man who liked what he saw, wanted it and had to have it. Immediately. And yet still he had held back, as if he had been told he could look but he could never touch.

So she had taken another risk and told him he could have what she knew he wanted. And now she was exactly where she wanted to be, in his arms, with him still deep inside her, her mind and body still recovering from being taken to the heights of desire and sent crashing over into ecstasy. A sigh of satisfied contentment escaped her lips.

Some wise old sage once said that fortune favoured the bold, and he was right. Fortune had certainly just smiled on her and rewarded her for her boldness in ways more glorious than she could have thought possible.

After her talk with Amelia and Irene she'd had rather high expectations, but what had just occurred was better than they had described. She had not realised making love would be so intense. Nor had she expected to feel so close to him, both physically and emotionally. When he had entered her, it had been as if they were joining as one. She had felt so cherished. So loved.

She stopped smiling. *Loved.* That was exactly what it was like. Now she knew why Irene and Amelia had called it making love. That was the emotion that had taken her over. A deep, abiding, satisfying love.

She nuzzled into him again, kissing his neck, loving the salty, masculine taste of him. She could stay like this for ever, joined to him as man and wife, man and woman.

His heart, which had been pounding against her chest, slowed down to a steady beat. His arms still tightly around her, holding her close, he rolled them over onto their sides and slowly withdrew from her.

They lay together, gazing into each other's eyes.

Love. Was that what she was seeing reflected back at her in those dark eyes? Had he felt it too? She had been confident enough to enter his room, confident enough to seduce him, but she knew she would never be confident enough to ask him that question. Was it because she feared what the answer might be?

She brushed away that question and smiled at him.

'Well, I must say doing one's wifely duty is rather pleasant,' she said with a light laugh. Joking always came so easy to her, and right now it was much better to make light of what had just happened between them than to focus on the powerful emotions still burning within her. 'I have to say I will be happy to do my wifely duty again at any time you wish,' she added, giving him what she hoped was a saucy smile.

He brushed back a lock of hair from her forehead, his face serious. 'I hope I didn't hurt you. I wanted you so much it was hard to hold back.'

He wanted her.

Did that mean he loved her as well?

'Oh, no, it was all so wonderful. Better than expected. No, don't ever hold back. And as for being hard, well, that rather is the point, isn't it, and I've certainly got no complaints.'

He smiled. He actually smiled. She had made him smile. She smiled back, certain she could not be happier.

'You do know how to flatter a man, don't you? And you said you failed that lesson at finishing school.'

'It's not flattery. It's the truth. It was wonderful.'

'There you go again. Well, flattery will get you everywhere.' He kissed her lightly on the lips and Georgina melted into him as her body once more tingled in response to his touch.

His lips left hers, but Georgina would not be having that. She still wanted more, much more. Now that she knew how he could make her feel, she was sure she would never be able to get enough of him.

Her hands curled around his neck and she pulled him back towards her, kissing him hard, her body stroking against his, letting him know what she needed.

His kisses moved to her neck and she sighed in pleasure as his lips caressed her soft, sensitive skin.

'I take it you would like to perform your wifely duty again?' he murmured in her ear.

'Mm, yes, please,' she said, running her inner thigh against the hard muscles of his leg.

His arms surrounded her and in one quick move she was on her back and his caresses and kisses were seemingly everywhere at once, causing her to writhe with almost unbearable pleasure.

'I'm going to need a bit of time to recover,' he said, between kisses. 'In the meantime, I think you're going to enjoy this.' His kisses moved lower. Wherever those wonderful lips went, Georgina knew she would enjoy it. His kisses stopped at her breasts, kissing each hard nub.

'I think you might be right,' she gasped out as he took each bud and suckled, sending powerful waves of pleasure shooting through her. She suppressed a moue of regret as his lips left her breasts. But no, she would regret nothing. She trusted him. He knew what he was doing and, whatever it was, she knew she would love it. His lips moved over her stomach, kissing and caressing. When he took hold of her legs and parted them, Georgina gave a little gasp of surprise and excitement. Was he really going to kiss her there?

He looked up at her, his expression questioning.

'Yes,' she murmured through her daze of desire. She was unsure what she was consenting to, but knew, whatever he did, it would be exactly what she wanted.

He parted her legs wider and looked down at her. A delicious sense of wantonness washed through her. He was looking at her most intimate part with such lust and it felt so wonderfully shameless.

He placed a leg over each shoulder and his head moved

between her legs, licking and nuzzling until Georgina could do nothing other than cry out in pleasure as rapturous waves surged up within her, rising higher and higher until they crashed over her, sending intense pleasure vibrating through her body, starting at the site of his tormenting tongue and consuming her entirely.

His arms wrapped around her, his strong body covering her, and he kissed her gasping mouth.

'Oh, yes, you were right. I did enjoy that.'

He smiled, and lightly kissed her lips again.

'So, if you've recovered, perhaps I can perform my wifely duty again,' she said, wrapping her legs around him. 'Now,' she added with a hint of desperation, arching herself towards him.

'This time I want to watch you,' he said, looking down at her as he pushed himself inside her, filling her up, making her feel whole.

Looking up into his lovely eyes, Georgina wrapped her legs tightly around him, her body immediately burning once more for him. Oh, yes, this was one duty she was never, ever going to tire of performing.

Completely exhausted, Georgina slipped into a blissful sleep. When she awoke the next morning she was still smiling. She rolled over to face the man sleeping beside her. Her husband. After last night's exertions he deserved a long, restorative sleep. She gently ran her finger along the muscles of his chest, causing him to moan slightly in his sleep. Was he dreaming of her? She hoped so.

She stretched, luxuriating in the feel of the sheets against her naked body. There was nothing she would rather do than spend the day in bed with Adam, but she had responsibilities. The children were expecting her to spend the morning with them. With one last, lingering look at the sleeping man, she moved gently to the side of the bed so she wouldn't wake him and retrieved her nightdress from the corner of the room where he had tossed it last night.

'Turn around,' came the command from the bed. 'I want to look at you.'

The nightdress draped from her hand, she turned to the man lying in the four-poster bed, staring up at her. She placed her hand on her heart as she looked down at the man staring up at her. Her husband. That magnificent man lying amongst the tousled bedsheets was all hers and they would be spending the rest of their lives together.

His hungry eyes slowly raked down her body and Georgina felt so beautiful. It was apparent in his eyes that he desired her and, oh, it was so glorious to be desired, and by such a man. As his gaze continued to stroke over her, her body reacted with a now familiar deep, throbbing want.

The temptation to give in was almost more than she could bear. Her body ached for him, her skin craved his touch, her lips tingled for his kisses. All she had to do was cross the room and join him in the bed, and he would stoke that flame that constantly smouldered for him.

But she couldn't. She had made a promise to the children.

'Have you had your fill?' she said, giving her nightdress a saucy little twirl.

He smiled up at her, a slow, sensuous smile that made her legs go weak.

'I doubt if I could ever get my fill of looking at you.'

'Well, I'm afraid that's all you're going to get until tonight, because I have other duties to perform now. I promised the children that we would start an inventory of all the trees in the woodland and rank them according to their climb-ability.'

He laughed. 'Climb-ability? Is that a word?'

'I don't know, but it should be.'

'You're perfect,' he said quietly, his eyes still slowly moving over her naked form.

'Stop looking at me like that! I have to go, and if you keep doing that, I'll get stuck in this bedchamber for the rest of my life.'

'How can I not look at you when you're so beautiful?'

The hunger in his eyes intensified and she took a step towards the bed. No, she couldn't. She had promised the children and, while it wasn't like her to be so responsible, especially when it meant forgoing her own pleasure, she would not disappoint them. She might have fallen hopelessly for this enticing man, but she also loved the children, and would not break her promise to them.

She lifted up her arms, pulled the nightdress over her head and wriggled it down her body. 'There, is that better?' she said when her head emerged. She swept her hand over her now covered body. 'Out of sight, out of mind, and all that.'

'Not really. I can still imagine what you look like under your clothes and that's almost as arousing.'

'Well, you're just going to have to keep thinking about that for the rest of the day, because I have things

I have to do.' She was being such a grown up. It was hard to believe those adult-sounding words were coming out of her mouth.

'Believe me, I will be thinking about your gorgeous body every minute of the day.' He pulled back the covers and his own body was revealed to her, in all its naked glory.

She couldn't help herself and did exactly what he had just done to her. Her eyes raked over his body, taking in those superb muscles. Her fingers twitched with the desperate need to run themselves over those hard, sculptured shoulders, down that firm, moulded chest, over his flat stomach and around the tight, powerful buttocks and thighs. She released a small groan, which caused his lips to quirk into a knowing smile.

When he crossed the room, took her in his arms and kissed her, she was incapable of doing anything other than sink against him, loving the feeling of his strong arms about her, loving the thought that this powerful, virile man wanted her as much as she wanted him.

And want him she did. Her hand moved to her night-gown, crumpling up the fabric, desperate to be free of the cloth that was separating her body from his.

The children.

The surprisingly responsible part of her mind crashed through the powerful pull of desire, reminding her of her promise.

'I have to go,' she said, dropping the fabric as he nuzzled her neck. 'I really do have to go.'

He released her and she tried not to be disappointed.

'Until tonight, then,' he said, gently stroking her cheek.

She looked up at him, her mind still in a daze. 'To-night,' she repeated, but remained where she was, as if her legs had forgotten how to move.

'The children,' he said, sending her a wry smile. 'Climb-ability? Remember?'

'Oh, yes, until tonight.'

She rushed towards the door, certain that if she remained in the room one minute longer she would forget her newfound sense of responsibility, would throw off her nightgown and do what her body was crying out for her to do—spend the day in bed, being made love to by a man whose touch was as addictive as the most powerful narcotic.

She entered her bedchamber, shut the door behind her and leant against the wall to compose herself. Tonight, he had said. Tonight, she would be back in his bed.

But for now, she had to prepare herself for the day ahead. She pulled the cord to summon her lady's maid to help her dress, then poured warm water from the blue and white china pitcher the maid had left, into the large wash bowl.

As she washed, she caught sight of her bed in the looking glass. It looked as if she had slept the night, but she hadn't, and would not be doing so again. Instead, she would be spending every night in the bed, and the arms, of her lovely husband.

Chapter Seventeen

Climb-ability? Adam smiled to himself as he rang for his valet. Whoever had heard of the word climb-ability?

He looked towards the door that led to the adjoining room. And who would have thought it would be Georgina who would be the responsible one? If he'd had his way, he would have sent a message to the children to tell them they would have to categorise the trees without Georgina's help.

Although he certainly would not inform them of the reason why.

But she was right, and if Georgina could be responsible then so could he. He would follow her good example and do something he had not done since he had brought Georgina into his household. He would join the family for breakfast. After all, he had no reason to avoid her now. He'd had what his body had craved so desperately. Now that he had satisfied that powerful desire for her, he could stop lusting after her like an out-of-control adolescent who wilted at the sight of a pretty young lady.

A dull pain clenched his heart, taking him by surprise—a pain that felt curiously like guilt.

What on earth was happening to him? He had done nothing wrong. She was his wife. She had come into his room. She had asked him to make love to her. It was what she wanted as much as he did. And he was a man, for God's sake. No man could resist what had been offered to him last night, even one who had vowed to love his first wife until the day he died.

His valet arrived to shave him and dress him for the day, and fortunately distracted him from his inner turmoil. He continued to push down all doubts when he left his bedchamber, strode downstairs and entered the morning room.

The children, Mrs Wainwright and Georgina were all seated around the oval table, and all five looked up at him as he entered. The children's smiling faces gladdened his heart. It was good to see them looking so happy, and it was the beautiful woman sitting in the soft morning light that he had to thank for that.

'You're just the same,' Edwin cried out as Adam moved to the sideboard to serve himself a hearty breakfast.

After last night he was famished, and he had every intention of piling his plate with sausages, scrambled eggs, toast and a generous helping of tomatoes and mushrooms. He couldn't remember the last time he'd had such a hearty appetite in the morning, but after last night's antics it was exactly what he needed, and he knew that his appetite was not caused by the long walk he had taken to get Georgina out of his system. It was the other way in which he'd tried to get her out of his system that had stimulated his appetite.

He looked over his shoulder at her and smiled. And thankfully he hadn't got her out of his system last night, so there was only one thing for it. He would have to try again tonight, and every other night that followed.

'He is, isn't he?' Edwin said to his sisters. 'He's exactly the same.'

'I'm the same as what?' Adam asked.

'Before you came in, we were discussing how different Georgie looks this morning,' Charlotte answered for her brother.

Adam stopped what he was doing, a silver serving spoon suspended in mid-air. He turned to look at his family. Georgina's lips were quivering, and she appeared to be fighting her smile from becoming a laugh.

'I don't know what you mean.' Adam turned back to the sideboard and continued to pile food on his plate so the children would not see his discomfort.

'Well,' Charlotte continued as if it needed to be spelt out, 'Georgie is all…sort of shiny, and she keeps smiling, as if… I don't know…and she's glowing or something. And Eddie's right, you are exactly the same. All shiny.'

Adam placed his plate on the table and exchanged a quick, conspiratorial look with Georgina and made a false grimace to say, *How on earth do we get ourselves out of this?*

'I believe it must be the new soap we've been using,' Georgina said, her eyes laughing.

'I think I need to start using that soap,' Mrs Wainwright said, causing Georgina's hand to shoot to her mouth in a failed attempt to contain her giggle.

Was that an innocent comment or a risqué joke? Mrs Wainwright's expression revealed nothing and she merely resumed eating her breakfast.

'So, I hear you're going to spend the morning rating trees for their climb-ability,' Adam said once he had recovered.

'Yes,' all three called out. Thankfully, the children were happy to move on to this more suitable topic.

'And we're going to do it sysmatically,' Dorothea said. 'That way, it can be part of our science lessons.'

'I think you mean systematically,' Adam said.

'Yes, that's what I said.'

Adam exchanged a look with Georgina, who merely smiled indulgently at Dorothea.

'As it is part of your science lessons, and it's such a serious endeavour, would it be all right if I joined you?' Adam asked, surprising himself.

'Yes,' came three loud responses from the children.

'But are you any good at climbing trees?' Georgina asked, her head tilted on one side as if it were a genuine question.

'Yes. It's *one* of the things I pride myself in excelling at.'

'And what would those other things be?' she said, her eyes large in mock innocence. 'Let me see, what else are you good at?' She tapped her finger on her chin and looked up at the ceiling as if in contemplation.

'I'm surprised you have to ask.'

'If there are other things you're good at, I believe you might have to show me before I'm completely convinced.'

She looked back at him and gave him a cheeky little smile that made him long for this day to pass so he could show her, again and again.

'I'm more than happy to show you any time, any place you want, if that is your wish.'

'Oh, yes, it is my wish. It most certainly is my wish.'

As they spoke, the children's heads moved from one to the other, as if following a tennis match, and Adam felt it wisest to change the subject.

'So, tell me about this science lesson of yours,' he said, turning to the children, which resulted in them all trying to talk at once, about how to rate a tree, about branch height and trunk width.

'That does sound very scientific. I can't wait to help you rate every tree in the woodland,' he said, when the children's chatter finally came to an end.

'I take it you no longer have important business that requires you to hide away in your study,' Mrs Wainwright said.

Adam merely nodded, not wishing to explain to Mrs Wainwright the reason for his sudden change in behaviour. Instead, he merely nodded and went back to discussing the day's adventure with the children.

Georgina watched Adam chatting happily with the children. He was a different man, and she took enormous pleasure in knowing she had done that. The power of seduction had unexpected consequences, and they were all good.

Breakfast over, the children excused themselves from the table and rushed off, desperate to be outside. Mrs Wainwright made her excuses and bustled off to do heaven knew what with the servants, while Adam took her arm and led her out into the garden.

This was all so glorious, better than she could possibly have imagined. She had been forced into this marriage against her will, but was now married to the most wonderful man, a man who had made her body sing repeatedly throughout the night and had promised to continue to do so, whenever and wherever she wished.

She moved closer to him and halted his progress. 'Quickly, kiss me while the children are distracted.'

She had expected an objection, perhaps a hesitation, but there was none. She was immediately in his arms, his body hard against hers, his demanding lips on hers. This was no quick peck, but the kiss of a man who wanted her desperately. A moan of pleasure bubbled up inside her. This magnificent, handsome man wanted her—wanted her with passion, with desperation. She kissed him back with equal ferocity, wishing the day could pass so she could be back in his bed.

They broke from the kiss. She looked up at him and saw the fire burning in his eyes—fire for her. A fire that sent the heat of her body to fever-pitch.

'Perhaps we should tell the children to assess the trees for themselves and we could return to bed,' she whispered.

Still encased in each other's arms, they looked towards the children, who had stopped walking and had turned to watch them. Georgina took in the three wide-eyed stares and three open mouths. She dropped her arms to her sides as if caught doing something wrong, and Adam did the same. But she was doing nothing wrong. She had merely been kissing her husband.

'Trees!' Eddie called out. 'You promised we'd climb trees.'

'It looks like we *are* going to have to wait until to-night,' Adam whispered, and lightly ran his hand across her buttocks, causing her body to thrum with delicious anticipation.

'Then I hope you make the wait worth my while.'

'On that, madam, you have my promise.' He sent her a devilish smile, took her arm in his and, leaning in close to each other, they walked over to the children.

They entered the woodland and each child ran to a tree and commenced climbing.

'Remind me again, what is scientific about this?' Adam said with a laugh. 'To me, it just looks like children climbing trees and having a good time.'

'Well, perhaps the experiment proves once and for all that girls can climb trees.'

They both looked at Lotte and Dora, who, despite the encumbrance of their dresses, had already scaled up the trunks of their respective trees, were balanced on branches and were looking up to see how they could climb to greater heights.

'If I had any doubts about that it would have been stripped away when my bride-to-be climbed down a drainpipe to avoid meeting me.'

Georgina laughed. 'Well, if I'd known at the time what would be in store I would have stayed in my room, like a maiden in a tower, and waited for you to whisk me away to your castle and have your wicked way with me.'

'So that's your fantasy, is it? Well, I've no problem with having my wicked way with you, but scaling up drainpipes?' He shrugged.

'What?' She laughed. 'You'd be no use in a gothic novel. Capturing innocent damsels is de rigueur in such novels. Until last night, that's how I've had to entertain myself, reading the gothic novels I found in the drawing room.'

His body went rigid beside her and she cursed herself. They were Rosalie's books, and the last thing she needed to do was remind him of his first wife.

'I need some help,' a small voice called out, breaking the uncomfortable silence that had descended on them.

They turned towards Eddie, who was jumping up and down and trying to reach the first limb of a tree.

'I'm coming,' Adam called out. He raced over to his son and lifted him up onto the first branch, then held his hand as he walked out along the branch.

Georgina joined them, watching the touching scene.

'We men have to stick together, don't we, son?'

Eddie paused, and nodded, his eyes fixed firmly on his feet.

'Good boy. We can't let these women think that they're the only ones who can climb trees.'

Georgina smiled as she watched him with his son. How could she not be in love with such a man?

Eddie reached the end of the branch and looked out at the surrounding woodland. 'I'm the king of the castle!' the little boy shouted out.

Adam smiled at Georgina, his hand still clasping his son's. 'I know exactly how he feels.'

Any discomfort she might have felt through inadvertently mentioning his wife's name floated away. He was once again looking at her in *that way*.

She did not need to worry. He wanted her. That look

proved it. And that shiver that his look always invoked once again cascaded through her body. This was what complete happiness felt like. And oh, it was wonderful, and she intended to do anything and everything in her power to make sure she continued to feel like this.

Chapter Eighteen

As much as she enjoyed spending time with the family—*her* family—Georgina was still pleased when it was time to go inside for luncheon. The children's tutor would soon arrive, and she and Adam would have a free afternoon, and she knew exactly where she wanted to spend that free time.

The suggestive smile Adam gave her across the table when no one else was looking made it clear that he was thinking exactly the same thing.

But it was not to be.

'This afternoon is always the time I discuss the week's menus with Cook and make time for the housekeeper and butler to raise any concerns regarding problems with the servants,' Agatha informed them as the footmen served the meal.

Georgina smiled at her. That was all very nice for her, but she had much better ways of whiling away the afternoon.

'I want you to also be present for those meetings from now onwards,' Agatha commanded. 'As you are now mistress of this house, it is essential you start to take responsibility for those tasks.'

Damn. Wasn't she being responsible enough? It would seem not, and the look on Agatha's face made it clear this was not up for debate. The delights she'd been looking forward to this afternoon would have to wait.

She sent Adam an apologetic smile.

'And I suppose I should occupy myself inspecting the roof in the west wing,' he said, and she could hear his disappointment. That was some consolation, she supposed.

'Good,' Agatha said. 'We will all be occupied gainfully this afternoon.'

Throughout the luncheon the children continued to discuss their tree-climbing prowess until the meal was over and the family dispersed to their respective tasks.

Georgina followed Agatha into the butler's pantry, where Cook, the housekeeper and butler were standing, waiting for the ladies of the house. Agatha indicated for them to sit, and Georgina sat beside her, wondering why on earth she had been dragged down into the lower part of the house.

Cook went through her suggestions for the menus, and Agatha insisted on asking Georgina's opinion on every dish, all of which seemed perfectly acceptable to her. Then they discussed the servants, and Georgina's only contribution was to suggest that if the scullery maid was unhappy, perhaps she should be allowed to work shorter hours and have more days off. Something which resulted in frowns from the butler and housekeeper, but a small smile from Agatha.

'Well, I think that went rather well,' Agatha said,

when the meeting was finally over and they were heading back up the stairs. 'I believe it won't be long before you are more than capable of running a household.'

Georgina frowned, in much the same way as the butler and housekeeper had when she'd made her helpful suggestion regarding the scullery maid. 'Oh, but I'll never be as good as you are at running a house. I think it's all a bit much for someone such as myself,' she said, using the helpless little girl voice that had always resulted in her getting her own way with her parents.

'I suspect there is nothing you are not capable of when you put your mind to it, provided it's something you want badly enough.'

Georgina looked at Agatha's face to see if there was a hidden criticism in her emphatic statement. Did she know that last night she had got what she wanted by seducing her daughter's husband? And if she did know, was she offended?

I'm his wife now, she wanted to cry out. *I have done nothing wrong.*

Still muttering to herself, she returned to her bedchamber to dress for the evening. Instead of selecting an ornate gown to impress her husband, this evening she decided to wear the gown with the fewest buttons and laces. That way, it would be easiest for Adam to remove. As she rolled on her silk stockings and tied on the ribbons of her garters, it was impossible not to imagine him rolling them off her later tonight. But she knew she had to keep such thoughts firmly in place until the time with the family was over.

She joined everyone in the drawing room, where they were already discussing the day's events.

'How was your meeting with the servants?' Adam asked as she took her seat.

'Very satisfactory, thank you,' Agatha responded for her.

'It was,' Georgina added. 'But I think the housekeeper and butler are being a bit hard on the scullery maid. Personally, I suspect that she has a beau and that's why she's so distracted from her work.'

'She has,' Lotte announced, leaning forward in her seat with a gleeful expression. 'He's the blacksmith's son, and she hopes that he'll propose soon.'

'Is that right?' Georgina said, turning to face the girl. She could see that Lotte shared her love of gossiping and the two of them were going to have to spend some constructive time together discussing the goings-on in the house.

'Yes, she goes all funny every time she mentions his name,' Dora added. 'A bit like the way you go every time you look at Father.'

'That's enough, children,' Agatha said. While Georgina did not like to see the children rebuked for gossiping, not when it was one of life's little pleasures, she was grateful that it had distracted everyone's attention from her suddenly burning cheeks.

'So, what did you learn in your lessons today?' Adam said, obviously just as keen to change the subject and save Georgina's blushes.

Dora groaned. 'It was science and it wasn't nearly as much fun as climbing trees.'

'But possibly more systematic and scientific,' Adam said with a laugh as he walked over to the sideboard to pour himself a glass of brandy.

Georgina tensed as he passed Rosalie's portrait.

'And I'm sure it was no worse than spending the day inspecting holes in the roof,' he said, lifting up the brandy decanter. 'After my afternoon, I believe I deserve this small reward.'

'Yes, do tell us all about the roof. I believe we'd all be fascinated to hear,' Georgina said in a rush, determined to hold his attention so he did not look down at the smiling woman in the silver frame.

He gave a small laugh. 'You're still fascinated by that roof, are you? Why, I will never know.'

Georgina tilted her head and forced herself to smile, as if indeed it was a fascinating subject. 'Well, it is the roof over all our heads so it's rather important.'

'I believe we can all avoid the west wing until it is fixed. The rooms have been cleared and the temporary repairs are being undertaken so there will be no further damage until the tilers are able to finish the job.'

'Well, that's good, isn't it, children?' she said, trying to involve them in her attempt to distract their father's attention from their mother's portrait.

He walked back to his seat and sat down, without once looking in the direction of his first wife, and she breathed a sigh of relief, then sent a silent apology to the portrait.

I know he loved you, but I'm his wife now, she secretly told the pretty woman on the sideboard.

Then she turned her genuine smile back to Adam, grateful that she had captured his full attention, and surely it would not be long before she had captured his heart as firmly as he had captured hers.

'You look pleased with yourself,' Adam said, crossing those long legs.

'Yes, well, I had a good day. You know, running the household and all that.' She waved her hand in a circle to indicate the household she now supposedly ran.

'I was occupied with the roof, the children with their lessons, and you and Mrs Wainwright with the household. We were all busy, but no one was doing what they really wanted to.' He sent a quick smile in Georgina's direction which caused her body to do that lovely tingling thing. 'But we can all be proud that we spent the day in a productive manner.'

'Pructive is still not as good as climbing trees,' Eddie added, causing everyone to laugh, and Adam to ruffle his son's hair.

'Perhaps we can climb trees again tomorrow,' Adam said.

'Maybe Father can become a buccaneer,' Dora said, which caused the other two children to cry out their agreement.

'Oh, and you too, Grandmother,' Lotte added politely.

'I believe my buccaneering days are well and truly over.'

'That settles it,' Georgina said. 'We'll induct your father into our gang tomorrow.'

That caused another cheer to ring out from the children, and their discussion on what sort of induction ceremony they should have was only interrupted when the footman announced that dinner was served.

Their loud chatter continued throughout the dinner and didn't stop until they returned to the drawing room.

'I'm rather fatigued,' Agatha announced as the others took their seats. 'I believe I shall retire early and I'll leave you to put the children to bed, Georgina.' With that, she turned and left the room. She really was passing over the running of the household to Georgina, but putting the children to bed was yet another task that she did not object to.

It was not long before Eddie was starting to nod off, and after their hectic day the girls were also starting to yawn.

'Right, bedtime,' Georgina announced.

Adam stood up and gently lifted his son into his arms, and Georgina took the girls' hands and led them up to their bedrooms. The nanny was waiting, but Georgina informed her that she could retire for the night, as she would undress the children and put them to bed.

The nanny bobbed a curtsey and disappeared into her room adjoining the children's.

While Georgina helped the girls out of their dresses and into their nightgowns, Adam carried the sleeping Eddie through to his room. Once the girls were snuggled down in their beds, she picked up the copy of *Alice's Adventures in Wonderland*, which the children had brought up to their room.

'Would you like me to read a bit more before you go to sleep?'

'Yes, please,' the two sleepy girls responded.

Georgina settled herself into a chair and opened at the page where the girls had left their bookmark, the spot where Alice is confronted with the dilemma of whether to drink the potion marked *Drink Me*.

A few pages in, she looked up and saw Adam standing at the doorway, watching her. She had been so caught up in the book she hadn't noticed him enter, and hoped he wasn't thinking her too much of a nincompoop for doing silly voices for each character.

But his soft expression did not suggest disapproval, quite the opposite. Was that the look of love? And if it was, was it directed at her or his two daughters?

'I think they're asleep now,' he said quietly, indicating the two girls in their beds.

'Oh, yes.' Georgina looked from him to the two girls. She had been so caught up in reading she hadn't noticed that her audience had nodded off. She put the book carefully back on Dora's bedside table and as quietly as possible crept out of the room and closed the door behind her.

'So, are you ready for bed as well?' he asked rhetorically, giving her a delightfully wicked smile.

'Oh, yes, I'm very, very tired and I need my bed, right now,' she said, lifting her arms above her head and stretching sensually. 'Or, more accurately, I think I need your bed. Right now.'

'You poor thing. Are you too tired to even walk all the way to our bed?'

She bit her lower lip and shook her head. 'Yes, I'm afraid I am.'

'In that case.' Just as she'd hoped he would, he lifted her into his arms and carried her down the hallway.

She covered her mouth so her giggles would not wake the children and snuggled into the muscular wall of his chest. The flames that had been smouldering within her all day started to burn, sending her temperature shooting up, and she knew there was only one way to quench that fire.

He raced her down the hallway and, when they arrived at his bedchamber, all but threw her onto the bed before ripping off his clothes and joining her. Then slowly, tantalisingly, he removed her clothing, kissing each area as it became exposed to him.

As they made love, Georgina knew her happiness was almost all-encompassing. The only thing that would make it complete was if he loved her the way she loved him, but, given the intensity of their love-making, she knew, just knew, that soon she would have that as well.

Adam lay back on the bed, holding Georgina in his arms, her long hair strewn across his chest. He was exhausted, although he knew that soon his desire for her would well up inside him again and he would be unable to resist the powerful need to lose himself in her glorious body, to forget everything except holding her, caressing her, making love to her.

He lightly kissed the top of her head and she curled in closer against him. Instead of quenching his appetite, each time they made love he wanted more, as if his appetite was insatiable.

All day he had been thinking about having her in his bed and had found it all but impossible to focus on anything else. He had almost been able to feel her soft skin on his fingers and taste her on his lips. Visions of her beauty had constantly intruded on his thoughts. And the reality had been even better than his imagination. As if she had bewitched him, she literally took his breath away every time he looked at her, and she so easily reduced him to an insatiable addict, desperate for more.

He had not expected this when he had taken her as his wife and saved them both from a worse future. He had been grateful at the time that she had agreed to their mutually beneficial arrangement. And by God he was still grateful. Grateful that she wanted to do her wifely duty, as she so amusingly put it.

He had not known what had driven him to ask her to marry him, apart from a desire to save her from being cast out by her father. There were plenty of other heiresses available who he suspected would have been even more accepting of being his wife in name only if it meant becoming a duchess.

But he had not made a mistake. He gently stroked her hair and lightly kissed her shoulder, causing her to wriggle against him in that sensuous manner he loved so much.

Georgina was turning into the perfect duchess, and she was more than happy to warm his bed at night, without expecting any more from him than physical love.

And physical love was all that he would ever be capable of giving her, so thank God she was under no illusions that he would be able to give more. If she had not wanted to consummate their marriage he would have accepted her decision, but he was a man, so he thanked the stars above that she wanted physical love as much and as often as he did. And he thanked the stars yet again that she was content with this new arrangement, aware that he would never truly be hers, as he was still in love with his wife—his *real* wife.

That stab of guilt that he'd fought so hard not to

feel all day pierced deep into his heart. He breathed in deeply to ease the pain, then gently ran his hand over her naked shoulder, down the curve of her back to her beautiful round buttocks.

'Well, that appears to have cured my terrible tiredness,' she said, her buttocks moving sensually in his hands. 'I suspect I could stay up all night now.'

He looked down at the woman in his arms, at her beautiful face, at those full breasts that were lightly caressing his arm, the nipples already tight, pointing up at him in invitation. By God, she was desirable and like an addict enslaved by a powerful drug he was incapable of resistance. And he didn't want to resist. He wanted her. She wanted him. Surely, that was all that mattered.

'So, now that I've been struck by this terrible insomnia, can you think of a way for me to occupy my time?' she said with a cheeky teasing smile as her fingers trailed a slow, tantalising line down his body.

'We could try this,' he said, wrapping his arm underneath her body and pulling her on top of him.

'Yes, this might work,' she replied, laughing, before kissing his lips and nuzzling his neck. Adam released a deep growl as her legs straddled him, her feminine folds rubbing against him, driving him wild with desire.

He looked up at her and saw the triumph in her eyes as she took him deep inside her. She knew she had him hopelessly under her spell, and she would get no argument from him. He *was* spellbound by her, completely and hopelessly.

He held her gaze as her hips began moving slowly, sensuously, then to an increasingly rapid rhythm, taking him higher and higher on an exhilarating, primal ride.

His hands cupped her beautiful breasts, tormenting the tight buds just as she was tormenting him. Through his own delirious passion, he watched her face. Her head was tilted back, her lips parted, panting. She was so beautiful when she was aroused, and that was something else he could never get enough of.

Just as he reached a pinnacle and was sure he could hold back no longer, she gasped loudly, her inner folds tightened around his shaft and his own ecstasy released inside her. She collapsed onto him, her heart pounding as rapidly as his own, her silky body damp with perspiration.

He wrapped his arms tightly around her, turned her over onto her back and kissed her hard and deeply. He knew he had lost himself to her, but also knew that lost was exactly where he wanted to be.

Chapter Nineteen

Despite getting virtually no sleep for the second night in a row, Georgina woke the next day full of energy. She resisted the temptation to stay in bed, knowing the children would be expecting her and Adam to join them at the breakfast table.

The children had no lessons that day and Georgina was sure they would be disappointed if they did not make good on their promise for the buccaneers to go off on one of their adventures.

They entered the morning room together, which seemed to surprise no one.

'We've got all sorts of good ideas for Father's initiation into our gang,' Eddie announced as they served themselves breakfast.

'And some of them are truly ghastly,' Lotte added with delight.

Georgina mouthed 'sorry' to him as they both heaped their plates high with food.

'You know what buccaneers really like to do on a day like this?' she said as she took her seat at the table.

The children looked at her with expectation, and she

pointed to the lovely sunny day through the large French windows. 'They enjoy going on picnics.'

The looks of expectation became quizzical.

'Is that something the servants could arrange at such short notice?' she asked Agatha.

'You're the mistress of the house now,' Agatha replied. 'You make the decisions.'

'Oh, but…um…' was all Georgina could say to that, suspecting this would involve more than just making the decision.

'You will need to go and inform Cook of what you require,' Agatha said, taking pity on her. 'It is usually preferable to arrange these things in advance, but Cook will hopefully be able to use whatever she is preparing for luncheon and pack it in picnic baskets.'

'Good.'

'I've never heard of buccaneers going on picnics,' Eddie said, looking dubious.

'Oh, yes, they always like to have a nice picnic on some deserted island before they bury their treasure. It's a well-known fact.'

Everyone except Eddie raised their eyebrows in question about this little known, and wholly made-up, fact, but Eddie went back to eating his breakfast, seeing her explanation as completely acceptable.

After breakfast, while the others prepared themselves for the day's adventure, Agatha pointed Georgina in the direction of the kitchen, leaving her with no option than to confront the formidable Cook.

You're the lady of the house, remember, she said to herself as she walked down the back stairs. *You're a duchess, a woman of substance, someone more than capable of organising a picnic.*

Cook turned out to be not quite as intimidating as she had expected and also helpfully suggested that Georgina have a word with the butler and housekeeper so footmen, carriages and maids could be arranged to ensure the food was transferred to a suitable site.

Having done that, Georgina returned to the family, feeling rather pleased with herself. 'It's all organised. We're going on a picnic,' she said to the children's cheers and a slight frown from Agatha.

'What?' she asked.

'You might wish to inform the children's nanny so she can dress them in appropriate clothing.'

Georgina looked at what the children were wearing—dresses on the girls, short trousers and a jacket on Eddie. It all looked perfectly appropriate to her.

'Their footwear,' Agatha said, pointing at Lotte and Dora's pretty embroidered shoes, bearing matching blue bows.

'Right. Come along, children.' If informing the nanny about suitable footwear was required, then that was what she would do. So she trudged upstairs, the children following.

Once they were all suitably attired, they finally assembled in the entranceway and waited while the maids helped them on with their coats and the footmen loaded hampers and blankets into the carriage. Agatha did a quick inspection, then finally nodded her approval at Georgina.

'I can see you are well on your way to becoming

the perfect mistress of your own home,' she said. 'Isn't she, Your Grace?'

Georgina didn't hear Adam's response as her attention was taken by the children, who were arguing over who would ride up in front of the carriage with the coachman.

'There's not enough room for all of you, so you're going to have to take turns,' she called out as she rushed down the steps towards them. 'Eddie, you can ride up the front on the way there and Dora and Lotte on the way back.' She turned back to Agatha. 'Eddie will probably be too tired on the way back.'

Agatha joined them and patted Georgina's arm while Adam nodded his agreement. 'Quite right, my dear,' she said. 'A good decision.'

Feeling as if she'd just passed a test with flying colours, Georgina took the footman's hand and entered the carriage, unable to stop from smiling. If Miss Halliwell could see her now, running a household, organising children and married to a wonderful man, and a duke no less, she would never have informed her parents that their daughter was a hopeless failure.

After a delightful trip across the estate, the carriage pulled to a halt close to a particularly pretty part of the river where a grassy area, surrounded by oak trees, swept down to the gently flowing water.

Adam took her hand to help her out of the carriage and gently kissed the back. 'No wading in the river today,' he said with a smile. 'No getting caked in mud.'

'No, today I promise I will act like a lady,' she said, raising her chin high and adopting her most imperious stance.

'Only during the day, I hope,' he whispered as she

alighted. 'I wouldn't want you being too ladylike at night.'

A delicious thrill gripped her. Perhaps she should write to Miss Halliwell and tell her how wrong she had been about Georgina. She wasn't as hopeless as she had said, and one thing she was particularly good at was giving her husband complete satisfaction in bed.

She giggled as she imagined the horror that would have crossed that old biddy's face, especially if she knew of some of the more interesting ways she had learnt to satisfy her husband, and he to satisfy her.

'Believe me, there is no danger of that,' she said, wondering if she could suggest a walk in the woods where she could show him just how unladylike she could be.

He lightly kissed her lips, his hand running down the naked skin of her arm, causing that deep longing for him to erupt again, and making her yearn to drag him off into the woodland right now and have her way with him.

But she would not think of that now. Or, at least, she would try not to think of that now.

While the children ran ahead, they strolled across the soft grass and Adam placed a guiding hand on the small of her back. When it slipped lower and moved across her buttocks, she knew that he too was thinking of the night to come, and she couldn't help but arch her back slightly in anticipation.

They reached the picnic setting and, trying to ignore those inappropriate thoughts, she seated herself on the blankets spread out on the grass. 'You can leave us, thank you,' she said to the head footman. 'I think we can manage by ourselves, can't we, children?'

Without answering, the children instantly started opening hampers to see what treats had been packed.

'You two are all shiny and glowing again,' Eddie said, then commenced gnawing on a particularly large chicken leg.

'They're always like that these days,' Lotte added, holding up a cucumber sandwich which was in danger of losing its contents.

'I know,' Dora said with a giggle. 'And they're always touching each other. Why do you keep doing that?'

'That's what husbands and wives do,' Georgina said, trying not to laugh.

'But I saw Father touching your bottom before. That's rude,' Eddie announced, which caused his two sisters to fall about laughing.

'Bottom, bottom, bottom,' Eddie repeated, obviously enjoying the way that word could make his sisters laugh.

'That will be enough from you, young man,' Agatha said, something Georgina suspected she was supposed to say, but she was laughing too much to do so.

Somewhat chastened, the children resumed eating, but she could see that Eddie was just itching to say his rude word again.

'When we've finished eating, I propose the buccaneers go on another of their rollicking adventures,' Georgina said before they had a chance to return to their favourite topic of discussing her and Adam's supposed shininess.

'But first we have to induct Father into our club and he has to prove he's worthy of becoming a buccaneer,' Dora said, causing raucous cheers to erupt from the other two children.

'We could toss him in the river?' Eddie said. 'Or make him climb up to the highest tree then jump down.'

Adam and Georgina looked at each other with matching looks of mock horror.

'Or perhaps I could give you sword-fighting lessons so you'll be able to defend yourself if another band of pirates attacks you.'

'Yes, sword fight,' Eddie agreed, and Georgina smiled as relief crossed Adam's face.

'Coward,' she mumbled.

'No, clever,' he responded quietly. 'The more we tire them out, the sooner they will go to bed tonight.' He gave her a suggestive smile, and she loved what he was suggesting.

Once the meal was finished, Adam had the children on their feet and marched them off to the nearby field, where he adopted the *en garde* position. The children tried to follow his lead, and a sword fight soon erupted, one that had much more enthusiasm than grace, and seemed to involve a lot more running up and down, whirling in circles and general mayhem than any sword fight Georgina had ever witnessed. While all this took place, Georgina, for once, was happy to sit back, watch and laugh at the antics, taking particular pleasure in Adam's exerted efforts to exhaust the children.

When he picked up a laughing Lotte and Dora under each arm and began running round the field with them, chased by an exuberant Eddie, who was seemingly trying to rescue the captured damsels, she did worry that he might be exhausting himself in the process. That would never do, as she had her own plans on how to try and wear him out, something she had thankfully failed to do so far. But there was no harm in trying yet again tonight.

'He's a changed man,' Agatha said, breaking in on her thoughts. 'And we have you to thank for that.'

She smiled at the older woman, touched by the compliment.

'It's been years since he's played like this with the children. You've really brought him back to life.'

Georgina's smile vanished, and she reached out and touched Agatha's hand, knowing that she must be thinking of her daughter.

'You must miss her terribly,' she said quietly.

'I do.' Agatha pulled her expression into the more familiar stoic one. 'But I'm pleased my grandchildren now have a happy, loving household.'

'I do love them,' Georgina said. 'It wasn't hard to fall in love with them because they're so, well, loveable.'

And it wasn't hard to fall in love with their father either.

She looked over at Adam, who had now collapsed in a heap, his children crawling all over him, the point of the game completely lost on Georgina, but obviously giving the children a great deal of pleasure.

She had fallen in love with him and now had exactly what she had always wanted. From that very first Season she had wanted to fall in love and marry, but had never met a man to whom she was in the slightest bit interested in giving her heart. Not until she had climbed down the drainpipe in a futile attempt to escape her destiny. She might have got the order slightly wrong. One was supposed to fall in love and then marry, but she had married, then fallen hopelessly, completely, passionately in love and now had a man she loved and children she also adored. This was possibly what perfection felt like.

Tommy's words seemed to whisper in her ear.

'*You've got what you wanted...*'

Well, to that she could now reply, *Yes, I have, and what is wrong with that?*

Adam lay on the grass, the children rolling over him, laughing loudly. He could hardly remember the last time he'd played with the children and taken such pleasure in their exuberance. Certainly not since Rosalie's passing.

That familiar tightness gripped his chest as an image of Rosalie making daisy chains with the girls crashed into his mind, before Eddie captured his attention by grabbing onto his shins and attempting to drag him along the ground.

'Aha, me hearties, the blighter is trying to best us,' Adam said, springing to his feet, and doing what he hoped was a passable impression of a pirate.

Eddie slashed at the air, in a chaotic but thankfully harmless manner, with a stick that had been converted to his sword. His sword-fighting was performed with as much vigour as his young arms would allow, while Adam pretended he was hopelessly outmanoeuvred and the girls ran around in circles, squealing as loudly as they possibly could. The reason for that particular behaviour eluded him, but the girls apparently could see some logic in what they were doing, so who was he to question the actions of the bold buccaneers?

Adam felt certain they would never tire of this game, but eventually their energies started to wane and they all headed back to the picnic blankets, where Georgina and Mrs Wainwright were chatting together amiably.

'So, who won?' Georgina asked.

'We did,' all three children answered, while Adam shrugged his shoulders. It was hard to know who'd won when he wasn't actually sure what the game was, and who was on whose side.

Georgina smiled and signalled to the coachman that they were ready to leave. The family packed up the picnic hampers, Georgina having earlier sent the other servants back to the house, and helped load everything into the carriage.

Just as they had expected, the day's activities had exhausted the children. Eddie fell asleep on the carriage drive back to the house, cuddled up against Georgina, and the girls were subdued, which they had rarely been since Georgina's arrival in the house. Even riding on top of the carriage did not result in the expected cries of delight, merely some muted comments of approval.

When they got back to the house, Mrs Wainwright suggested it would be best if the children had their dinner in the nursery as they were far too tired to dine at table, and summoned the nanny to take the sleepy children to their beds.

'I'll come and tuck you in once you're undressed,' Georgina said as the children departed up the stairs, although Adam suspected the moment their heads hit the pillows they would be asleep.

Mrs Wainwright also announced she would not be dining with them this evening and would take a tray in her room, then she disappeared, leaving them alone in the hallway.

'Shall I tell Cook that we are also rather weary and would like to have trays sent up to your bedchamber?' Georgina said, placing the back of her hand on her forehead in a dramatic rendition of weariness and causing Adam to laugh.

'Oh, God, Georgina, you're right. I am hungry—very hungry,' he growled in her ear.

'In that case, you'd better get to bed as well and I'll go and tell Cook to have something sent up to your room.'

It's not food I'm hungry for, he wanted to call out as she hurried off down the hallway towards the kitchen, but a passing footman caused him to hold his tongue.

It was hard to believe that the young woman who was organising him and his family was the same reckless Georgina he had met at the side of the road only a few months ago. She was turning into an efficient manager of his household, not to mention her care for his children. It seemed that wonders would never cease.

While she organised their meal he walked up to his bedchamber, taking the stairs two at a time, anxious to experience more of those wonders that never ceased to amaze him.

Chapter Twenty

The next morning, and every morning that followed, when Georgina woke up, if she wasn't already snuggled up to Adam, that was the first thing she would do. Was there a more perfect way to start the day than in the arms of the man you loved? If there was, Georgina couldn't think what it might be.

And each morning her feelings of love for him increased, along with her certainty that Adam was in love with her. He hadn't said it yet, not in actual words, but every kiss, every act of affection, every time he gave her *that look*, said it louder than words ever could. Although it would be nice to hear those three little words, but Georgina just knew it was only a matter of time. She just had to do what she previously had been incapable of doing, be patient, and she would get what she wanted.

There was always the option of forcing the issue by being the first one to declare her love, just as she had forced the issue by appearing in his room dressed only in her nightgown, but she would not do that. It was going to be so much more special if it came from him first.

And when it did, she just knew her life with him would be even more wonderful than it was now and her happiness would be complete.

He opened his eyes, stretched, smiled at her, and her certainty that he would soon say those three little words surged through her, along with other insistent feelings that only he could satisfy.

His strong arms encased her, and as she melted into his body she realised that her initial thought on waking had been incorrect. There *was* a better way to start the day than being snuggled up to the man you loved. You could start the day by making love to the man you were hopelessly, totally, incurably in love with. And that was exactly what she intended to do.

Her body sated, her mind awash with adoration for the man who made her so happy, she lay in bed and watched Adam as he stood at the washstand and ran water over that magnificent body. It was so tempting to rise from the bed and lick those rivulets of water as they trickled down his superb muscles.

He turned and looked at her, his gaze sweeping over her body. She just loved that hungry look in his eyes and moved sensually in the bed, letting him know the effect he was having on her.

'Don't tempt me,' he said, his gaze still on her. 'Remember you promised Lotte and Dora you would begin their preparation for the Season, and I said I'd help Eddie with his reading lessons.'

'You're right,' she said and climbed out of bed. She had been unable to resist Lotte and Dora's constant pleas, but was unsure what she was actually going to teach them.

'Are you sure you trust me with that task? After all, I hardly had the most successful of Seasons, did I?'

'You managed to catch me,' he said, taking her in his arms and kissing her. Georgina melted into the kiss. It wasn't quite how she remembered their non-courtship. But now was not the time to quibble over little details.

He deepened the kiss, but Georgina reluctantly pulled away.

'Who's trying to tempt whom now?' she said with a little laugh, wondering briefly whether the first lesson could wait a bit longer, before pushing that thought away. 'I need to wash and dress and the children will be wondering what is keeping us. Eddie will probably think you're busy touching my bottom again.'

He laughed, and lightly patted her naked derrière. 'You're right, you need to get dressed, but I'll be wanting you back in my bed and looking just like that again tonight.'

She looked down at her body and smiled. It was amazing how comfortable she had become with being naked in front of him. It felt so natural and was a long way from that first time she had entered his room dressed in her nightgown, feeling nervous and anxious about her own attractiveness. Now, every time he looked at her, she felt more desirable and more powerful, knowing he was incapable of resisting her.

'If you approve of it so much, perhaps I should appear like this in public,' she said, doing a little twirl and looking at him over her shoulder in a coquettish manner. 'I'm sure I would be the belle of every ball I attended.'

He wrapped her gown around her shoulders. 'Don't you dare. That is for my eyes only.'

And your *body is for my eyes only,* she thought, fastening the gown as her eyes raked over his muscular form. You *are for me, and me alone, and that is the way it will always be.*

After breakfast, the family gathered in the drawing room, where Georgina was supposed to give her first lesson on how to conduct oneself during the Season, while Eddie and Adam neglected the book in front of them and watched on in amusement.

'Right,' she said, handing each girl a large book. 'This lesson involves walking around the room with a book on your head.'

'Why?' Lotte asked, looking down at the dictionary in her hand.

'Good question,' Georgina said. 'It's so, should the occasion demand, you can steal books from people's bookshelves without them noticing.'

His daughters stared at her, wide-eyed, and Adam had to suppress a laugh. 'I've never attended finishing school,' he said. 'But I believe that particular exercise has something to do with adopting the correct feminine posture, not theft.'

'Oh, yes, your father's right,' Georgina said. 'Right, here you go.' She placed a heavy tome on each girl's head, which instantly tumbled to the ground.

'It also makes you light on your feet,' she said. 'As you'll get plenty of practice jumping out of the way of falling books. Right, let's try again.'

Adam pulled Eddie onto his lap as they watched the entertainment, the reading book long forgotten. Slowly, the girls got the hang of the exercise and the number of squeals of fright and jumps in the air as the books crashed to the floor diminished. Despite Georgina's joking, he could see his little girls turning into elegant young ladies before his eyes.

Georgina looked in his direction, smiled and raised her eyebrows as the girls performed perfect circuits of the room, their heads held high, their shoulders back and their movements graceful.

He smiled back in approval. It was miraculous. Once again, she was surprising him—as she had done since she'd first arrived at his estate, and continued to do every day, and especially every night.

'Right, you've mastered that,' she said, turning back to the girls. 'I suppose we should discuss the art of conversation next.' She gave a mock scowl.

'You're not going to take Lotte and Dora outside to talk to shrubs, are you?' he said, laughing at the prospect.

The two girls removed the books from their heads and stared at him.

'What?' he asked, looking around the suddenly quiet room. 'That's what Georgina said she had to do at Halliwell's Finishing School—talk to shrubs.'

'You called us Dora and Lotte, not Dorothea and Charlotte,' Dora said, breaking into a smile, a reaction that rippled round the room, until all three females were beaming at him as if he had done something miraculous.

'And I'm Eddie, not Edwin.'

Adam looked down at the young boy smiling up at him from his lap and tousled his son's already messy hair. 'All right, Eddie, Dora and Lotte, let's all concentrate on our lessons, shall we?' Adam said, trying to adopt a stern manner, but the smile quirking his lips made that impossible. 'And Eddie, you haven't even tried to read your book.'

'You've changed,' Dora said, and Lotte and Eddie nodded their agreement.

'Yes, you've become much nicer since Georgie joined our household,' Lotte added.

'Have I? Georgina must be doing something that is good for me.' He sent her a quick wink and was pleased to see a flush of delight on her cheeks. 'So, she's the perfect person to teach you how to be proper young ladies.'

He laughed as Georgina lifted her eyebrows in disbelief.

'Are you sure about that?' she said.

'Well, how to be proper young ladies in the drawing room and how to behave during the Season,' he said, joining in her laughter.

'You didn't used to laugh as much as this before you married Georgie,' Lotte said, looking from him to Georgina and back again.

'No, and you used to spend all your time staring at the little lady in the blue dress and looking sad,' Eddie added, pointing at the miniature of Rosalie on the sideboard.

Adam's smile died instantly as the full impact of Eddie's words hit him hard, like a thump in the chest.

'You mean your mother,' he croaked, his throat suddenly dry and raw.

'No, Georgie is my mother,' Eddie said, still pointing towards the sideboard. 'I mean the little lady in the blue dress who sits over there.'

Eddie slipped down off his lap, crossed the room,

picked up the portrait of his mother and placed it face down. 'That's better. She's not my mother, Georgie is. Now you can always smile at my real mother, and not look sad at the little lady.'

Adam could hardly make sense of what his son was saying. All he knew was that the boy had forgotten about Rosalie, his real mother, just as Adam had forgotten about her, his real wife—the woman he had vowed to love until the day he died. The woman he had hardly thought about since that first night he'd had Georgina in his bed.

Eddie turned and smiled at everyone in the room, then his bottom lip quivered. 'What's wrong? Why is everyone looking at me like I've done something naughty?'

'You haven't been naughty,' Agatha said, crossing the room and taking the young boy's hand. 'Children,' she said, turning to face the girls, 'that's enough lessons today. Let's go outside and play.'

Eddie cheered and raced to the door, pulling his grandmother by the hand, while Dora and Lotte remained standing in the middle of the room, staring at Adam. Georgina wanted to make this right for his children but could think of nothing to say. All she could do was register the weight that had suddenly descended on her body. She gripped the back of the nearest chair, the floor seemingly no longer solid beneath her feet.

'Come on, girls,' Agatha called again. Lotte and Dora followed their grandmother out of the room and the door shut behind them.

'He's just a little boy,' she choked out. 'He doesn't know what he's saying.'

As if she hadn't spoken, as if he was no longer aware of her presence, he crossed the room and picked up the miniature and stroked a finger along the portrait. 'I am so sorry, my darling,' he murmured. 'I will never forget you. I will not stop loving you. My wife, my one true love.'

Georgina's breath caught in her throat, her heart appearing to shatter into tiny pieces. She placed her hand on her chest in a fruitless attempt to ease the pain as she watched the man she loved declaring his eternal love to another.

She was jealous. How could she not be? Those were the words she wanted him to say to her, longed for him to say to her every time he took her in his arms. But it wasn't just jealousy that was consuming her. There was something else. He was in agony, and she hated seeing him that way. It was unbearable to see the man she loved suffer so, even if it was pain caused by another woman. The woman he still thought of as his wife. The woman he still loved.

As quietly as possible, she left the room, closing the door softly, although he was so absorbed in staring at the portrait in his hand she doubted he would have noticed if she had stomped out and slammed the door behind her.

That was what she would once have done when she didn't get her own way, but it was not what she wanted to do now. And, even if she did, what would be the point? No amount of tears and tantrums could make a man love her when he was in love with another.

She stopped outside the drawing room, leant against the wall and fought to slow her gasping breath.

Adam did not love her. That was now clear. She had seduced him into making love to her, but nothing she had done, nothing she could do, would make him love her the way she loved him. As painful as it was, that was something she would have to accept and live with. And her heartache would also have to be her secret. She loved the children too and did not want them to know the extent of her anguish. They'd had too much sorrow in their lives to suffer any further.

She closed her eyes and drew in another series of deep, slow breaths, fighting to ease the painful sorrow in her chest. It didn't work. It seemed this pain was something else she was going to have to learn to live with.

Pulling herself off the wall, she straightened her shoulders in the same manner she had instructed Lotte and Dora and, keeping her head high, strode down the hallway and out through the entranceway.

In the garden she could see Agatha attempting to engage them in a game of tag, with limited success. Eddie was running around like the innocent child he was, while Lotte and Dora made a half-hearted effort to pretend they were enjoying themselves.

The two girls looked at her with concern as she crossed the lawn towards them. Even Eddie looked abashed, knowing something was wrong but unsure what it was. She put on her sunniest smile, placed her arm around Eddie's shoulder and kissed the top of his head.

'So, what game are we playing today?' she asked, hoping she sounded sufficiently chirpy.

'We didn't really feel like playing,' Lotte said.

'What?' Georgina exclaimed. 'How can you not feel like playing? What else is life for, except to play?'

That was exactly how Georgina had felt before she'd met Adam and the children, that life was just one long game that she loved playing. Even when she'd lost, she'd always been able to see it as a win. When men had rejected her during the Season because she did not have the right background, she had laughed off the insult, and seen them as the ones who had lost. When men had courted her for her dowry, she'd seen it as a wonderful excuse to have fun at their expense. But now she had lost the game with the highest stakes of all and knew there was no way in which she could turn this into her own personal victory.

She had married Adam knowing that he did not love her, and that he was still in love with his first wife. The scene in the drawing room had not revealed anything she had not already known. So she would just accept it, get on with life and make certain that her sadness was never, ever passed onto the children.

'It looked to me like you were playing tag,' she said, still smiling as brightly as she possibly could. 'So, let's continue doing that. And you're it,' she said, patting Eddie's arm and running off.

Eddie chased her around the garden, and Georgina squealed each time he nearly caught her, doing her best impression of someone having a jolly good time.

Eventually, the girls joined in, and soon they were all running around in circles, as a happy Eddie chased them on his little legs.

Agatha sent her a grateful smile and soon retreated

back to the house, just as Eddie caught Georgina and triumphantly tagged her leg.

'You're it,' he proudly announced.

'Not for long,' she declared, 'and when I catch you, I'm going to gobble you all up. So, who's going to be my first victim?'

Roaring like a lion and waving her 'paws' in the air, she chased the children, pleased when the girls started to laugh loudly as they dodged around hedges and shrubs.

While she pretended that nothing had changed for the sake of the children, Georgina knew that everything had changed. The man she loved did not love her—would never love her. The man she had married would never see her as his true wife. She was merely the woman he had been forced to marry because circumstances demanded, the woman he took to his bed, the woman he would make love to but never actually love.

With a smile on her face and a pain in her heart, she kept playing with the children, wondering what her future would hold, now that she knew her husband would never truly love her the way she loved him.

Chapter Twenty-One

When luncheon was served, Georgina forced herself to maintain her sunny disposition while she braced herself for seeing Adam again. How she was going to react to being in his company she had no idea, but she had no need to wonder. He did not join them for luncheon and he remained absent for the rest of the afternoon.

Despite her own anguish, she couldn't help but worry about what he was going through. She wished she could go to him, to comfort him and soothe away his grief, but knew that such tenderness would not be welcome. Or worse, he might believe that she was merely trying to seduce him again. That she was trying to divert his attention from the woman he really loved as she shamefully knew she had done in the past.

Tommy had been right when he'd said on her wedding day that she'd got what she wanted. If she hadn't wanted to marry Adam, she would have found a way of getting out of it.

She'd denied it at the time, but deep down she knew she had wanted him. She had wanted him to marry her

and then she had wanted him to take her to his bed. Her
father had inadvertently helped her achieve the first,
and when it had looked as if she wasn't going to get the
second, she had presented herself to him and made an
offer she knew no man was likely to turn down. And, in
doing so, she had made him betray his vow to his wife
and caused him such heartbreaking agony.

That had never been her intention, but her intention
had most certainly been to get exactly what she wanted,
and never once had she thought about anyone else but
herself. As she always had.

'Are you all right, Georgina?' Agatha asked quietly.

Georgina was snapped out of her reverie and realised
she was holding her empty fork in the air and had been
staring into space.

'Oh, yes, perfectly all right. I'm just not so fond of...'
she looked down at her plate to see what she was eating '...chicken pie.'

'I thought it was one of your favourites,' Eddie said.

'You're right. Silly me. And this pie is particularly
delicious,' she said and took a generous mouthful. She
smiled as she chewed, wondering why it tasted like
sawdust, and why no one else seemed to have noticed.

Forcing it down her throat, she wondered whether
Adam had been served a meal. She also wondered what
he was thinking. Was he blaming her? Did he now despise her for seducing him away from Rosalie? Did
he know she had deliberately distracted him whenever
there was a danger of him looking at her portrait? Did
he hold her responsible for the children forgetting about
their mother? And if he did despise her, was he right
to feel that way?

She continued to move the food around on her plate. To her immense shame, she had even once considered hiding Rosalie's portrait so he would not think of his first wife, but think of her, and only her. She hadn't done so, but, even if she had, it would not have stopped him loving Rosalie, or caused him to love her.

Tommy wasn't entirely right. She hadn't got the one thing she *really* wanted, despite trying her damnedest. Adam's love. She had tried everything and had failed. From now onwards she was going to have to accept that fact and their relationship would have to return to the one they'd originally agreed on when they'd first married. One that involved no kissing, no touching, no lovemaking. Her heart sank, but her mind knew this was as it should be.

Luncheon over, the children's tutor arrived and they disappeared into the rooms for lessons. Finally, Georgina could let go of her artificial smile. She retired upstairs to the privacy of her bedchamber, massaging her sore jaw as she went. It was surprising how much strain an unnatural smile could cause if you held it for too long.

Seeing the bed she had not slept in for some time, she felt the tears she had been holding back all morning course down her cheeks, and she threw herself on the bed, pounding the pillows in frustration. This was where she would be sleeping from now onwards. Alone. She would not be going to Adam's bedchamber. As much as she craved his touch, she could not make love to him now. She could not express the depth of her love for him when she knew he was still in love with another woman.

Her crying was interrupted by a gentle tap on the door. She jumped off the bed and ran to the looking glass, wiping away her tears with the back of her hand, quickly blowing her nose on her lace handkerchief and attempting to repair the damage to her hair.

'Who is it?' she asked, annoyed at the choking sound of her voice.

'It's Agatha. Are you sure you are all right?'

Her heart clenched in disappointment. How could she possibly think that Adam might follow her to her room? When she'd left him staring at his wife's portrait, he had neither noticed that she was still in the room nor registered when she had left. He simply no longer saw her.

'Yes, I'm all right, thank you,' she said with forced cheerfulness.

'Are you sure?'

'Yes, I'm perfectly fine, honestly,' she lied, overdoing the cheerfulness just a tad. 'I'm just quite tired so I think I'll rest this afternoon.'

Agatha made no reply and Georgina put her ear to the door, wondering if she was still there.

'I'm so sorry, Georgina,' she said quietly. 'My son-in-law has always been unworthy of a woman's love.'

Georgina's heart clenched more tightly as Agatha's boots clicked off down the hallway. Did Agatha also blame her for trying to make Adam forget his wife, and for causing the children to forget their mother? And was it blame she fully deserved?

Adam spent the afternoon in the drawing room, Rosalie's portrait in his hands. He knew he'd have to leave eventually, but feared that if he was no longer looking at her lovely face, he would yet again forget all about her. That was something he could not bear to do. But he knew he could not stay in the drawing room for ever. His reaction to Edwin's comments had upset his family and he needed to put things right.

He could not blame his son for what he had said. It was not Edwin's fault that he had forgotten all about the woman who was his mother. While it had wounded him deeply, his son's words were understandable.

Edwin had never known his mother. She had merely held him in her arms a few times before the strain of childbirth had claimed her and taken her from her husband and children.

But while his son forgetting was understandable, Adam's behaviour was inexcusable. Since the moment he had found Georgina in his bedchamber he had hardly thought of his first wife, and when he did, he had pushed the memory of her away so he could indulge himself in the sensual pleasure he was experiencing with his new wife.

Edwin's words had unintentionally made the betrayal of Rosalie painfully clear.

When was the last time he had looked at her portrait? That was something he could easily answer. The day before he'd first had Georgina in his bed. Before that night, he had gazed at her portrait several times each day, his grief hitting him anew each time, the memory of what he had lost coming back to torture him.

Not only had he not looked at her portrait, but the memory of her laughter, of her sweet, gentle ways, was no longer constantly on his mind.

How could he have betrayed her memory so quickly

and so totally? But he had not only broken his vow to Rosalie, he had also mistreated Georgina, neither of which had been his intention.

If only he had not been so damn attracted to Georgina. If he had married a woman who he did not want to bed every time he looked at her, who did not make him laugh so easily, whose company he did not take so much delight in, perhaps he would not have cast his first wife away so quickly. But he could hardly blame Georgina for being who she was. It was not her fault she was so beautiful, so desirable. It was his fault for succumbing so easily.

Nor could he blame her for the way he lost himself so completely when he made love to her. It was not her fault that he could no longer think straight each time he surrendered himself to the exquisite pleasure of her touch.

He was a terrible, terrible man. He had let his desire for one woman drive out his love for another—a love which he had sworn would be eternal.

'I do love you, Rosalie,' he said to the portrait clasped against his chest. 'I will always love you.' But even those words sounded false to his ears. How could they be true when he was still thinking about another woman, still imagining her touch, still remembering the taste of her lips, her feminine scent and the silky softness of her skin?

He placed his head in his hands, the portrait sliding to his lap. He had thought himself a good man, but he had behaved appallingly. He had forgotten the woman he loved because he had been losing himself with a woman he had arranged to marry but had never intended to be anything other than his wife in name only. And, damn it all, he still wanted her, wanted to have her in his arms, to feel her touch, her kisses.

Adam doubted he could hate himself any more than he did now if he tried. Neither woman deserved him. They both deserved a man so much better than he could ever be.

Chapter Twenty-Two

That night Georgina had to face Adam over the dinner table. She forced herself to keep smiling, determined that the children would think everything was still the same, even though everything had changed.

'Did you have a pleasant afternoon?' she said to Adam, keeping her voice polite and cheerful and hoping he would play along with this pretence for the children's sake.

'Yes, thank you,' he replied as he shook out his napkin and placed it on his lap. 'And you?'

'Oh, yes,' she replied. 'I retired to my room and used the time while the children were at their studies to catch up on some reading.'

She sounded ridiculously sunny and was fooling no one, least of all the children. Lotte and Dora were staring at her as if fearing she had lost her senses. After the comfortable way they had been with each other, the way they had laughed and even touched each other at every opportunity, no one could fail to notice that they were now being overly polite, like strangers attempting to make a good impression. Even Eddie was looking at them with a curious expression, and Georgina prayed he would not make another inappropriate comment, the way young children were apt to do. If he mentioned the way Adam touched her or made another joke about his father touching Georgina's bottom, she was sure she would not be able to contain the tears that she was holding back.

Adam would not be touching her again, and she would never again feel the casual stroke of his hand that told her that they were a couple, that they were lovers, as comfortable with each other's bodies as they were with their own.

'Perhaps you'd like to tell your father what you learnt in your lessons today,' she said, forcing herself to keep smiling.

All three children frowned at her.

'What's wrong with —' Eddie started to say before he was interrupted by Agatha.

'Do as Georgina said. Tell your father what you learnt today.' The terseness of her voice made it clear that she would tolerate no argument from the children.

While the children discussed how boring they found mathematics, Georgina nodded along, and could see that Adam was equally distracted, but he fortunately made noises in all the right places, and Agatha filled any awkward silences with questions and comments.

The difficult dinner over, they retreated to the drawing room, where Georgina remained on eggshells, worried that someone would mention the portrait on the sideboard. She fought not to look in that direction and could tell that everyone else in the room was doing the same, even Eddie.

The painfully polite conversation continued, and Georgina was grateful when it became time for the children to go to bed. Maintaining a cheerful façade, she settled them into bed and read some more of *Alice's Adventures* until they finally drifted off.

Then she knew what she had to do. This awkwardness could not continue, if for no other reason than it was confusing the children. She had to talk to Adam.

Ignoring the churning in her stomach, she forced her feet to take her back to the drawing room. She entered to find Adam alone, once again gazing at the portrait of his beloved wife. His eyes quickly moved away as she entered and he sent her an awkward smile.

'I believe we need to discuss what happened today,' she said, surprised at how strong she sounded.

He nodded while exhaling a long sigh. 'Yes. I am sorry, Georgina.'

She sat down in the wing chair facing his. 'You have nothing to apologise for. I knew when I married you that this was merely a marriage of convenience and that you were still in love with your wife. It perhaps should be me who is apologising, for forgetting what this marriage is.'

'No. It was I who forgot,' he said, looking in the direction of the miniature haunting the sideboard.

'Be that as it may, we are married and we need to discuss what sort of marriage we are to have.'

'If you choose to leave, I will understand,' he said. 'I have treated you appallingly. You deserve so much more than what I can offer you. If you wish for a divorce, I will declare myself to be the guilty party.'

She stared at him, astounded that he could even suggest such a thing. 'There will be no divorce and I will not be leaving. It would be too hard on the children. Rightly or wrongly, I am becoming an important part of their lives, and yes, Eddie, and possibly Dora and Lotte, are coming to see me as their mother.'

He drew in a deep breath but said nothing.

'They've already lost their real mother. I will not be responsible for them losing another.'

'As you wish,' he said, staring down at his hands, clasped between his knees.

'But that still doesn't settle what sort of marriage we are now to have.'

'I will abide by whatever arrangement you want.'

I want you to love me, she wanted to scream out.

'I believe it would be best if we now sleep in our own bedchambers,' she said, sounding certain, even though the thought of never feeling his touch again was making her heart and body ache.

He nodded and her heart further shattered within her chest.

'I am sorry, Georgina,' he said, finally looking at her. 'I never meant to deceive you, or to deceive myself.'

'I have already told you that you have nothing to apologise for,' she said quietly. 'You did not deceive me.'

I deceived myself. Tommy was right. I have always got everything I wanted. I wanted your love, therefore thought I would get it, even though you told me you could not love again.

Georgina's father had always eventually given in, even if it took some pouting, the slamming of doors and a few temper tantrums for him to concede defeat. Her mother had usually held out longer, but eventually she too had always succumbed to Georgina's demands.

Even at Halliwell's, where they were supposed to train this wilfulness out of her, she'd managed to turn everything to her advantage.

But the one thing she now knew she wanted more than anything in the world, she simply could not have.

And she would be throwing no more temper tantrums. It seemed, finally, she would be doing what Miss Halliwell had tried to get her to do, what her father had tried to insist on—she would act like an adult.

She would accept that her fate was to live in a loveless marriage, something she had been determined to avoid. Well, that was not entirely true. This marriage would perhaps be easier if it *was* loveless. Instead, she was in a marriage where there was plenty of love, but none of it was directed towards her.

'I'll say goodnight then,' she said, standing up. He too stood up and for one desperate moment she thought he might be going to argue with her. That he was going to say that he wanted them to remain lovers, that he craved her touch as much as she craved his.

'Goodnight, Georgina. Sleep well,' he said, destroying all illusions.

As she left the room, Georgina knew her marriage was now what it was always meant to be—an arrangement, nothing more.

Adam slumped down into his chair the moment Georgina left the room. He now had exactly what he'd wanted when he'd first become aware of the necessity of taking another wife.

Didn't he?

He'd needed a wife whose marriage settlement was

sufficiently large to save the estate. Georgina's dowry had not only paid off the excessive mortgages, it had ensured that everyone who lived on the estate had a secure future, that the house could be repaired and he could now provide generous marriage settlements for Charlotte and Dorothea, so they would have their choice of husbands.

He'd wanted a wife who would care for and love his children. Georgina loved his children and they loved her in return, there was no doubt about that. And he'd wanted a wife who would expect nothing from him, who would respect the fact that he loved another woman, would always love that woman and would never betray her. Now he had that as well.

Yes, he had everything he had set out to achieve when he had first headed to London to partake in the Season. And yet he could not have felt more empty inside, as if he had lost everything.

Adam was very familiar with the feeling of guilt. He had felt deep guilt when Rosalie had died. He had blamed himself for her death. As much as they'd both wanted a son, as much as he loved Edwin with all his heart, he should have taken every precaution to ensure that she not get pregnant again. If he had, his lovely Rosalie would be here with him now.

And guilt was what he was feeling now, mingling with intense shame. He had needed a wife but should never have chosen Georgina, for so many reasons. She was a woman who needed to be with a man who could love her and make her happy. That would never be him. By marrying her, he had deprived her of that opportunity, and he had done so for his own selfish reasons.

When he'd become aware that he must marry again, that had been one of the conditions—he would only marry a woman who was content to marry a title, who wanted the honour of being a duchess and cared nothing for being in a loving relationship. He had known that was not Georgina, and yet he'd ignored that knowledge.

But, worse than that, he should never have made love to her. That had never been part of their arrangement. And, damn it all, despite being racked by the agony of guilt and regret, he wanted to go upstairs, throw open the door of her bedchamber and bury himself in her arms.

He really was a man beneath contempt.

He looked over at Rosalie's portrait, his self-disgust intensifying. He had never deserved that lovely young woman, and he did not deserve Georgina. And thank goodness Georgina had the strength and the maturity to put their marriage back on the tracks it should never have wandered off.

From now onwards, they would live together as man and wife in name only, just as they had originally agreed. He would remain faithful to his wife. He looked towards the door through which Georgina had departed.

But was that fair to Georgina? Once again, was he thinking only of himself, of what he needed to do to loosen the knots in his chest, to relieve the agonising pain in his stomach?

He deserved this punishment. Georgina did not.

She was such a sensual woman it would be cruel not to allow her to continue to explore that sensuality. It just couldn't be with him.

Bile burning up his throat, he came to a decision.

He would have to tell her that he had no objection to her taking a lover. It was what so many members of his class did. In arranged marriages, once the woman had produced the necessary heir, they were often given the same freedom as their husband to find love and satisfaction elsewhere.

He groaned and placed his head in his hands. He and Georgina would have to live in the same manner as so many others did. It was the least he owed her. She had saved his estate, was providing motherly love for his children, and she deserved to find her own love and happiness.

The knot in his chest tightened several notches at the idea of Georgina with another man. If the thought of it caused this much pain and made him rage against that imagined man, how would he cope when she did take a lover?

How would he cope, knowing that another man was holding her, caressing her, making love to her? And, worse than that, how would he cope if it became more than just a physical relationship and she actually fell in love with that man and he fell in love with her?

He stood up and paced rapidly around the room, the desire to hit something, anything, especially this imaginary man, welling up inside him and consuming him like a raging fire.

If merely thinking of her with another man could cause his body to burn with anger and resentment, how on earth was he going to cope when she actually did take a lover, when his beautiful, enchanting Georgina was giving her smiles, her laughter, her joy and…his teeth clenched together so tightly, pain shot through his jaw…her body to another man?

He stopped walking, closed his eyes and forced himself to breathe slowly and deeply. Endure it he would. The ongoing agony he would suffer would be no less a punishment than he deserved for all that he had done to Georgina—to both women.

He would focus on what he had, not what he could never have. Georgina had promised she would never leave his children. That was something he believed would not change. She so obviously loved them, and they her. That care and love was something for which he would be eternally grateful. And if he was to prove that he still had some decency left in him, then he would show his gratitude by granting her the freedom to find the love she deserved.

He slumped into the nearest chair. He would be brave and strong, and at the next opportunity he would tell Georgina of his decision, and then he would just have to find a way to live with it.

Chapter Twenty-Three

Week after strained week had passed without Adam informing Georgina that he had no objection to her taking a lover, should she choose. With one very good reason. He *did* have an objection, even if he had no right to it.

When alone, he practised how he would say it. Straight to the point, making it clear that this was a mature, sensible arrangement for both of them.

And yet, every time he found himself alone in her company, the words would not come. His throat would restrict, as if stopping them from emerging, his heart would pound so loudly he could hardly hear his own thoughts. Then the moment would pass, and relief would wash through him, until that sense of relief was once again chased away by guilt and shame.

He had promised her freedom when they married, now he needed to make good on that promise.

He had to forget his own feelings and set her free. She had a right to be happy. He wanted her to be happy. He could not make her happy so she should find happiness elsewhere. That was logical, but nothing about his feelings, nothing about the way his body ached every time he imagined her with another man was logical. And so he continued to say nothing, and every time he tried and failed to inform her of his decision it reinforced just what a selfish man he was and always had been.

He had selfishly not made enough effort to try and talk Rosalie out of her desire to give him a son. At the time he had known it was what she wanted, but he still should have put his foot down, told her that the risk was too great, instead of giving in to her wishes. And now he was selfishly stopping a woman who had given him so much from finding happiness elsewhere.

And it was obvious that she was not happy. She still laughed, joked and played with the children, but she had a careworn look, one that he had caused. With him she was always excruciatingly polite, and that in itself spoke volumes. Georgina was not polite. She was cheeky, irreverent, mischievous. But now it was as if she were in the company of a very important person and had to be on her best behaviour at all times.

He doubted that even as a child, when Georgina had found herself in such circumstances, she would actually have been so deliberately polite. And that made her courteous manner even harder to bear. He had taken a lively young woman, destroyed her spirit and turned her into this paragon of good manners. That was yet another crime against his two wives he could add to the growing list.

Each evening, after Georgina had put the children to bed, she retired to her own bedchamber, alone, and had even ceased to come back downstairs to say goodnight to him. That did not surprise him. Those exchanges had become the most awkward of all their encounters and a reminder of what they had briefly shared but would share no longer.

And that was exactly what had happened this evening. He had been left alone in the drawing room, contemplating how his inexcusable behaviour was destroying that lovely young woman who deserved so much more from life than what he could offer.

This had to stop. He looked towards the door. He would go upstairs and tell her right now that she did not have to continue living like this, that she could be free to live a life separate from him, and if that included finding a man who could make her happy then so be it.

He shook open the newspaper. It was getting late. He would definitely do it tomorrow. First thing in the morning. This had gone on too long. He had to put an end to her unhappiness.

The door opened and he braced himself. It would not be tomorrow after all. He would have to be true to himself and do it right now.

Mrs Wainwright entered the room and he released his held breath. Thank goodness. He had a day's reprieve.

His former mother-in-law stood in the middle of the room, scowling at him in that familiar manner.

'I thought you had gone to bed,' he said.

'Well, you thought wrong. Again.'

Such criticism was nothing new. She had disapproved of him for marrying Rosalie. Her reaction had irritated him, but now he knew her to be right. If Rosalie had married a man of her own class there would have been no pressure to produce an heir. She would have stopped having children once it had become obvious that her body could not cope with another childbirth. She would still be alive and happy with another man.

'It's time we had a talk,' she said, her glower intensifying. 'I've given you plenty of time to sort out this problem and you haven't done a damn thing about it. So it's time for you to listen to a few home truths.'

Adam nodded, knowing that he deserved this lecture. He signalled to the facing wing chair so she would be comfortable while she berated him, but she chose to remain standing, forcing him to do the same, like a naughty boy about to receive a much-deserved reprimand.

'What are you going to do about your wife? You know she's miserable, don't you?'

Adam exhaled loudly. This was none of Mrs Wainwright's business and he certainly was not going to inform her that he had decided it best that Georgina find happiness with another man. That was a private matter between him and Georgina. Or, at least, it would be a private matter when he finally developed the fortitude to discuss it with her.

'I am fully aware of the problems in my marriage,' he said, adopting a suitably stern tone. 'And I believe I am more than capable of solving them myself.'

She huffed out a humourless laugh. 'It doesn't look that way to me. For God's sake, man, just admit that you love your wife.'

He looked over at the miniature on the sideboard. 'I do love her. You know that I do.'

'Not my daughter. Yes, I know you love her. I mean your wife, Georgina.'

Adam stared at her, aghast. 'No. I do not... I will never... I love Rosalie, with all my heart and soul.'

Mrs Wainwright shook her head from side to side, her expression growing ever more disdainful.

'I made a vow,' he said, for some reason desperate for her to understand. 'A deathbed vow that I would love Rosalie until I die.'

'And you're keeping that vow. I know that.'

Adam released his breath, pleased that she understood and this conversation was now over.

'But you also love Georgina,' she added.

His breath again caught in his throat. He looked towards the sideboard. 'I love Rosalie. I will always love Rosalie.'

Mrs Wainwright sank into the chair with a deep sigh. 'You really are a fool, aren't you? How these bright young women ever managed to become enamoured of such a nincompoop I'll never know. Sit down,' she said, indicating the facing chair. 'And I'll explain this in simple words that even you will hopefully understand.'

Adam did as he was commanded, but remained perched on the edge of the chair, as if wanting to flee from this unwanted conversation at the first opportunity.

'You loved my daughter. Yes?'

'Of course,' he said, bracing himself, uncertain of where this conversation was heading.

'And did she love you?'

'Yes, I believe she did.' He smiled, remembering all the times she had said those words to him. 'I know she did.'

'Did she try and make you happy when she was alive?'

'Yes. We were very happy and very much in love.'

Surely even the disapproving Mrs Wainwright would know that.

'Did she take pleasure in seeing you miserable?'

'No, of course not. What a thing to say. That's not what love is. You only wish happiness for the other person.'

'Exactly.' Mrs Wainwright raised her hands, palm upwards, as if that explained everything.

He shook his head. She surely knew that he and Rosalie had been in love and treasured each other's happiness, so why was she looking at him as if he were an imbecile?

She sighed. 'I can see from that blank expression that you still don't understand. My daughter loved you, heaven help her. She wanted your happiness as much as her own, probably more. Since she died you have been miserable. I understand that. You were grieving the loss of the love of your life. Just as I was grieving the loss of my daughter. But since Georgina entered this house you have again laughed and taken pleasure in life.'

Adam swallowed the lump in his throat. Yes, he had taken pleasure, in ways he never should have.

'I know,' he said, looking down at his hands, clasped tightly in his lap.

'That is precisely what my daughter would have wanted for you. And if you don't realise that then I suspect you never really knew her at all.'

His head shot up and he glared at the judgemental woman sitting across from him.

'How…how can you possibly say that?' he stammered, trying to form the words that would express his outrage at such an accusation. 'I knew Rosalie better than I have ever known anyone in my life.'

'So tell me, what sort of woman was she? Was she a woman who wanted you to be happy?'

'Yes, of course she was.'

'Was she a woman who wanted her children to be happy?'

'How can you even ask that? She wanted that more than anything in the world.'

She sent him a self-satisfied look, as if she had won the argument. But she had done no such thing. All she had done was told him something he already knew.

She shook her head slowly. 'My goodness, how these intelligent women could fall in love with a man who is so dim-witted I will never know.'

'Women?'

'Yes, *women*. Both your wives fell in love with you, although why I'll never understand. And it looks like you know this one as well as you knew my daughter.'

'Now, look here,' Adam said, standing up. He'd had enough of her insults and was not going to listen to another word of this lecture.

'Sit back down and stop pouting.'

Adam glared at her. He had never pouted in his life.

'It was obvious to me that Georgina was in love with you from the moment you brought her home as your wife. And it would be obvious to anyone with a ha'penny worth of sense that she has fallen deeper in love with you with every passing day.'

'No, you're wrong. She never wanted to marry me. This was an arrangement forced upon her, just as it was forced upon me by circumstances outside our control. Her father—'

Mrs Wainwright rolled her eyes, bringing his explanation to an end. She was obviously not going to listen.

'Men are such fools, and you more than most,' she said and released an exasperated sigh. 'She's in love with you. I know it's hard to understand, I certainly can't understand it myself, but there it is. And I'm sure my Rosalie would approve of that love wholeheartedly.'

'But—'

'No buts. And it doesn't take a great deal of insight to see how much your love for Georgina has grown since she first arrived in this house as your new wife.'

'But…' He looked from Rosalie's portrait to Mrs Wainwright, no longer sure what he was going to say.

'And that's as it should be. Do you think Rosalie would want you to mourn her for the rest of her life, for you to be miserable, for her children to be miserable, for this house to be one laden with grief? Is that the sort of woman you think my Rosalie was?'

'No,' he murmured, looking back towards the sideboard.

'Rosalie would be filled with joy that Georgina has come into this house and lifted the pall that has hung over it for the last five years. She would love seeing Georgina playing with the children, making them laugh and filling their days with happiness. Don't you agree?'

'Well, yes. It goes without saying she would want to see her children happy.'

'And she would want to see you in the arms of another woman, knowing that you are happy, married again and in love. To think otherwise would be a disservice to my daughter. It would suggest you think of her as a mean-spirited woman who wanted the man she loved to remain unhappy for the rest of his life. Do I need to say it again? If you think that, then you never knew my Rosalie, never really loved her.'

He stared at her, lost for words.

'Am I right?'

'Yes,' he said, slowly nodding. 'Yes,' he repeated, a heavy weight seemingly lifting off his shoulders. 'Yes, you are right.' He looked over at Rosalie's portrait then back at Mrs Wainwright.

'Then go and make things right with your new wife. Go and show her how much you love her, how important she is to you, and how much you have changed since that lovely, high-spirited young lass was foolish enough to agree to marry you.'

Chapter Twenty-Four

Mrs Wainwright left the room, leaving a stunned Adam staring into space.

In love with Georgina?

Was that what he was feeling? Was that why every emotion felt so intense? Was that why the thought of her with another man caused bile to burn up his throat and almost choke him? Could it be true that when he was consumed by an insatiable desire for her, it wasn't just because he wanted to make love to her, it was because he *was* in love with her?

He looked over at the sideboard. With Rosalie, it had been so clear when he had fallen in love with her, but at the time he had been an innocent young man of nineteen meeting a beautiful, enchanting, equally innocent young woman. With Georgina, it was different. He was a man weighed down by grief and responsibility. He had three children to care for and an estate in peril. There had been no joy in his heart when he'd set out to find a wife, no thoughts of courtship or wooing, as there had been when he'd first met Rosalie. Marriage had been a practical matter that they had both undertaken due to necessity.

And yet…

Mrs Wainwright was correct. He *was* a fool. From the moment he'd first met Georgina he had been unable to stop thinking about her. He had convinced himself that it was because she was always present. At that one ball he had attended, every time he'd turned around, there she'd seemed to be. And yet he had given not a passing thought to any of the other women he'd met at that ball, and would struggle to remember their names, never mind what they looked like. But from the moment he had first met Georgina she had been firmly in his thoughts, and there was more than just her appearance he could conjure up. He could remember her laugh, her smile, her scent, those dimples in each cheek that appeared every time she smiled, the different hues of blue in her eyes.

And he had not hesitated when he'd heard her father giving her an ultimatum. He'd told himself at the time it was because their marriage would be mutually beneficial. It was—but it was so much more. It was what he wanted, even if he had refused to admit it at the time.

It was a love that had made him miserable, simply because he'd refused to admit it, had refused to believe that he was entitled to love again, and to be happy again.

He looked back towards the door through which Mrs Wainwright had departed. She was also correct about her daughter. Rosalie would not have wanted him to be unhappy, just as he could not have borne the thought of Rosalie's unhappiness. Nor did he want Georgina to be unhappy, and yet she was, all because of his foolish behaviour.

He could not be certain that Mrs Wainwright was correct when she said that Georgina was in love with him. Although, if she was, he'd have to agree with his former mother-in-law that it would be foolish for such an intelligent young woman to fall for a man such as he.

But *if* she was in love, there was only one way to find out for sure. He would have to ask her. He walked across the room and picked up the portrait of Rosalie.

'I'm sorry, my love,' he said, gently stroking her cheek. 'It *was* an insult to your memory to ever think that you would not want this house to be full of love and laughter. And I know you would approve of Georgina. I should never have doubted that.'

He lightly kissed the portrait, placed it back on the sideboard and left the drawing room. Smiling for the first time in what felt like an age, he took the steps up to the bedchambers two at a time. When he reached the landing, he stopped.

All he had to do was knock on Georgina's bedchamber door and profess his love for her, but Mrs Wainwright was correct about one more thing. He needed to show Georgina that he was a changed man. That she had changed him, for ever and for the better.

He was not the man she had met on the side of the road. He no longer wanted to be that dour man who had judged her so unfairly for being impetuous, a risk-taker and a woman wholly unsuitable to be his wife and a mother to his children.

She needed to see that he was no longer that uptight man who had no appreciation of her sense of fun, the man who did not value the gift of joy and laughter she had brought into this house, or the love she had given his children and the affection she had shown him.

He quickly retraced his steps back down the stairs, out through the entranceway and around the side of the house. He looked up to Georgina's bedchamber. Light from her candles was spilling out into the dark night. Good, she had still not retired. Mrs Wainwright had said he should prove to her that he had changed and that wise, if somewhat cantankerous, woman was right.

He grabbed hold of the drainpipe and gave it a firm tug. It held. He looked up at her window and his firm resolve wavered. It was a long way up. Had he ever done this before? If he had, it was not since he was a young boy and he was definitely out of practice.

He released the drainpipe. Perhaps there was another, less drastic way of showing how much he had changed? One that didn't risk life and limb.

He took a firm hold of the drainpipe. No, as they said, faint heart never won fair lady. He would not think of the danger.

Trying not to grunt at the exertion, he heaved himself up to the first bracket. So far, so good. He looked up. When was the last time the brackets had been maintained? He ran his thumbnail along the nearest brick. Had the mortar holding the bricks together turned to dust through lack of attention? He was about to find out.

He shimmied up to the next bracket, then the next one, the ground moving further and further away. Then discovered a flaw in his plan. The next bracket was missing. He reached out his foot, trying to find a foothold in the bricks. None presented itself. So he scrambled over to the other side of the drainpipe, hoping to have better luck there.

'What on earth are you doing?' Georgina's voice came from high above him. 'You're making enough noise to waken the entire county.'

He looked up. She was leaning out of the sash window, her long hair hanging loose around her face, the candles creating a halo effect on her blonde hair.

He was like a mortal gazing upon an angel. He sighed. Had he ever seen a more heavenly sight?

'Well, what are you doing?' she repeated. His angel did not sound amused.

'Um…is that not obvious? I'm climbing up the drainpipe.'

'Why?'

'To see you.'

She looked over her shoulder. 'There is a door in my bedchamber, you know?'

'I'm making a point…a romantic gesture,' he said, reaching out his foot and waving it in the air as he searched for that elusive foothold.

'A what?'

'A romantic gesture. But I think I might be stuck.'

She stared at him, her brow furrowed, and then she laughed. That sound made his precarious position worthwhile.

'You're hopeless, aren't you?' she said, still laughing at him. 'I could shimmy up this drainpipe with my eyes closed.'

'Perhaps you're going to have to give me some lessons.'

'I think it might be best if you admit defeat and climb back down and use the stairs.'

'Never,' he said, wrapping himself around the drain-pipe and doing an impression of the monkey he had seen at the zoological gardens, or was it more like a snake? Whatever it was, he moved in an ungainly manner up to the next fixed bracket and breathed a sigh of relief when he reached that sanctuary. With the remaining brackets thankfully in place, he was able to scale the rest of the drainpipe with relative ease, and he finally reached her window.

'I told you I could do it,' he said, peeping over the windowsill.

'After that performance, I don't think you should be auditioning for a place in the circus any time soon,' she said, a delightful smile on her lips.

He gripped the windowsill to pull himself in and another problem struck him. How did one climb from a drainpipe, over a jutting windowsill and into a bedroom?

'I think you're going to need my help,' she said, leaning out and grabbing hold of the top of his trousers. 'I hope this holds and your tailor didn't skimp on the stitches or this is going to be highly embarrassing for you.'

With that, she gave an almighty tug while he did his best to gain a footing against the wall and a handhold inside the room. She placed her foot on the windowsill and, with much huffing and puffing from both of them, dragged him into the room.

They collapsed in an untidy pile on the bedroom floor.

Entwined in each other's limbs, they remained where they'd fallen, both breathing heavily. Adam wondered if he was the only one to be reminded of other times when they had lain wrapped together in exhaustion.

When his heartbeat resumed something that resembled a normal beat, he stood up, offered her his hand and pulled her to her feet.

'That was meant to be more like the balcony scene from *Romeo and Juliet* and less like something from a French farce,' he said, still holding her hand and trying to regain as much of his dignity as he could.

'Lucky for you, I enjoy French farces.' She looked towards the window. 'And that was more farcical than most.'

She looked back at him in expectation. Adam suddenly realised that he should have given more thought to what he was to say and less thought to his supposedly grand entrance. After all, this was the most important conversation he was going to have in his life.

'Will you marry me?' he said, causing her to stare at him wide-eyed, as if he had lost all sense of reason.

'Um…we are married. Remember? The church? The white dress? Standing at the altar making our vows?'

'No, I want you to marry me. I want us to be man and wife, not just in name only.'

She looked over at the bed. 'I believe we've done that already as well.'

'Oh, Georgina, I'm making a mess of this, aren't I? In the same way I've made a mess of everything since I followed you out onto that terrace and made that first clumsy, insulting proposal.'

'You mean when you stepped out to get some air and *found* me on the terrace,' she said, eyeing him sideways.

'No, I followed you. I saw that you were distressed

and I was concerned for your wellbeing, then I heard your father's threats.'

'You were concerned about me?'

'Yes, and then I made that foolish proposal, so now I want to do it properly.'

He dropped down onto one knee and took her hands before she could distract him with any more questions.

'Georgina, I love you.'

She gave a small gasp, her eyes growing large.

'I love you with all my heart and soul. Since you came into my life I've learnt how to laugh again. You turned my world from one that was dull and grey to one that is vibrant and filled with colour and light. I'm nothing without you and I want you in my life. I need you in my life. I love you. Will you be my wife?'

She nodded, rapidly and repeatedly.

'That is the proposal I should have made to you when I first asked you to marry me, but I was too stupid to realise I had fallen in love. I was too wrapped up in my grief to realise that the most wonderful woman in the world had come into my life.'

'And if you had made a proposal like that, I would have given the same answer as I did the first time. Yes, although this time perhaps I could add, yes, yes, a thousand times yes.'

'So can we start again? Can we have a marriage that is based on love, not on convenience?'

'Yes, yes, yes.' She stopped smiling, her brow furrowed. 'But…'

'What's wrong, my love?' he asked, his heart suddenly lurching in his chest.

'If we are to start again, then there is something you

must know,' she said, biting her lip. 'When I accepted your first proposal, I told myself it was because of Father's threats. But that was wrong. Father would never have really gone through with his threat. He would never have tossed me out on the street. He simply isn't that sort of man. I could have saved you from this marriage, but I didn't because, even though I pretended it wasn't so, I was in love with you and wanted to be your wife.'

He stared up at her from his bent knee position, surprised at this revelation.

'I'm so sorry, Adam,' she said. 'I know this changes everything.'

'It changes nothing. My love for you sparked into life when I first met you, and it seems it was the same for you. It's just that neither of us was able to admit what was really in our heart.'

'So you forgive me for tricking you into marrying me?'

'There was no trickery, and if there was, you would merely have tricked me into doing what my heart wanted, even if my head did not realise it. So there is nothing to forgive.'

'Oh, Adam, I do love you with my heart, head and soul, and yes, I want to be your wife.'

They continued to smile at each other.

'Um… I think you can stand up now,' she said.

He laughed and stood up, still holding her hands, still looking into those beautiful eyes. 'You are so beautiful,' he whispered. 'You have such a beautiful spirit.'

She sent him a cheeky smile. 'And?'

'And a beautiful face.'

'And?'

'And a beautiful body that I just can't get enough of.'

'Well, that's something you can always try to do,' she said, then bit her bottom lip, a pretty blush on her cheeks.

Her jokes made him smile, but he needed to focus. There was so much more he needed to tell her. He could not let himself become distracted by her laughter, nor by what he was desperate to do with that beautiful body.

'Georgina, I'm sorry it took me so long to realise that what I felt for you was love,' he said, imploring her to understand. 'I always knew that you were a beautiful young woman, and I tried to dismiss my feelings as nothing more than physical desire. But when we made love, the emotions that welled up inside me were so intense they frightened me, so I pushed them away. I tried to tell myself it was nothing more than lust that I was feeling, and that was so wrong. Now I know what I was feeling, what I *am* feeling, is a deep, intense, unfathomable love.'

He clasped her hands to his heart. 'I never wanted to fall in love again, and that is why I tried to push those feelings away. I wanted a wife I would not love, out of a misguided loyalty to Rosalie, but you made that impossible.'

She smiled back at him. 'I've always had a contrary nature.'

'I know, and never, ever change that.'

'Oh, as someone who is contrary, I suppose that will have to be the first thing I'll have to change.'

He laughed, wrapped his arms around her waist and kissed her laughing lips.

'Georgina, I do love you so much,' he said when his kisses had finally stopped her laughter.

'So, do you think we can now consummate our new marriage?' she said with that delightful cheeky smile he loved so much. 'Or after your exertions on the drainpipe do you think you've got the energy left for…?' She tilted her head towards her bed.

'Believe me, I will always have enough energy for that.'

With that, he scooped her up in his arms and carried her to the bed, determined to prove to his wife just how energetic he could be.

Epilogue

Just as she did every Sunday, Georgina gathered the children up, ensuring they were dressed in their best clothes, and with Adam on her arm strolled to the local churchyard to lay flowers on Rosalie's grave.

Adam knew that Rosalie would have loved Georgina, just as he did, and just as their children did.

Mrs Wainwright, or Agatha as she now insisted he call her, had returned to her own home not long after Adam and Georgina had conducted a mock marriage in the garden gazebo for the children's entertainment.

Lotte and Dora had made wonderful bridesmaids, and Adam could see that they would soon be turning into delightful young ladies. Georgina had continued their weekly class to prepare them for their debuts, lessons that seemed to involve more laughter and mayhem than actual instruction.

During the service, Eddie had taken his role as best man very seriously. That was until he'd dropped the ring and sent them all scrambling around on the floor for it, with much laughter and butting of heads.

It was possibly the most chaotic and the most enjoyable wedding Adam had ever attended. And that was how their married life continued, with plenty of chaos and plenty of laughter.

Adam had worn a dove-grey suit for the wedding and, as his valet had once advised him, added colour with a gold brocade waistcoat, while Georgina wore a simple white gown, but adorned her hair and the girls' hair with wreaths of flowers, so they'd looked like carefree nymphs from a fairy tale.

At the end of the service, Agatha had told him she was sure that Rosalie was smiling down on them, enjoying the fact that the man she loved was now happy and that her children were cared for and loved. It had touched him more than he would have thought possible.

Agatha had also informed them that Georgina was now more than capable of running her own household, so there was no need for her supervision.

Georgina had been riddled with nerves, certain that such an undertaking was beyond her, but, to everyone's surprise, including Georgina's, Agatha was proven correct yet again. She'd soon proved herself a more than capable mistress of the house. After a few months she'd even decided she was capable of hosting dinner parties, although, to be on the safe side, the first party had been for her friends, Amelia and her husband, Leo Devenish, Irene and her husband, Joshua Huntington, the Duke of Redcliff, and Emily Beaumont, the only unmarried friend from her time at Miss Halliwell's Finishing School.

Georgina had expected there to be hitches that her friends would either politely ignore or turn into part of the fun, but everything had gone smoothly. And that had become the first of many social events she'd hosted, turning a house that had been in mourning for far too long into a house full of people, laughter and pleasure.

Agatha continued to visit regularly to see her grand-children, but from that day on it was always as a guest, and she left the management of the house and the ser-vants entirely to Georgina. On each visit, she also never failed to remind Adam how good Georgina was for him, and how grateful he should be to Agatha for pointing out to him that he had fallen in love with his wife.

Adam *was* grateful, but he did not need Agatha to remind him of how much he was in love with Georgina or how good she was for him. He was reminded of that fact every time he looked at his beautiful, impetuous, adorable wife.

* * * * *

*If you enjoyed this story,
make sure to pick up the other
books in Eva Shepherd's
Rebellious Young Ladies miniseries*

Lady Amelia's Scandalous Secret
Miss Fairfax's Notorious Duke

*Whilst you're waiting for
the next book, why not read her
Those Roguish Rosemonts miniseries?*

A Dance to Save the Debutante
Tempting the Sensible Lady Violet
Falling for the Forbidden Duke

COMING NEXT MONTH FROM

H HARLEQUIN

INTRIGUE

#2199 A PLACE TO HIDE
Lookout Mountain Mysteries • by Debra Webb
Two and a half years ago, Grace Myers, infant son in tow, escaped a serial killer. Now, she'll have to trust Deputy Robert Vaughn to safeguard their identities and lives. The culprit is still on the loose and determined to get even...

#2200 WETLANDS INVESTIGATION
The Swamp Slayings • by Carla Cassidy
Investigator Nick Cain is in the small town of Black Bayou for one reason—to catch a serial killer. But between his unwanted attraction to his partner Officer Sarah Beauregard and all the deadly town secrets he uncovers, will his plan to catch the killer implode?

#2201 K-9 DETECTION
New Mexico Guard Dogs • by Nichole Severn
Jocelyn Carville knows a dangerous cartel is responsible for the Alpine Valley PD station bombing. But convincing Captain Baker Halsey is harder than uncovering the cartel's motive. Until the syndicate's next attack makes their risky partnership inevitable...

#2202 SWIFTWATER ENEMIES
Big Sky Search and Rescue • by Danica Winters
When Aspen Stevens and Detective Leo West meet at a crime scene, they instantly dislike each other. But uncovering the truth about their victim means combining search and rescue expertise and acknowledging the fine line between love and hate even as they risk their lives...

#2203 THE PERFECT WITNESS
Secure One • by Katie Mettner
Security expert Cal Newfellow knows safety is an illusion. But when he's tasked with protecting Marlise, a prosecutor's star witness against an infamous trafficker and murderer, he'll do everything in his power to keep the danger—and his heart—away from her.

#2204 MURDER IN THE BLUE RIDGE MOUNTAINS
The Lynleys of Law Enforcement • by R. Barri Flowers
After a body is discovered in the mountains, special agent Garrett Sneed returns home to work the case with his ex, law enforcement ranger Madison Lynley. Before long, their attraction is heating up...until another homicide reveals a possible link to his mother's unsolved murder. And then the killer sets his sights on Madison...

YOU CAN FIND MORE INFORMATION ON UPCOMING HARLEQUIN TITLES, FREE EXCERPTS AND MORE AT HARLEQUIN.COM.

HICNM0124

Get 3 FREE REWARDS!

We'll send you 2 FREE Books <u>plus</u> a FREE Mystery Gift.

FREE Value Over **$20**

Both the **Harlequin® Historical** and **Harlequin® Romance** series feature compelling novels filled with emotion and simmering romance.

YES! Please send me 2 FREE novels from the Harlequin Historical or Harlequin Romance series and my FREE Mystery Gift (gift is worth about $10 retail). After receiving them, if I don't wish to receive any more books, I can return the shipping statement marked "cancel." If I don't cancel, I will receive 6 brand-new Harlequin Historical books every month and be billed just $6.19 each in the U.S. or $6.74 each in Canada, a savings of at least 11% off the cover price, or 4 brand-new Harlequin Romance Larger-Print books every month and be billed just $6.09 each in the U.S. or $6.24 each in Canada, a savings of at least 13% off the cover price. It's quite a bargain! Shipping and handling is just 50¢ per book in the U.S. and $1.25 per book in Canada.* I understand that accepting the 2 free books and gift places me under no obligation to buy anything. I can always return a shipment and cancel at any time by calling the number below. The free books and gift are mine to keep no matter what I decide.

Choose one: ☐ **Harlequin Historical** (246/349 BPA GRNX)   ☐ **Harlequin Romance Larger-Print** (119/319 BPA GRNX)   ☐ **Or Try Both!** (246/349 & 119/319 BPA GRRD)

Name (please print)

Address   Apt. #

City   State/Province   Zip/Postal Code

Email: Please check this box ☐ if you would like to receive newsletters and promotional emails from Harlequin Enterprises ULC and its affiliates. You can unsubscribe anytime.

Mail to the **Harlequin Reader Service:**
IN U.S.A.: P.O. Box 1341, Buffalo, NY 14240-8531
IN CANADA: P.O. Box 603, Fort Erie, Ontario L2A 5X3

Want to try 2 free books from another series! Call 1-800-873-8635 or visit www.ReaderService.com.

---

*Terms and prices subject to change without notice. Prices do not include sales taxes, which will be charged (if applicable) based on your state or country of residence. Canadian residents will be charged applicable taxes. Offer not valid in Quebec. This offer is limited to one order per household. Books received may not be as shown. Not valid for current subscribers to the Harlequin Historical or Harlequin Romance series. All orders subject to approval. Credit or debit balances in a customer's account(s) may be offset by any other outstanding balance owed by or to the customer. Please allow 4 to 6 weeks for delivery. Offer available while quantities last.

Your Privacy—Your information is being collected by Harlequin Enterprises ULC, operating as Harlequin Reader Service. For a complete summary of the information we collect, how we use this information and to whom it is disclosed, please visit our privacy notice located at <u>corporate.harlequin.com/privacy-notice</u>. From time to time we may also exchange your personal information with reputable third parties. If you wish to opt out of this sharing of your personal information, please visit <u>readerservice.com/consumerchoice</u> or call 1-800-873-8635. **Notice to California Residents**—Under California law, you have specific rights to control and access your data. For more information on these rights and how to exercise them, visit <u>corporate.harlequin.com/california-privacy</u>.

HHHRLP23